AMERICAN HERO

A QUESTION OF JUSTICE

RACHEL LEE

D0058040

Silhouette®
INTIMATE™MOMENTS®
Published by Silhouette Books
America's Publisher of Contemporary Romance

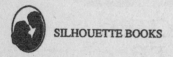 SILHOUETTE BOOKS

ISBN 0-373-07613-4

A QUESTION OF JUSTICE

RACHEL LEE

wrote her first play in the third grade for a school assembly, and by the age of twelve she was hooked on writing. She's lived all over the United States, on both the East and West Coasts, and now resides in Florida.

Having held jobs as a security officer, real-estate agent and optician, she uses these, as well as her natural flair for creativity, to write stories that are undeniably romantic. "After all, life is the biggest romantic adventure of all—and if you're open and aware, the most marvelous things are just waiting to be discovered."

To my sister Pat, for giving me courage when I most
needed it, and for some of the best advice I ever had.
And to Cris, always.

ACKNOWLEDGMENTS

My deepest gratitude to Nathaniel Brown for hours
of research into Wyoming Statutes regarding rape,
and for all the advice on procedure.
Most especially, thanks for all the insight into the
personal conflict criminal defense attorneys face daily.
Without your perceptions, this book would have
been a hollow bell.
And, of course, any errors are mine.

Chapter 1

"Counselor, do you have any questions for the witness?"

"Yes, Your Honor, I do." Rising from the defense table, Sandy Keller picked up her pad and tried not to look into the sullen face of her young client. Les Walker, she felt, was going to lose on the basis of his scowl alone, never mind a damning accumulation of circumstantial evidence. In the meantime, all she could do was give him the best defense she could make out of this lousy case.

Conard County Deputy Sheriff Micah Parish sat in the witness box. He wore his inky black hair to his shoulders and bore the stamp of his Cherokee ancestors proudly on his face. She'd cross-examined him in other trials and had no illusion that it was going to be easy to undermine his testimony.

"Deputy Parish, you lifted a fingerprint from the checkout counter at Freitag's Mercantile the night of the robbery, which was later determined to be my client's."

"That's correct."

"How many other fingerprints did you lift from Freitag's Mercantile that evening?"

Micah tilted his head slightly, but met her gaze steadily. "I don't recall the exact number."

Good answer, she thought, but she wasn't going to let him get away with that. It was her responsibility to make it perfectly clear to the jury that a fingerprint, in and of itself, proved very little. "Let's see if we can narrow it down a little. You lifted more than one set of prints, is that correct?"

"Yes."

"More than . . . oh, a half-dozen different prints?"

Micah nodded slowly. "I'm sure there were more than a half-dozen different prints, yes."

"More than a half-dozen." She glanced at the jury as she drove the point home and was glad to see they were following intently. "More than a dozen?"

"I'm not sure. I'd need my notes."

"Well, for now we'll go with 'more than a half-dozen.' Tell me, Deputy, do fingerprints come with time and date stamps?"

She was looking past Micah at the jury, but from the corner of her eye she saw him stiffen. The jury, too, seemed to grow more intent as they realized that something interesting was happening. Slowly she turned her head and looked at Micah. "Deputy?"

There was a kind of wariness around his dark eyes now, something only someone who saw him often would be able to detect. "I don't understand the question, Counselor."

"I thought it was quite clear. Do fingerprints come with a time and date stamp, like a videotape?"

"No."

"Then you can't say precisely when those fingerprints were left on the counter?"

"No."

"Which means you can't say for certain that my client didn't leave that print there much earlier in the evening . . . during normal business hours, perhaps?"

He shifted ever so slightly in his chair, and she saw the glimmer of admiration appear around his mouth, a not-quite smile. "No, Counselor, I can't say that for certain."

"In fact, Deputy, all you can say is that my client was in Freitag's Mercantile at some time recently. Is that correct?"

"Yes."

"And just how many people pass through Freitag's on a given day?"

"Objection!" Sam Haversham, the prosecutor, was out of his seat like a shot. "Counsel is asking the witness to speculate."

Sandy turned toward Judge Williams. She could have argued, but her point had been made, and the jury knew the answer already. "I withdraw the question, Your Honor." She faced Parish once again. "Deputy, were you able to identify all the fingerprints you found at Freitag's?"

"No, ma'am."

"So... someone else also touched the counter beside the cash register?"

"Yes."

"Someone you can't identify?"

"Yes."

"Like the real robber?"

"Objection!" Haversham was on his feet again.

"I'll rephrase, Your Honor." Now she looked directly into Parish's dark eyes. "Deputy, could one of those unidentified prints belong to the real robber?"

That thin, almost-smile again. "Yes, that's possible, but..."

"No further questions, Your Honor."

Turning sharply away, satisfied that she had done the best possible job she could in demolishing the importance of that fingerprint, she returned to the defense table. It wasn't that she wanted to get a guilty person off—she hoped she never did that—but it was her job to make sure the jury evaluated the evidence correctly. To make sure that they didn't put more weight on a fingerprint than was justifiable. After all, among the other fingerprints on the counter at Freitag's might well be one of theirs.

Glancing toward the rear of the courtroom, she nearly stumbled as she recognized the craggy face of a man who was seated in the very back row. Garrett Hancock? No, it couldn't possibly be. What reason could a Texas Ranger have for sitting in a Wyoming courtroom, listening to a burglary case? None. Absolutely none.

She slipped into her chair and tried to pay attention as Sam questioned Parish again, trying to undo the damage she had done.

She couldn't afford to get distracted. This case was a dog; she didn't stand a chance in hell of getting this young miscreant off, but she still had to give him the best defense possible. That was her job, her duty and her moral responsibility.

But awareness of Garrett Hancock burned at the base of her skull like a maddening itch, and she had to force herself to focus on the trial. A trial that she had advised Les Walker would be a waste of time and probably get him a longer sentence. It wasn't as if she had any defense to offer other than that Les's mother was willing to testify that her son had been in his bedroom at the time the robbery was committed. Considering that the sheriff had found Les in possession of all the stolen goods, considering that he'd purchased a used motorcycle for almost exactly the sum of money that was missing from Freitag's... Well, Mrs. Walker was probably going to be ignored by the jury as a biased witness.

Sam Haversham finished questioning Micah, and Sandy declined the opportunity to do a re-cross. She had, after all, said all that needed saying with regard to the fingerprint. The jury would keep it in perspective now, and that was all she could ask . . . or wanted to.

"You may step down now, Deputy Parish," Judge Williams told him. "Mr. Haversham?"

"Prosecution rests, Your Honor."

"In that case, seeing as how it's nearly three, this court will adjourn until ten tomorrow morning." She brought her gavel down sharply.

"All rise."

Standing, Sandy watched the judge depart the courtroom. A moment later her client was leaving, too, in the company of two deputies.

"That was some hatchet job you did on Micah," growled a low voice in her ear.

Sandy whirled around and found herself face-to-face with the Texas Ranger. A torrent of conflicting feelings flooded her, ranging from pleased surprise that he evidently remembered her from their brief meeting nearly two years ago, to dismay that he was evidently annoyed at her.

And then anger drove everything else away, clearing her head and putting her on her mettle. "It wasn't a hatchet job, Ranger. You know as well as I do that a fingerprint can tie a defendant to the scene of the crime, but it doesn't prove a damn thing."

"It proves plenty. Besides, Micah says the kid has a record a mile long."

"Do you eat eggs for breakfast, Mr. Hancock?" He was good, she thought, surprised that her abrupt change of subject didn't throw him. He didn't so much as blink.

"Yeah, as a matter of fact, I do," he said.

"Well, there's a plate in my sink right now with egg yolk on it. I can therefore infer you must be the person who ate eggs at my house this morning?"

"No, but—"

"Just because a person has committed six rapes doesn't mean he committed a seventh. Or, in this case, a prior record for petty theft doesn't mean my client committed *this* burglary."

It took a moment, but slowly one corner of his mouth hitched up just the tiniest bit. "Point taken. But with all the other evidence—"

"It is my job to make sure that my client is tried on the basis of evidence, Mr. Hancock, not inference or supposition. That fingerprint does not prove my client robbed the Mercantile. All it proves was that he was there at some time. Just that simple. And I have to make sure the jury doesn't give it more importance than it honestly deserves."

"You defense lawyers are always getting crooks off on technicalities."

He was scowling at her now, and she scowled right back. She'd stopped letting men intimidate her many years ago. "Considerably less often than you law officers like to think. Ninety percent of the people who are convicted are actually guilty of the crime. What frightens me is that the other ten percent aren't. All I'm trying to do is make sure the jury is convinced beyond a reasonable doubt and maybe keep some of those ten percent who are innocent out of jail. That's all."

Turning, she scooped papers into her open briefcase and wondered why she had ever thought, even fleetingly, that it might be nice to see this man again. Two years ago she had been impressed by the sensitivity he had shown toward Faith Parish who, until she had fled to Conard County and met Micah Parish, had been the abused wife of a San Antonio, Texas, police officer. Garrett Hancock had come up here to extradite Faith's former husband, and Sandy had been assigned the unenviable task of representing the abusive cop as defense counsel.

She'd been impressed with Garrett then, but now she wasn't so sure. She had no use for cops who didn't understand the importance of defense attorneys.

"You ready to go, Garrett?" asked the deep voice of Micah Parish.

"Sure. Just renewing my acquaintance with Ms. Keller, here."

"That's right, she was Frank Williams's attorney." Micah gave Sandy one of his almost invisible smiles. "You'll have to come up and have dinner with Faith and me while Garrett is visiting."

She managed a smile and a noncommittal response, and then watched as Micah and Garrett left the courtroom. So the ranger was visiting the Parishes. Well, that explained what a Texas Ranger was doing in a Wyoming courtroom. After a moment, ignoring a sense of disappointment, she returned to packing up her papers. By lunchtime tomorrow, Les Walker was probably going to be convicted. She seriously doubted the jury would be out any longer than it would take to poll the members. For all Garrett claimed that criminals were always getting off on technicalities, in reality it didn't happen very often.

Well, he'd thoroughly soured her mood, she thought as she tramped across the courthouse square toward her office in a small white clapboard house just off Front Street. The house had been left to her many years ago by an uncle and had proved to be a perfect office location.

Nina, her secretary, was busily typing a brief on the computer when Sandy stepped in the side door. A glance over Nina's head told Sandy that no one was in the waiting room, which meant she could kick off her shoes and enjoy a cup of coffee before plunging into anything more.

"Hi, Nina. Anything up?"

"Yes'm." The young woman glanced up with a wry smile. "Sheriff's office called. They've got another client for you."

"It can't be my turn again already!" The county legal society volunteered its members for duty as public defenders on a rotating basis. There weren't very many attorneys in Conard County but there also weren't very many crimes. Sandy hadn't been expecting to get called to serve again so soon.

"This one isn't *pro bono*," Nina said. "Sheriff Tate asked if you could come over ASAP. They've made an arrest, and the suspect is asking for you."

A defendant with money? That was a rarity! "Just as soon as I have a cup of coffee," Sandy told her.

"How'd it go in court?"

"About the way I expected."

Settled behind her desk, she kicked off her pumps and wiggled her toes gratefully. There was no discomfort quite like having to wear high heels all day, and it seemed to get tougher with each passing year. Maybe, at forty-seven, she ought to admit it was time to come down from three-inch to two-inch heels.

Placed in the middle of her green blotter was a stack of mail, all neatly opened and unfolded by Nina, envelopes clipped to the back of the enclosures. Ordinarily the mail was the very first thing she dealt with when she returned from court, but today she decided to let it go.

She enjoyed criminal defense work more than any other facet of the law, but it was also mildly depressing to expend so much effort knowing it was unlikely she would win. By nature she was a winner, not a loser, and every loss galled her, even a loss like the Walker case, where she hadn't stood a chance in hell.

There were two contests in every court case. The first was the plaintiff against the defendant, in this case the State of Wyoming versus Les Walker. That one mattered professionally.

But there was a second contest that was purely personal, and every trial lawyer knew it. It was Sandy Keller versus Sam Haversham, one-on-one. Who was the best? It was ridiculous to look at it that way, and she knew it, but inevitably, at a gut level, she took defeat as a personal judgment, even though it was nothing of the sort. Juries decided on the basis of evidence, not on the basis of which lawyer they liked best. Still, it would take her a day or two to shake the feeling. It always did.

Which made this a perfect time to go see her new client. Maybe she would get revved up enough to carry herself through the inevitable loss tomorrow. Of course, maybe she wouldn't want to touch this one with a ten-foot pole, either. That was the nice thing about a paying client—she could always turn him down.

But first the cup of coffee. On stocking feet, she padded back out to Nina's office and poured herself a mugful from the pot on the warming plate. Both she and Nina were inveterate coffee drinkers. Around here, the pot was never allowed to go dry.

"Did the sheriff say what the guy was arrested for?"

Nina's fingers paused over the keyboard, and she looked up. "Nope. I got the feeling they're trying to keep it quiet."

"Oh, goody." She spoke sarcastically, but the truth was, her interest was immediately piqued. If the sheriff was try- ing to keep a lid on it, it must be something big. Maintain- ing an appearance of indifference, she padded back to her office.

But her stomach fluttered with uneasy anticipation. She'd deferred major cases before, but it had been a while, and there was always a mixture of excitement and fear—excite- ment at the prospect of a meaty case, and fear that she might not be adequate for the task.

It wasn't as if major criminal cases crossed her desk every day of the week...or even every year. Nor did she want them to. Part of the reason she had returned to Conard County after working for several years in the larger world was be- cause life here was more tranquil. Living on a perpetual adrenaline high didn't appeal to her.

But once in a while it felt good. Like now. She stuffed her feet into her shoes and reached for her briefcase. The desire to dawdle over her coffee had completely vanished, re- placed by awakening curiosity. No point spending time in speculation. All she had to do was trot over to the jail and find out what was up.

The tension at the sheriff's office was high, noticeable the instant she stepped through the door. It wasn't so much that people were scurrying around and talking as it was that there were more people than usual and that they were unusually quiet. Something big had happened, but nobody was talk- ing about it. That alone was enough to set off her alarm bells.

Velma Jansen, the dispatcher, didn't even bother to rus- tle up a smile. "Nate's expecting you, Sandy. Just head on back."

The sheriff's office was halfway down a narrow hallway with a window at the far end. The window looked as if it hadn't been scrubbed since the building was erected, and years of grime and smoke had virtually frosted it. The office door was open, and the sheriff, Nathan Tate, rose the instant he saw her on the threshold.

"Afternoon, Sandy. Micah tells me you did a good job of demolishing the fingerprints on the Les Walker case." One corner of his mouth hitched up in a faint smile that said he was trying to be pleasant. Everything else about him said he was finding it difficult.

Nate and Sandy had grown up together and gone to school together, and ever since had been tussling about the law from different sides of the criminal courtroom. Ordinarily their disagreements were good-natured and minor. Last winter Sandy had been his divorce attorney, very briefly, until he and Marge had sorted things out. Now they were back to their usual "law" and "lawyer" positions.

Sandy smiled. "Micah knows I was right. There's a limit to what a fingerprint proves."

"Good try, but it won't get the kid off."

She shrugged. "My job is to make sure he gets a fair trial. I think I went through this just a little while ago with that Texas Ranger, Garrett Hancock. Is he up here on business?"

"No, just came up to visit Faith and Micah. Maybe you remember, he was the one who investigated Faith's former husband?"

"I remember he came up here to take Frank Williams back to Texas with him. I didn't know he was close to Faith, though."

"They got to be pretty good friends after Garrett stopped Frank from stabbing her to death."

Sandy shook her head. "I never did hear that whole story."

"Get him to tell you. It's no big secret. Right now, I got other things on my mind, so why don't you just pull up a chair? Can I get you coffee?"

"No, thanks, I just had some. Nina says you have a paying client for me."

"Apparently so." Nate settled behind his desk and leaned back, a powerful man with a sun- and wind-reddened face and dark, gray-flecked hair. "Before I start talking as the sheriff, I want to say something as a friend. You want to think real hard before you take this case, Sandy. Oh, I know all the stuff about how even Ted Bundy was entitled to a fair and legal defense, the best defense possible, but you need to consider very carefully, anyway, because this is a case that's going to take a toll on you. It'll be a personal toll for sure, but it will probably also be a professional toll. You might never be able to practice law in Conard County again."

Sandy felt the skin across the back of her neck tighten. "What's he accused of?"

"It appears he raped a five-year-old girl."

Sandy didn't immediately go upstairs to meet her potential client. Nate got called away for a few minutes to handle something out front, so she sat where she was, staring at the wall behind his desk. A topographical map of the county had been enhanced with little pins and flags, but she hardly even saw them.

Accused of raping a five-year-old girl. She could well understand why Nate wanted her to think about it before taking the case. When word of this got out, indignation was going to run high, and the anger would unquestionably spill over on the defense attorney. She would be a fool to dismiss the potential fallout without weighing it and determining whether she was prepared to deal with it.

Rising, she walked to the window and stared out at the gray spring day. It looked as if it might snow again tonight, she thought absently. It was high time the weather started warming, but it appeared that it was going to be a tardy spring.

If the accused went to trial, the public attention would be incredible. Nothing like this had happened in Conard County in her memory, and the rape of a child was always guaranteed to rouse people's anger. Folks here might never forgive her for defending this guy. They would certainly never forgive her if she managed to get him off, and in a case like this...well, there was so much potential for legal missteps that even if the guy was convicted there was a good possibility he could get off on appeal. A child wasn't the best witness, and if there had been any mismanagement of evidence...

She shuddered inwardly. Defense attorney for an accused rapist. Again she shuddered, trying to slam the lid down on a coffin that she'd buried many, many years ago. Could she be certain that she would give an accused rapist the best defense? After all, she knew what it meant to be a victim. All that had happened a very long time ago, and she considered herself well past it, but...what if her feelings prevented her from providing the best defense she could?

That was the other side of this decision. Could she be sure that old ghosts wouldn't prevent her from doing the best job for him? Because that was essential. If she took this case, she had to do the best job she was capable of and set her personal feelings aside.

No easy task, sometimes.

"Sorry to keep you waiting so long."

Nate's voice drew her out of her reverie, and she turned around, managing a small smile. "That's all right. I needed the thinking time."

"You're going to need more of it when you hear the whole story," he said, resuming his seat behind the desk and motioning her back to hers. "It's not pretty. I'll give you the background first, and then we'll get to the reasons we arrested your client."

"Not my client yet."

"Sorry. It's been a long night and an even longer day. The suspect. I'll tell you about him when I get there in the story, okay?"

She nodded.

"You heard that little Lisa Dunbar was missing?"

"I heard about it this morning before court. Someone said she hadn't come home from school last night."

"That's the gist of it. Her mom works, and the eldest daughter baby-sits after school. Only last night, the older girl, Debbie, decided to go to a friend's house instead of coming home from school on the bus with Lisa. The bus driver said Lisa got off the bus alone at four. I don't know if you're familiar with the Dunbar place?"

Sandy shook her head. "Not really. It's been a while since I've been out in that part of the county."

"Well, the bus lets the kids off at the ranch gate, but it's more than a mile walk up the road to the house. Lisa evidently got snatched somewhere along there. There was absolutely no sign that she had gotten home. Mom came home about six-thirty, found both girls missing and no sign they'd come home, and she called us. The eldest girl turned up about twenty minutes later, dropped off by the friend's mother. All she knew was that Lisa had gotten on the school bus to come home."

Nate shook his head. "Kids. It was a kid thing for her to do, to let her sister come home alone, but now she's a mess, too, because she's old enough to feel responsible for what happened to Lisa. Old enough to realize it might never have happened if she had come home with her."

"She can't know that," Sandy said. "There's no way she can know that, Nate! Both girls might have been assaulted."

Nate nodded. "I don't think this was done on the spur of the moment, either. Somebody knew those girls came home at that time and had to walk up to the house from the road. Lisa wasn't a target of opportunity. No way."

Sandy turned her head and looked out the window at the chilly, gray day. The trees in the courthouse square had only just begun to bud. It would be a damn shame if a frost killed them.

No, chilling as the thought was, she didn't believe Lisa Dunbar had been a target of opportunity, either. It wasn't as if she'd been abducted from somewhere full of kids, such as a playground or a mall. Nate was right. Someone had wanted that girl. Maybe both girls. "How old is the sister? Debbie, isn't it?"

Nate nodded. "Thirteen."

"Old enough to watch her sister, young enough to get sidetracked by a friend." Sandy shook her head and stood up, pacing to the window and rubbing her upper arms with her hands. "It's getting colder out there."

"Yeah. We're supposed to get a frost tonight. It'll kill the trees."

"Maybe. Okay, the mom called you, and the search began?"

"That's it. We verified that she'd gotten on the bus, that she'd gotten off at her stop and that she hadn't been seen by anyone since. It was already getting dark by then, but we started a search of the ranch, thinking maybe she'd wandered off the road chasing a jackrabbit or a deer or something. It wouldn't be the first time."

"No." There had been a case not too long ago where a child that age had wandered off from a campsite following an animal. Search parties had located him some six hours later, unharmed but scared.

"It was cold last night. Nobody wanted to halt the search for fear she might die of exposure. We started getting really uneasy, though, after a few hours, because Lisa knows the ranch. She may be only five, but there aren't too many places she could wander to within a short space of time and not find her way back. You know how ranch kids are."

"Born with a sense of direction." She'd been one herself. By the age of five she'd wandered freely over quite a large area and had known her way home. Her brother's grandchildren were now doing the same thing at similar ages.

"She'd been missing more than two hours by the time her mom phoned us, and by the time it had been dark for a few hours...well, everyone was pretty much certain she'd been hurt somehow, and nobody was quitting. Then, in the early hours this morning, her book bag was found on Willis Road."

Sandy drew a deep breath and turned around to look at Nate. "Quite a way from home."

"Exactly. No more speculation after that. We knew she'd been kidnapped, and we knew she'd probably been hurt. We moved the search over to that area . . . and found her."

He passed his hand over his face and shook his head. "Actually, *I* found her, on the creek bank south of Willis Road. She was naked, nearly unconscious from hypothermia, and it was obvious she'd been raped."

"Obvious?"

"She'd been bleeding, Counselor. No five-year-old girl bleeds that way from any other cause."

She drew a long, shaky breath and wrapped her arms more tightly around herself. "Did she identify her attacker?"

"He was dark, had black hair, long in the back. . . . Something like that. I took it down, and it's being typed up for the report now. I'll see you get a copy."

"What was her state of mind?"

"Disoriented, crying. . . ."

It might well classify as an excited utterance, then, she thought, which meant Nate's memory of what the little girl had said could be admitted into evidence, rather than being dismissed as hearsay. She would have to make a motion on that, try to prevent it. . . .

And that was when she realized she had almost made up her mind to take the case. She was already planning her moves. Good Lord, did she really want to defend a child molester?

"Where is she now?"

"At the hospital."

"Nobody's questioning her, I hope."

Nate shook his head. "I'm the only one who has. Sam Haversham and her family are looking into getting a good psychologist to talk to her. In the meantime, everyone's leaving her alone and just letting her talk if she feels like it. I hear she doesn't much feel like it."

"She's got to be in a terrible state of shock."

"I'd think so."

Sandy expelled a long breath. "I take it you arrested the suspect on the basis of her description? It isn't a very good description, Nate."

"Give me some credit, Sandy." He spoke mildly enough, but his eyes held a haunted look that she didn't like. "One of the searchers found signs of recent digging on the property across the road from where we found Lisa. We dug up her clothes. That's when I made the arrest. The guy fit her description, and her clothes were hastily buried on his property."

"What does *he* say?"

"Not a word. From the moment we read him his rights, he hasn't said anything except that he wants you for his attorney."

"Who is it?"

"Craig Nighthawk."

She shook her head. "I don't think I know.... Wait. Isn't he that truck driver who bought Hattie Maguire's acreage a few years back?"

"That's him. Always quiet, kept to himself.... Hell! Up until today I never much thought about him one way or the other." He rapped his fingers impatiently on his desk and then sprang to his feet. "Look, I know you're probably going to take this case. You were always a scrapper, and maybe you think you like a quiet life, but I know better. I'm trying to keep a lid on this mess, trying to keep folks from knowing what happened....

"Hell, Sandy, the kid's only five. There's no reason the whole damn county has to know she was raped. If word gets out that some kid was raped, everyone will connect it with Lisa Dunbar being missing overnight. I'm hoping if we can keep it quiet for a while we can at least protect the kid's identity."

"I'm with you." She managed a thin smile. "She's suffered enough damage. But do you *really* think you can keep it quiet? You've arrested somebody. There must be dozens of people who know that."

"I was the one who found the little girl. I called for a couple of my deputies, but none of the other searchers saw her or know that she was raped. Just me, Micah, Les and the doctors and her family know what really happened. And I'd like to keep it that way as long as possible."

"You've got my word I won't spill the beans. As far as I'm concerned, she's a Jane Doe. So... any other evidence?"

"We're doing tissue samples—she may have scratched her attacker—checking her clothes for hairs... anything that might carry a genetic imprint. I don't know if they've found sperm samples or anything like that. I know the doctors were going to swab for samples. If anything turns up, Sam will let you know. Assuming you take the case."

Sandy sighed and looked over her shoulder at the darkening day. Should she or shouldn't she?

"I'll talk to him," she said finally. "I'll talk to him before I decide."

"It won't be pretty. People could get really angry at you if you defend him."

She faced Nate straight on. "I won't let that decide me, Nate. Sure it'll be uncomfortable, but everyone is entitled to a fair trial, and the last I heard, everyone is presumed innocent until convicted. That's the point of a trial, isn't it?"

"But principles can be cold comfort sometimes."

"Yeah." She wondered if she was going to be able to live up to hers.

The Conard County jail was above the sheriff's office in an armored room on the second floor. It was a small jail, having only six cells and a conference room where attorneys could consult with clients, and where the sheriff could question suspects.

By the time Nate took Sandy upstairs, Craig Nighthawk was already there and waiting, guarded by a deputy. When Sandy stepped into the room, the deputy nodded and left. She heard the bolt being shoved home with a solid thunk, and then she was locked in with a man who might well be a child molester.

Craig Nighthawk didn't say anything to Sandy, but his dark eyes never left her as she pulled out a chair on the far side of the table and sat facing him. Well, they were even, she thought, not saying a word as she opened up her briefcase and pulled out a legal pad and pen.

"I'm Sandy Keller, Mr. Nighthawk," she said finally. "I understand you've asked for me to be your attorney, but I haven't decided yet whether I'll take your case. If I decide not to, anything you tell me will not be covered by attorney-client privilege...which means I could conceivably be subpoenaed to testify. Do you understand what that means?"

He nodded, his eyes never wavering. Sandy decided he did indeed understand her, so she continued.

"Don't tell me anything you wouldn't want me to have to tell someone else. Now, I don't know why you asked for me, but maybe you can give me a reason why I should take your case."

He never moved so much as a muscle, but she had the distinct impression that he leaned across the table toward her. His intensity was palpable. "I can give you a reason," he said. "It's simple. I didn't do it."

Chapter 2

"**H**e didn't do it."

Nate scowled at her. "Come on, Sandy! You weren't born yesterday! How many times have you heard someone say that when you knew damn well they were guiltier than sin!"

"Plenty. And I never believed them... until now. I'm telling you, Nate, this guy didn't do it. Now you can ignore me, or you can get busy finding out who *did* do it."

He settled his hands on his hips and blew out a frustrated breath. "Sandy, be reasonable. If we come up with some evidence that indicates he didn't do it, I'll get to work on it, but right now the evidence points to him, and he's got plenty of reason to lie about it."

"Nate..."

"Look. We'll collect all the evidence there is. We're waiting for the results from the lab, and we're searching the area out along Willis Road for any additional data we can find. I promise you, if anything turns up that might exonerate Craig Nighthawk, you'll hear about it. We're not in the business of burying information. And we're not in the business of sending innocent people to prison, either."

"Then—"

He shook his head. "Let me finish. We're also not in the business of proving guilt or innocence. That's the job of the lawyers. We collect the evidence, period. We'll let Nighthawk go if we find reason to. In the meantime, if that isn't good enough for you—if you want somebody to *prove* Nighthawk's innocence—maybe you'd better hire a private investigator."

A short while later, standing out on the sidewalk in front of the sheriff's office, she felt the frigid wind cut through the wool of her blue suit. This morning it hadn't been cold enough for her to need more than the suit jacket. Now she wished she had her ski parka on.

She also wished she wasn't wearing three-inch heels on feet that were aching, and that she'd had her hair cut and restyled into something more sophisticated than the bob she'd been wearing for so many years, and that she'd colored it so the gray wouldn't be so obvious... and that she weren't foolhardy enough to believe in the innocence of a man who had no more defense than his own words: "I didn't do it."

She was going out on a limb, she realized. Just because she had looked into a man's eyes while he claimed innocence—and believed him—she was preparing to take an immense risk. Every instinct told her that Craig Nighthawk was telling the truth. *He* believed he hadn't done it. *He* believed in his own innocence, and because he believed it, so did she.

But it had been one hell of a long time since she'd been young enough and passionate enough about anything to *want* to go out on a limb. Awareness of the risks gave her a queasy feeling even as it heightened her senses. But what else could she do? If she believed the man was innocent, she could hardly turn down the case. It wasn't as if defense lawyers grew on trees around here.

The air tasted of snow, she thought, and turned toward her car. Snow. Again. Much as she loved living in Conard County, after six months of winter with only the prospect of a cold spring, she was beginning to think Florida sounded good. Any place far enough south that it wouldn't snow in April and May. Easy to visualize a white beach, blue water and warm sunshine. So easy to imagine stretching out on that beach and listening to the lapping of waves on the shore.

Instead she'd been foolhardy enough to agree to defend an accused rapist for no better reason than that he said he hadn't done it. Good grief, she needed to be committed!

"Ms. Keller."

For just a fleeting instant she experienced a wild urge to ignore Garrett Hancock. She still felt bristly from their encounter after adjournment and wasn't sure she wanted to get freshly irritated. What made her turn, however, were even more fleeting urges and images, furtive feminine feelings she hadn't allowed herself to indulge for so many years.

She was attracted to the man. She'd recognized that the very first time they met. At the time it hadn't seemed like a problem, simply because he was only in town for a couple of days. She'd thought of him once or twice since, with the kind of vague disappointment that accompanied a missed opportunity.

When she'd recognized him in the courtroom earlier, all those vague feelings had rushed to the foreground, reminding her that it was indeed possible for Sandra Keller to be attracted to a man, despite all her resolutions to the contrary. One lousy marriage ought to be enough to warn anybody off, she'd always believed. Still believed. So why did her heart skip a beat at the sound of this man's voice?

The smart thing, she told herself, would be to tell him to get lost. He clearly didn't have much admiration for defense attorneys, and she was past the stage in her life where she had any desire to defend herself to anyone. Why defend herself to a man who would be heading back to Texas in a few days anyway? Even if she ignored her own good sense and tangled herself up with him, it would come to nothing.

But despite all her resolutions, despite knowing better, she turned around with a cautious smile. "Ranger."

Garrett's face was sharply etched, strongly masculine. Textured by wind and sun, it was ageless. He was lean and fit, about six feet in height, and his cowboy boots added another two inches. A good-looking man overall, but his most remarkable feature was a pair of electric blue eyes. They seemed to stand out in his dark face, to glow with an internal light of their own. They probably could look as glacial and forbidding as Arctic ice, but right now they looked... as wary as she was feeling. He was uneasy about speaking to her, she realized, and felt herself relax. Neither one of them was comfortable, and for some reason that made her feel better.

"I was on my way to Maude's to get dinner when I saw you," he said. "Would you join me?"

A moment of common sense nearly caused her to decline, but before she could frame a polite refusal, she heard her own voice saying, "Thanks, I'd like that."

Maude's was only a block off the main street, facing Good Shepherd Church. The menu hadn't changed in forty years, and the food was still the best-tasting down-home cooking to be found anywhere. The hour was early enough that they had the place mostly to themselves, and Garrett settled them in the booth against the front window so that they could look out at Good Shepherd and the slowly darkening afternoon.

"Snow again tonight," he remarked. "Don't you folks ever get tired of it?"

The question was friendly, as was the faint smile around his startling blue eyes, so she smiled back and admitted, "Often, but that doesn't stop the snow."

He chuckled and passed her one of the menus that was tucked between the ketchup and mustard bottles. "Back home in San Antonio right now, most folks are already using air-conditioning."

"Right now that sounds pretty good." She knew Maude's menu by heart, and after a quick scan of the day's special, she put it aside. "Will you be visiting the Parishes long?"

"I'll be around for a week or so, I guess. I may stay longer. I'm on convalescent leave, so my time's pretty much my own. I'm not sure whether I'll hang around here or head down to Colorado and look up some old friends."

"Convalescent leave? What happened?"

He gave her a wry smile that brought a twinkle to his eyes. "I'd like to tell you some exciting story about a shoot-out, but the simple truth is I was in an auto accident. A drunk driver ran a red light."

"How awful! Are you going to be okay?"

"Oh, I'll be a hundred percent again before long. I just need some time for all the repair work to settle in enough that it doesn't twinge all the time."

"Were you hospitalized for long?"

"A couple of weeks."

Which meant he'd been terribly hurt in the accident, Sandy thought. She wanted to commiserate, to ask exactly how badly he'd been injured, but she didn't feel she knew him well enough. Her silence was just beginning to grow awkward when Maude interrupted it with a demand for their orders.

After Maude stalked off, Garrett spoke with a kind of gruff embarrassment. "I'm sorry I gave you a hard time over your cross-examination of Micah about the fingerprint. I get frustrated sometimes with the way the law works."

She was willing to accept the olive branch—cautiously. "I think we all get frustrated about it sometimes."

"That crack about people getting off on technicalities was a cop's gripe, but one I know isn't fair. We grouse about it a lot, but basically all those technicalities just make us do our jobs better."

"That's the idea." Smiling at Maude when the older woman set mugs of coffee in front of them, she received a glare back. It didn't faze her; that was Maude's usual demeanor. "The standard of proof in a criminal case—'guilty beyond and to the *exclusion* of every reasonable doubt'—

demands it. The alternative is 'guilty until proven innocent.' I don't think any of us wants to see that."

One corner of his mouth lifted. "Better that one guilty man should go free than that one innocent man should go to jail, eh?"

"That's the general idea. But it's more than that. If we make each criminal case a battleground for doing it right—for doing it *constitutionally*—then we protect the rights of everyone. Or, to put it another way, if the state can't convince a jury with *legally* collected evidence that a person is guilty beyond any reasonable doubt, then the person is not guilty. Unfortunately, sometimes that means a criminal will go free. Most of the time it doesn't, because the police and prosecutors do their jobs legally." She wanted to sound cool and objective, but instead sounded earnest and intense, something she thought more suited to a young woman than one of her years. At her age she ought to be adopting some of the armor of cynicism, but she somehow never seemed quite able to do that. Get her on the subject of the constitution and the law, particularly civil liberties, and she became as impassioned as any idealist.

Because she *was* an idealist at heart. She truly believed every criminal court case was a constitutional battleground, and that regardless of the guilt or innocence of the defendant, the constitutional right to a fair trial was the real issue each and every time. That was how she could fight as fiercely for a guilty defendant as for one she truly believed innocent . . . as she believed Craig Nighthawk was innocent.

She wished there was some way she could discuss the case with Garrett. Wished, actually, that she could tell Garrett Hancock that she was defending Nighthawk, and that she believed he was innocent. But she wasn't free to discuss the case, in part because of attorney-client confidentiality and in part because she wanted to help protect Lisa Dunbar's identity. Best just to stay away from the entire subject.

"It's been good to see Faith Parish again," Garrett remarked, saving her the problem of changing the subject. "I don't know how familiar you were with what happened there—"

"Well, I was supposed to represent Frank Williams at his extradition hearing, but then he escaped and tried to kill Faith, and Micah killed him...." She shrugged. "I heard he was abusive and had tried to kill her once before."

"That's right. I'd been investigating him for drug running, and he was indicted on a bunch of counts. After he got out on bail, I got this itchy feeling that something was up, so I started following him again. He made a beeline for Faith, intending to kill her. By the time I broke into her apartment, he'd inflicted multiple stab wounds."

"My God!" She hadn't known and couldn't imagine why anyone would want to treat tiny Faith Parish that way. Thinking of Garrett breaking in just in the nick of time, thinking of how badly Faith must have been wounded and how close to death she must have been, made her stomach feel queasy. It was one thing to read about it happening to a stranger and quite another to hear about it happening to someone you knew and liked.

"Sorry. You don't need the gory details. The point is, I got to know Faith pretty well after that. She felt grateful, and I felt protective. My sister was in a situation like that for a couple of years, and I know just what hell it is. And, of course, Frank was intent on killing her, and I was afraid he might get another chance."

"They didn't let him out again on bail after that, surely!"

"No." Garrett shook his head. "Maybe you don't recall. He escaped from custody. That's how he got up here after her. I came up once because we got a request for Frank's rap sheet from the Conard County Sheriff, and I thought he'd been picked up for something up here...which wouldn't have surprised me, because I knew Faith had come up here. Turned out Micah was just checking up. A few days later, I was back up here because Frank *had* turned up and been arrested."

"And then he escaped from the jail and tried to kill Faith again. I'm not normally a bloodthirsty person, but I think the world is better off without Frank Williams."

Garrett gave her a crooked smile. "Careful, Counselor. You'll start sounding like a cop rather than a lawyer."

She smiled back, thinking that maybe he was okay after all. Despite her impression earlier in the courtroom, it appeared Garrett Hancock didn't take himself too seriously. She liked that in anyone, man or woman. "You said your sister had been in an abusive relationship. Is she okay now?"

"Yeah." He patted his breast pocket absently, the automatic gesture of a man looking for his cigarettes. When he didn't find them, he became aware of what he was doing and suddenly grinned. "Bad habit. I quit smoking a couple of years ago, but when I get tense I still find myself looking for my cigarettes. Yeah, my sister's okay. She dumped the guy years ago. The really scary part of it was that her husband had her convinced that she was to blame."

"That's common enough, I hear."

"Apparently so." He shrugged one shoulder. "I'm afraid this is a major concern of mine, so stop me if I get on my soapbox about it."

"That's okay. I don't mind soapboxes. I have a few of my own."

The faint smile returned to his lips. "I guess you do, Counselor."

Maude interrupted their conversation to serve them, muttering something about how the fries might not be just right because the kitchen boy had turned off the deep fryer earlier, and that grease was never quite ready when the thermostat first said it was.

"They look great, Maude," Sandy hastened to assure her. "Just the right golden brown."

"Well, you let me know if they're soggy. I've never served a soggy fry in forty-nine years, and I don't aim to start now!"

When Maude had disappeared back into the kitchen, Garrett's eyes crinkled in the corners. "She's quite a character, isn't she?"

"Always has been. She was just like this when I was a little kid. I don't think she's changed by so much as a hair."

A knock on the window drew their attention, and they turned to see one of the deputies smile and wave before he moved on down the street.

"I like it here," Garrett said abruptly. "If I live long enough to retire, I could easily see coming up here."

"No way, Ranger. You'll be like everyone else at that age—looking for a warm, sunny climate to make life easy and slow."

"I live in one of those climates right now."

"Well, I guarantee that when you're sixty-five the idea of shoveling snow won't appeal to you."

He laughed. "It doesn't appeal to me right now. But the folks here do. Guess that's why I keep coming back."

"It's why I stay. I practiced for a while in a large firm in Cheyenne, but I got tired of the pace, tired of the office politics and infighting. It was such a relief to come back here and live a civilized life."

"*Civilized.* That's a good word for it. Folks here seem to have time to be courteous. You don't find that much in cities anymore. San Antonio's a friendly town, and so's Austin, but not as relaxed as Conard City."

"When there're only five thousand people in an area the size of this county, you get to feeling like family pretty easily. It's great. Really great." She looked down at her plate and wondered why she hadn't just ordered a salad. She didn't really feel hungry. So that Garrett wouldn't feel awkward, though, she had to eat at least some of it.

"I take it you grew up here?"

She looked at him. "I sure did. Conard County born and bred. My older brother inherited the family ranch north of town and still makes a living on cattle."

"But you wanted bigger things?"

"Not bigger so much as just different. I've always enjoyed a good challenge, a good problem to solve. There are plenty of problems to solve in ranching, but not my kind. I was reading casebooks in high school. The law is endlessly fascinating." She paused to eat a fry. They *were* soggy, which gave her an excuse not to eat very many of them. "What about you?" she asked Garrett. "Native Texan?"

"Born and raised. My father was a ranger, too, so I guess you could say it runs in the family." His eyes crinkled at the corners as he smiled at her. "'One riot, one Ranger' was a motto I was raised with. Made me into a self-reliant cuss, I guess. My sister will tell you I'm the most frustrating man on earth to talk to or to get information out of." He shrugged. "Can't help that I'd rather listen than talk. I learn more that way."

Sandy was surprised into a laugh. "I'm sure you do. It also keeps other people from learning very much about you."

His smile broadened a shade. "Silence is often mistaken for wisdom. My mama used to tell me that. If you don't tell people every thought in your head, she'd say, they'll think you're smart." He chuckled, and Sandy joined him. "I guess I was a chatterbox when I was little."

"Did you feel pressured to become a ranger?"

"By my dad, you mean? Nah. He used to say he didn't much care what his kids did, as long as they were law-abiding and productive citizens. I didn't exactly set out to be a ranger, either. I joined the FBI initially, because I wanted to work in counterintelligence. Spent about ten years in the Washington area, then decided I really wanted to be living down home in Texas."

He gave a slight shrug of one shoulder. "Anyhow, there were a variety of reasons why I wasn't very content with the bureau, so I took a position with DPS, the Texas Department of Public Safety. State police. That was okay, but for some reason, when the test for ranger came up, I couldn't resist taking it." He grinned. "Got selected, too. Dad was proud enough to bust, and I kind of felt I'd finally gotten to where I wanted to be. Still feel that way. Looking back, I figure I wanted to be a ranger all along."

"That's how I feel about law—it was the only thing I wanted to do. It wasn't exactly an approved career for a woman at the time, but nobody had told me I couldn't do it. I *did* get a little frustrated when I went to work for that firm in Cheyenne and they wouldn't let me do any trial work. They tried to keep me concentrating on family law. I raised a fuss and finally got my own way, but I seriously doubt I'd ever have made partner." She shrugged indifferently. "In the end, it didn't matter, because I was unhappy there."

"Micah said you have a son."

"Yes, I do. He's graduating from college this year. Then he's planning to go on to medical school." She couldn't prevent the smile that rose to her lips. "I'm terribly proud of him."

"I imagine you are. I was never lucky enough to have kids. Or get married, for that matter."

"Do you regret it?"

"Not having kids? Not really. It's one of those things I just never thought about. Mainly because I never married, I guess. And I never married because I never found a woman I loved who could put up with my life-style. When I get involved in a case, I lose track of time, even the day of the week."

"I do that, too. Some things just can't wait." Like the rape case she had just taken on. She glanced out the window at the dark evening and saw that the first snowflakes were beginning to fall. She had so many things to deal with that she would probably go back to the office this evening and start thinking about which pretrial motions she could file to buy time and control what evidence would be admitted. And she would need to get hold of Sam Haversham and find out just what he knew and was planning.

"You're taking the rape case, aren't you?"

Garrett's question jerked her sharply back to the present, and she looked at him. "What do you know about that?"

"More than most folks, I guess. I was part of the search party, and I wasn't far behind when Nate found the little girl. I heard they made an arrest this afternoon. I figured that's what you were doing at the jail. Am I right?"

She nodded slowly. "Nate wants to keep this under wraps for a few days, at least, so that the little girl's identity doesn't come out."

"I know. Believe me, I wouldn't discuss it with anyone except you or one of the other deputies. Are you sure you want to get mixed up in this, Sandy? It could get really messy."

"That's a chance I have to take." She hesitated only a moment before adding, "I honestly don't think they've got the right man."

He whistled softly. "Now, that *will* get messy. Do you have any evidence for that?"

She shook her head. "Gut feeling."

"Sandy..."

She shook her head. "You look into that man's eyes when he tells you he didn't do it, and then you tell me he's lying."

He leaned back in his chair and regarded her steadily for long, silent moments. "Okay," he finally said. "Okay. You believe him. How are you gonna prove it? From what I'm hearing, the deck is heavily stacked against him."

"I'm going to need to find an investigator, I guess. But first I want to see what the physical evidence turns up, particularly the analysis of body fluids. The whole thing may become moot."

"Always that chance. But where around here can you find a private investigator?"

"God knows. I'll probably have to bring in someone from elsewhere."

There was another noticeable pause before he cleared his throat and said, "You could ask me. I wouldn't mind taking a little busman's holiday. I'm going out of my gourd with next to nothing to do." One corner of his mouth curved up. "I guess I'd better develop some hobbies before retirement hits me between the eyes, but for right now... right now I'd like to be busy doing what I do best. So if you decide you need someone..."

"I might take you up on it, Ranger." There wasn't a doubt in her mind that he would be the best investigator she could hope to find. He might be difficult to deal with at times, and he might get under her skin, but he was definitely the best man for the job... assuming he could keep an open mind.

"This would be different from your usual investigative work," she reminded him. "You're used to looking for evidence to prove someone's guilty, not trying to find proof that someone didn't do it."

"Comes down to the same thing in the end, Counselor. I've almost never worked on what you could call a cut-and-dried investigation. A lot of the time I start out with a handful of clues that don't point to any particular person. I use that evidence to give me some idea of who might have done it. Sometimes I come up with several suspects, and then have to get together enough information to nail one of them. This really wouldn't be any different. I'd look for something that didn't fit with the theory that this guy did it, and from there I'd start looking for who might have done it. You don't just look for proof of innocence—you look for evidence of who *really* did it."

"I don't need proof of innocence to get him off. I just need enough to raise a reasonable doubt in the minds of the jury."

"I know. But look at it from *his* perspective, Counselor. What good is it going to do to get him off if he can't live in this county because everyone still believes he's guilty? Nope, you'll have to find out who really did it if he's ever going to have a normal life again." He looked down and then raised his startling eyes to hers once again. "Assuming, of course, that he really *is* innocent. I could conceivably find more evidence that he's guilty."

"I'm aware that possibility exists." Of course it did. While she was inclined to believe Craig Nighthawk's protestation of innocence, she was experienced enough to know that he might be a world-class liar. As much as instinct told her that he was innocent, some little corner of her mind remained warily apart, alert for any indication that she was being used or misled.

"It always exists." He picked up his cup and took a swallow of coffee. "Most of the time the cops arrest the right guy, Counselor."

"But not all the time, Ranger. Ten percent of the time they arrest the wrong guy."

He nodded. "This may be one of those times. I'll have to see the evidence before I can say. I *do* have a great deal of respect for Nate Tate's police work."

"So do I. But there are a couple of things we have to get clear here, Garrett...in case I *do* take you on as an investigator. The first thing is, you're not the judge or jury. You don't decide anything from the evidence. If you make up your mind about this man's guilt or innocence from the evidence that's already been collected, you won't be any good to me. The other thing is attorney-client privilege. If you work for me, you'll be working for the accused and privilege will cover all your communications with him and all my communications with you about anything he tells me. You won't be able to repeat any of it anywhere."

"Even if he says he did it."

"Even if. So you'd better figure out if you can live with that."

He didn't answer immediately. In fact, he didn't answer at all. When he walked her back to her car, he said only, "I'll think about it, Counselor."

He wouldn't be able to live with it, she thought as she started her car and watched him walk down the street toward his own. He was a lawman, accustomed to a suspect's every admission to build a case against him. He wouldn't like the idea of privilege extending to an admission of guilt. But then, few people found that notion palatable. It was something an attorney learned to live with, but something only a lawyer or a priest could understand.

Feeling thoughtful and just a little blue, she backed out of the parking slot and turned her Volvo toward her office. She had a lot of thinking to do, and she would do it best among her law books.

Nina had cleaned the coffeepot and set everything out neatly for the morning. Sandy took advantage of it and started a fresh pot of coffee. It was going to be a long evening, she thought. The arraignment and bail hearing had to take place within seventy-two hours of Nighthawk's arrest, and she would need an argument to get a reasonable bail for him. She figured Sam Haversham wasn't going to want the man released at all and would argue for extraordinary circumstances.

Judge Williams would be inclined to give Haversham what he wanted, too, given that even by Nighthawk's own admission, his only tie to Conard County was the property he'd bought out on Willis Road. It would have been helpful if he'd paid the mortgage off, but as it stood, he had twenty-eight years left on a thirty-year mortgage. Hardly an unbreakable tie for a man accused of first-degree sexual assault. He didn't have any family in the area, didn't belong to any local church, didn't have friends who could vouch for his reliability. He was an enigma, and even after talking to him, Sandy didn't feel she knew a darn thing about him.

He was at least part Indian, to judge by his appearance and his name, and by the fact that when she had asked about a church affiliation he had said he belonged to the Native American Church. Which wouldn't help his case at all if word got out, because peyote was one of their sacramental practices, and to most white folks that would mean he was a drug abuser. Thank goodness his religious affiliation wouldn't be legally admissible in court . . . not that that would necessarily keep people from finding out.

Nothing was going to help him, she found herself thinking sourly. Nothing. Judge Williams would probably deny bail because of the seriousness of the charges and the fact that there was no way to guarantee that Craig Nighthawk would hang around for the trial.

And that might truthfully be best. She didn't think his hide would be worth a plugged nickel once folks around here found out he'd been charged with raping a five-year-old. If Lisa Dunbar's dad didn't go after him, some other hothead would. Frontier justice hadn't been gone so long in these parts that it was forgotten. And too many folks just naturally assumed that only the guilty were arrested—which was far from the truth, but not something that could be argued with a lynch mob. No, Nighthawk was probably considerably safer where he was.

He wasn't going to like it, but she decided she would suggest to him that he should refuse bail even if it were granted. It wasn't as if he would be able to work if he were out of that cell. He was an interstate trucker, and there was no way on earth he could haul loads cross-country when he was forbidden to leave the county, which he would be while out on bail. No advantages and plenty of disadvantages to freedom, then.

Sighing, she reached for one of her casebooks and looked up the Ironshell case. That was a rape case involving a minor, too, and there had been an interesting decision by the Federal Appeals Court having to do with excited utterances. And that was an issue she needed to address before the trial, to see if she could find a way to get the judge to bar Nate Tate's recollection of Lisa's statements.

She wasn't holding her breath on this one, though. And if Nate were allowed to repeat Lisa's description of her attacker, Craig Nighthawk wasn't going to stand a chance in hell . . . unless they could find out who really had committed the crime.

Thumbing through the casebook, she hardly saw the words on the pages before her. In her mind's eye she was seeing Garrett Hancock as he had looked sitting across the table from her in Maude's. Hard to believe that the man she'd had dinner with was the same man who had accosted her in court earlier and practically accused her of using technicalities to get the guilty off.

Hard to believe he had volunteered to help her investigate this case. She would have taken him for the type to believe that the sheriff must have arrested the right man. And maybe he was. Maybe he was just offering to help because it would be interesting, not because he believed he would turn up anything that would exonerate Nighthawk.

Did it make any difference what he believed? Texas Rangers were sort of the FBI of Texas, renowned as investigators, called in to handle the most difficult major cases. She couldn't ask for a better investigator. And she felt that Garrett had enough integrity to do the job right, regardless of what he believed.

Well, she told herself, this all might become moot if the physical evidence proved that Nighthawk couldn't have done it. A sperm sample might settle the entire case.

Maybe.

In the meantime, she had to ready every weapon in her arsenal, and the first thing she had to do was see how she could get the judge to suppress Nate's testimony about what Lisa had said. And then, if she and Garrett were going to investigate this case on their own, they were going to need time, which meant finding a way to postpone the trial date for as long as possible.

Forcing her attention back to her law books, ordinarily one of her favorite occupations, proved surprisingly difficult. Garrett Hancock's face seemed to float before her on every page, a handsome man who couldn't possibly be interested in her, and who had to be too young for her, anyway.

"Lord, Sandy," she muttered under her breath. "Getting the hots for a good-looking guy at *your* age. Don't you know better?"

Apparently she didn't.

Chapter 3

In the morning, just as she had anticipated, the jury listened with stony faces to what little defense her client and his mother could provide. Twenty minutes after withdrawing to the jury room, they were filing back into the courtroom with their verdict of guilty. Les Walker returned to the county jail to await sentencing.

Back at her office, she found that the Nighthawk case was moving forward. That morning at the ex parte hearing, the judge had approved the prosecutor's complaint against Craig Nighthawk, which essentially meant that Sam Haversham had established, to the court's satisfaction, probable cause for Nighthawk's arrest. Another message told her that the bail hearing would be held that afternoon at three-thirty. A copy of the complaint filed by the D.A. would be delivered to her that morning.

And Nina, having learned from Sam Haversham's secretary what the case was about, was frowning disapprovingly.

"You shouldn't touch this case," Nina scolded, following Sandy into her office. "You have to *live* in this county. If you get that man off, nobody will ever forgive you!"

Sandy dropped her briefcase on her desk and wondered if there might be some legitimate reason to try to get in touch with Garrett Hancock today. The sad fact was that she'd fallen asleep thinking about him last night and awakened this morning with his face before her eyes. She had it bad, and somewhere between her first cup of coffee and getting to court this morning, she had managed to convince herself that the best cure would be an overdose of the man. The reasoning sounded weak, even to her.

"Look, Nina," she said, facing her secretary of twenty years, "if he gets off, I won't be the only one involved. There'll be a judge, and probably a jury."

"Do you think anyone will care about that? Nope. They'll be sure you pulled some fancy legal trick."

"Of course," Sandy said dryly, "there couldn't be any possibility that the man is innocent."

"Of course not—" Nina broke off abruptly and stared at her boss with widening brown eyes. "Are you saying this guy didn't do it?"

"That's what he says."

Nina shook her head sharply. "No! Damn it, boss, that's what they *all* say!"

"Not all of them. Very few, in fact. But it doesn't matter, anyway, Nina. I don't believe all of them. I *do* believe this guy."

"So what's the deal? He has three unimpeachable witnesses who can place him halfway across the continent at the time of the rape?"

Sandy ignored Nina's sarcastic tone and replied levelly, "No."

"Then you don't have a case. Sandy, Nathan Tate is a good policeman. If he says the evidence shows this guy did it—"

"Nate could be wrong," Sandy interrupted ruthlessly. "He may be good, but he's not infallible. Nor do they have a whole lot of evidence at this point. From the verbal information I've been given, I'm almost surprised the judge approved the complaint.''

''Well, that doesn't mean a whole lot, either,'' Nina said tartly. ''What *is* going to mean a whole lot is what folks around here will think!''

Sandy blew out an exasperated breath and flopped into the chair behind her desk. ''I'll tell you what's important, Nina! What's important is that the Supreme Court of these United States has said that under the Sixth Amendment, the accused has a right to counsel. The right to an attorney. Craig Nighthawk, whether he's guilty or innocent, is entitled to the best defense an attorney can provide for him.''

''You don't have to be the attorney!''

''That's not the point! The point is that he's entitled to one. He asked for me. But even more importantly, the point is that guilt or innocence is not decided by me, nor is it decided by *you*. Neither of us is judge or jury, and the mere fact that Nate Tate arrested this man is the poorest excuse I can think of for a conviction! Innocent people *do* get arrested, and without a fair trial there's no way to be certain beyond a reasonable doubt that *any* person is guilty! Nina, you've worked with me for nearly twenty years. I'm sure you understand that by now.''

Nina shook her head and sighed exasperatedly. ''Forget I said that. The point *I'm* trying to make is that you might have to leave this county if you win this case! Let some other lawyer do this.''

Sandy felt herself softening as she always did when someone expressed concern for her; she'd certainly had little enough of that in her life. But now was not the time to be swayed. Her principles were at stake here. ''Nina, I appreciate your concern, but I'm going to defend this man. Someone has to do it. If that means I have to leave Conard County—well, that would be a shame. I prefer to think my neighbors are wiser than that, though.''

A Question of Justice 45

"Oh, they're wise enough," Nina muttered. "Wise enough. In a year or two they might get over it. But what about you in the meantime?"

"That's a risk I have to take."

"Well, I just hope you know what you're getting into."

"I do. Believe me, I do." Sure she did. She was putting everything she had striven for on the line. Conceivably she could lose everything she had worked for. Oh, not because the anger of her neighbors would make life too uncomfortable. No, because they could simply go elsewhere for their legal services. Boycott her. And this county was small enough that a boycott would probably succeed.

But this was ridiculous, she told herself, flipping open her briefcase. She was borrowing trouble. None of those things had occurred yet, and they might well never occur, especially if she could come up with sufficient evidence to get Nighthawk acquitted.

The phone on her desk rang once, a signal that Nina was putting a call through directly, without asking first if Sandy wanted to take it. Which meant the caller was either the Sheriff's Department, Sam Haversham or her son, Gerard. She was hoping it was Gerard. Instead it was Nate Tate.

"I thought I'd give you your druthers," he told her. "We're serving a search warrant on Nighthawk to examine his house and land. Since he's incarcerated, we're going to serve *you.* Do you want us to just drop it by your office, or—"

"I want to be present at the search."

Nate sighed. "I somehow figured you would. What's the point? You know I'm not going to plant anything."

"I want to see what you find, if anything. I want to see where you find it. And I want to know where you haven't looked."

"We're pretty much going to look *everywhere,* and it's going to take a few hours at the very least. The Dunbar girl's panties haven't turned up, among other things."

"Well, I have to be in court for the bail hearing at three-thirty, and before then I need to talk to my client."

"That sure as hell puts us on a *tight* time schedule." She could hear him drum his fingers on his desk, a rapid tattoo. "Okay. Come on over to see Nighthawk, and I'll serve you the warrant. Then we'll head out to his place. Come three o'clock, I'll bring you back in for the hearing...and I'll give my deputies a coffee break."

He didn't have to do any of this; as far as the law was concerned, Craig Nighthawk's house could be searched on that warrant with no one present except the deputies. Nate was certainly bending over backward for her, and she said so.

"No big deal," he said gruffly. "Believe me, I want this crud convicted for what he did to that little girl, and I want him sent up for a good long time. But I *don't* want his conviction to get overturned on appeal because I did some stupid little thing wrong."

Fifteen minutes later she was in the conference room of the Conard County Jail, waiting for Craig Nighthawk to be brought to her. Sam Haversham had left an envelope for her with the dispatcher, knowing that Sandy would be over sometime today to see her client before the first hearing. While she waited, she reviewed the formal complaint as it had been filed, with the attached copy of Nate's report. Her scalp prickled uneasily as she read.

"Do you know who hurt you, Lisa?"
"Bad man."
"Do you know his name?"
"No name. No name." Child became hysterical, crying and sobbing, needed to be calmed down. Questioning resumed some five minutes later in mother's presence.
"Can you tell me what he looked like?"
"Yes."
"Tell me, Lisa. What did the person who hurt you look like?"
"Big and mean."

"What color was his hair?"

"Black."

"Was it long or short?"

"I don't know."

"Did his hair come down this far? (Chin) Or this far? (Shoulders indicated)."

Child nodded that hair was shoulder-length.

A nod. On the basis of a nod, Craig Nighthawk was in jail. He certainly wasn't the only man in Conard County who had shoulder-length black hair. Sandy shook her head and read further.

It seemed that Lisa had indicated the man's face was "mashed," which the sheriff took to mean he was wearing some kind of mask. His face was dark, she said, but not black. The mask or the assailant's skin...they couldn't be sure, could they? Just because Craig Nighthawk had deep brown skin... She shook her head again.

The judge considered the evidence, meager as it was, to be sufficient to justify the arrest of Craig Nighthawk. But probable cause for an arrest was a far cry from winning a case in court. If the D.A. couldn't come up with any more than this, Craig Nighthawk would likely be freed at the preliminary hearing in a few weeks.

And then he would probably have to leave the county for a long, long time. Garrett had been correct, she thought. Nothing less than complete vindication was going to give Nighthawk his life back.

The door swung open to admit Craig Nighthawk, escorted by a deputy.

"Ring the bell when you're through," the deputy told Sandy, then left the room. The sound of the heavy bolt being driven home was loud in the silence of the conference room.

"How are you managing?" Sandy asked Nighthawk.

"Okay." He shook his head. "Not okay. I'm so mad I could bust a gut!" He jumped up from the table and started pacing. "I didn't do it. I didn't *do* it! What am I doing stuck in a stinking jail cell?"

It was sure going to be fun to try to convince this man to refuse bail if it was offered—which she doubted it would be. Watching him pace, she felt a great deal of sympathy for his plight and could understand the anger he must feel. But that wasn't going to get them anywhere.

"We need to talk, Mr. Nighthawk. We need to discuss matters calmly if we're ever going to get you out of this mess."

He paused, his back to her; then, with a stiff nod, he resumed his seat. "Sorry. I'm just real angry, and there's nobody but you to let off steam with."

"I can understand. I *do* understand. But we have more pressing things to deal with right now. Your anger may have to wait a while."

He gave her another nod, and a sigh escaped him. "Okay. What do we have to deal with?"

"A couple of things. First off, when I go downstairs the sheriff is going to serve me with a warrant to search your house and property for some specific items, among them the victim's underclothes. I told him I expect to be present during the search, so I'll be spending most of the day out there."

"All right. Damn it, maybe they'll believe me when they don't find anything! That kid was never in my house! Never on my property! At least, not with *my* knowledge."

"Well, it'll help if they don't find any more evidence that can implicate you even remotely. But by being there I can know exactly what they find as soon as they find it...assuming they find anything. That's especially important because I want to hire a private investigator, and he'll want to know what was searched and what wasn't, among other things."

"A private investigator."

Sandy waited a moment, letting him assimilate the idea. "It'll be expensive."

"Yeah. What isn't? You think it's necessary?"

"Let's just say I'd feel a whole lot better with someone
out there trying to find proof of your innocence, rather than
just trying to confirm what they already believe."

He looked away from her, as if restraining himself, then
nodded. "It's a hell of a choice, Ms. Keller. Run the risk of
spending most of the rest of my life in jail, or spend every
penny I've ever saved trying to stay free. Either way, it's
going to cost me damn near everything."

There wasn't much she could say to that, so she just
waited for him to deal with his feelings. When he finally
looked at her again, he appeared calmer. "Okay. Whatever
it takes. Where are you going to find a private eye?"

"There's a Texas Ranger vacationing up here. He says
he'll do it." Beneath the table she crossed her fingers, hoping Garrett hadn't changed his mind. "They're highly
trained investigators."

"I didn't know there were any Texas Rangers left."

"Ninety-six of them, I hear."

"Well, okay. Hire him. What else?"

"You'd better brace yourself, because you're not going to
like this at all."

"I haven't liked a whole hell of a lot since Sheriff Tate
knocked on my door and told me I was under arrest for the
rape of a little girl. What could be worse?"

"Not accepting bail."

The silence in the room was suddenly profound. Seconds
dragged interminably while Nighthawk didn't twitch so
much as a muscle. Sandy had expected almost any kind of
reaction but this. She'd been ready to deal with rage and
shouting, but not complete, stony silence.

When Nighthawk spoke, his voice was completely level.
Expressionless. "Why would I refuse bail?"

"In all honesty, I don't expect you'll get it, but if you do,
I want you to refuse it. Quite frankly, Mr. Nighthawk,
you're safer in jail. Word of the charges against you is going to spread across this county like wildfire after the hearing this afternoon."

"And my life won't be worth a plugged nickel."

"It's an unfortunate possibility that someone might try to take matters into their own hands, yes."

He nodded. "Yeah. Yeah, it's a possibility." His mouth drew into a tight line, and he shook his head, as if the injustice were beyond words. "Just how long do I have to sit in this cell? Damn it, I didn't do anything wrong!"

His frustration was palpable. Sandy felt a great deal of sympathy for him, but there wasn't anything that could be done. "I'm sorry, Mr. Nighthawk. Truly. But the judge approved the complaint against you this morning, and at present there is absolutely *nothing* we can do except try to find evidence to prove you didn't do this. Until then, the safest place for you is in the Conard County Jail, sorry as that is. I wish it weren't that way, but if wishes were horses..." She shook her head and left the old aphorism incomplete.

"I know. I have to face reality." His jaw worked tensely for several moments before he spoke again. "Indians learn that early."

"I don't think your arrest has anything to do with your race, Mr. Nighthawk."

He fixed his dark eyes on her. "No, I don't think it does. That isn't what I meant. Surprisingly enough, I don't think my race motivated the sheriff. That's about the only positive thing I have to say about any of this mess, though."

Sandy nodded. "Okay, then. I'll accept the warrant, check it out and accompany the sheriff out to your place for the search. If I can get the investigator to go with me, will that be all right by you?"

He shrugged. "At this point I don't seem to have any privacy left. Why not? Anybody you want can go through my stuff. The sheriff's going to do it anyway. What's another person or two?"

She didn't need him to spell out the feeling of violation this had left him with. The tragedy was that he didn't deserve any of this. At least, she hoped he didn't.

Ten minutes later she went downstairs to get the warrant and was glad to find Garrett Hancock down there talking to

Nate. Too good-looking for his own good, she told herself as she felt her heart give a little leap. A striking man, not conventionally handsome, but certainly enough to catch *her* eye. Yeah, she really needed this right now.

"What did you decide?" she asked him point-blank.

"I'm still volunteering."

"Then you're hired."

Nate interrupted the rapid exchange. "Hired for what?"

"Garrett's working for the defense as a private investigator on the Nighthawk case."

Nate turned and looked fully at the Texas lawman. "Why?"

"It'll keep me out of trouble while I'm here."

It was evident to Sandy that Nate didn't like the answer, but there wasn't much he could say about it. "Just remember you're a private citizen up here."

"I won't forget, Nate."

Nate turned to Sandy. "And don't you forget he's not a licensed P.I. Call him a research assistant or something, will you?"

"No problem. And I presume you don't have a problem with him coming along when you perform the search?"

Nate shook his head. "Fine by me. Just keep out of the way, both of you."

Willis Road was about twelve miles out of town and a long way from Lisa Dunbar's home. Garrett owned a four-wheel-drive Explorer, better for the rural roads after last night's snowfall, so they agreed to take his vehicle rather than her Volvo. With a smile he handed her the keys.

"You know a heck of a lot more about driving on snowy roads than I do."

His willingness to admit that warmed her. In her experience, admittedly not the broadest in the world, men were reluctant to admit a woman might know more about or have more skill at anything except cooking and cleaning. Her ex-husband, an attorney at the Cheyenne firm where she had worked, had been like that. He had considered her utterly inept, little more than a glorified legal secretary. It wasn't until they'd been married several years that she had finally realized his attitude toward her had been based on her sex, not on her knowledge or her ability.

Since then she had seen many examples that proved her husband was far from atypical. Some men seemed to be determined to deprive a woman of every vestige of self-confidence, as if only her total dependency on them could satisfy them. Sometimes it was just a subtle but corrosive condescension that slowly ate away at her belief in herself; other times it was open scorn. Coming as it did from someone the woman loved, it was eventually crippling. It had taken her years to reconstruct her self-esteem and self-confidence in her legal abilities alone. In other areas she had never recovered.

Not every man seemed threatened by a woman's knowledge or skills, of course. Nate Tate certainly wasn't, nor was Sam Haversham. And Garrett Hancock's remark about her ability to drive on snow seemed to indicate he was not that kind of man, either. It was nice to think he was confident enough of himself not to be threatened by other people's abilities.

Not that it mattered, she reminded herself sternly. He was heading back to Texas in a couple of weeks, and it was absolutely certain that he intended to head back alone. There was no point in allowing herself to even think otherwise.

Besides, even if he weren't heading back to Texas, he still wouldn't want her. She was a plain woman in her late forties who knew from long experience that men didn't find her attractive. And this one, who must be a decade younger than she was, couldn't possibly be interested in her at all. He was just being nice because he regretted his outburst after the adjournment yesterday.

That settled in her own mind, she forced her attraction to Garrett into the back of her mind. For the umpteenth time. Her attraction to him had a damnable way of resurrecting itself.

* * *

There was little enough in the scenery to hold Garrett's attention as he and Sandy drove out to Craig Nighthawk's place. He wasn't sure why he'd been crazy enough to volunteer for this job, but he had a pretty good idea that it involved one slightly bristly lady lawyer—the one sitting beside him, to be precise.

Oh, he was three kinds of fool for even thinking about it. He knew damn well that she wouldn't be interested in going to Texas, and he wouldn't be interested in giving up the rangers, so there was no point to it. He'd never been one for brief affairs.

But if the the only problem in a relationship with Sandy were whether she would move to Texas, he would have been willing to take it on. A compromise satisfactory to both of them might have been difficult, but not impossible.

No, it was experience that made him reluctant to pursue his attraction. He'd had two serious relationships in his life, both of them with women he'd been ready to marry. One of them had lasted right up until a week before the wedding, when he'd been involved in a shoot-out that had convinced Janine she couldn't live with a man who put his life on the line, even if it only happened once in a blue moon.

The other relationship had been just as damaging. Maybe more so, because it had struck at the kind of person he was. Being a cop was not something he did for forty hours a week. It was his life. He ate, slept and breathed it when he was on a case that required it; anything else and he would never have been a ranger. Shortly after he'd gotten engaged to Wanda, he'd become involved in a big drug case that had demanded his every waking hour and some of his sleeping ones, as well, for a couple of months. Then, no sooner had they closed that investigation than he'd been assigned to a major police corruption case that had kept him on the streets till all hours of the morning. Within six months, Wanda had returned his ring, leaving him devastated.

Since then he'd considered himself a confirmed bachelor, steadfastly refusing to give any woman access to his heart. The simple fact was, when he fell, he fell hard, and being rejected left him feeling gutted. He was a two-time loser who was bound and determined never to give another woman a good shot at him. The thought brought a wry smile to his lips and drew his attention back to the woman beside him. He should be feeling safe, he thought. She wouldn't give up her career to come to Texas, and from what he'd heard, she hadn't even dated much in the twenty years since her divorce. She probably didn't want to put her neck in that wringer again any more than he did. That being true, she posed no threat.

He couldn't quite put his finger on whatever it was about her that attracted him. He'd been pondering the matter, because he didn't like to act without a clear-cut reason and didn't like to feel things he couldn't explain. Part of an investigator's mind-set, he sometimes thought—there had to be a reason for everything.

She was a little older than he was, maybe five years. Didn't bother him at all, nor did it surprise him that the age difference didn't bother him. Such things had ceased to matter to him a long time ago. What he did notice was the sparkle in her fine hazel eyes, eyes that had the clear-sighted gaze of the honest and honorable. He liked those funny little half eyeglasses she perched on the tip of her nose whenever she had to read, and wondered if she'd picked them to make herself look more sober and serious, especially in court. He'd gotten his own first pair of reading glasses just a couple of months ago and understood the dilemma involved in choosing something that changed your face so radically. Yeah, she'd probably picked hers to enhance her image in court. They were kinda cute, he thought.

He liked the way she hadn't colored her gray-streaked hair. It took guts for a woman to admit her age, but Sandy Keller made no bones about it that he could see. The gray in her hair was pretty, as pretty as the smile lines around her eyes and framing her mouth. He never could understand why Madison Avenue forced the smooth face of youth onto the world. Character and living were what built a face and told a story. You could look at Sandy Keller and see that she was a warm, generous person who liked to smile. And who frowned when she concentrated, to judge by the little line between her brows.

So he liked what he saw. He even liked the way her waist had thickened a little since back when he'd met her the first time. Made her look more womanly. It was a waist a man could enjoy squeezing. And when all was said and done, the woman had a hell of a calf and looked sexy as all get-out in those narrow little skirts she liked to wear to court.

It had tickled him to death the other day when he'd caught her slipping her shoes off under the defense table and rubbing the arch of one foot with the instep of the other. Poor little lady probably needed a foot rub like mad by the end of a day on those heels of hers.

And then there was her intelligence. He'd never liked a woman with a block of wood for a head. Or a man, for that matter. A little native intelligence was always helpful. In this woman's case there was considerably more than mere native intelligence. He wondered if she had any idea just how bright she really was. Probably not. She didn't seem to be at all full of herself, which was another thing he liked a whole lot about her.

She probably didn't know it, but her eyes would settle on him sometimes and then leap quickly away, as if she were afraid of being caught looking—and that told him as clearly as anything that she wanted him, too. Otherwise she wouldn't have been afraid of being caught looking at him. And that realization pleased him more than he felt really comfortable with.

Simple fact was, nothing could come of this, and he damn sure didn't want to get involved, anyway.

But that didn't stop a man from noticing and didn't stop him from wishing. Nor did it stop a woman, he thought with an inward smile as he returned his attention to the snow-covered countryside. He wondered if Sandy might be interested in a little innocent fun over the next couple of weeks. He didn't think she was the type to go to bed with a man she didn't feel committed to, but then, he wasn't that type, either. So maybe they could just date casually and make this cold gray spring a little warmer. Make the evenings a little more pleasurable. A harmless flirtation.

Sounded good to him.

Craig Nighthawk's house was set well back from the road, not visible to passing traffic. Nor was any activity along the road visible from the house and barn. Garrett commented on that as they turned off Willis Road and into the untouched driveway, identifiable only by the open gate at the roadside and the parallel rows of snowdrifts left by a winter's worth of plowing. Sandy followed the three sheriff's vehicles, feeling as if they were bucking from one rut to the next. Nighthawk needed to grade his driveway.

"What difference does that make?" she asked Garrett, her voice breaking as they struck yet another rut.

"Just that someone could have come off that road and buried something on Nighthawk's property, and chances are he'd never see 'em."

"And?"

"And it's just bugging me that the little girl's clothes were found on his property. Ask yourself, Counselor, if you'd bury the evidence on your own property."

Sandy shook her head. "*I* wouldn't, but don't forget the guy who gave the bank teller a holdup note written on his own deposit slip."

"Or the one who used a taxi for his getaway car and gave the driver his home address." Garrett chuckled and shook his head. "I know. I've met plenty of them. Does Nighthawk strike you as stupid?"

"Actually, no."

"Me neither."

"When did you meet him?"

"During the search for the little girl. We let him know we were searching his property for a missing kid. Came right out to help. Of course, a guilty man would have done the same. That doesn't mean anything at all. But I had a chance to talk with him for a few minutes here and there, and he didn't strike me as a fool. Or as a nervous man, come to that."

"And you've been thinking about that."

"Yep. Since we talked about it yesterday, I've been thinking over how he acted the night of the search, and it just doesn't strike me as the behavior of a guilty man. I've been wrong before, though."

"I'd like to find the truth. Honestly, Garrett, I'd really like to find the truth. That's something a defense attorney rarely knows and isn't supposed to care about. Defending someone rarely involves seeking the truth about what happened. My job is to make sure the defendant gets a fair trial under the law, and the decision made by the jury is one of guilt or innocence. I imagine most of the time we get a pretty clear picture of what actually happened, but that's a far cry from trying to discover the *truth*. And my job, or the prosecutor's job, is certainly not to *prove* the truth." She shook her head slightly. "Just once I'd like to know what the truth is, and in this case more than ever. If that man is innocent, this is one time when *innocence* will have to be proven beyond and to the exclusion of any reasonable doubt. Like you said last night, he'll never have any chance at a normal life here otherwise."

"So we do our damnedest to find the real culprit?"

"That's the idea." She glanced at him. "Did you think I wanted you to do something else?"

He shifted a little on the seat. "I just wasn't sure what I was supposed to do if something comes up that looks bad for your client."

"*Our* client, Ranger. Our client. What you do is tell me about it. I don't believe he did it, Garrett, but if he did, well…I want to know that, too. This time I definitely want to know that."

"That could make things uncomfortable for you."

"I'm not worried about that. But attorney-client privilege only covers what my client tells me. It doesn't cover physical evidence. I can't obstruct justice any more than the next person."

"That considerably relieves my mind."

She glanced at him and smiled. "I kinda thought it might. No, we're no more in the business of suppressing evidence than anyone else. Just remember, anything Nighthawk tells us *is* privileged, and we can't repeat it."

"I can live with that."

Craig Nighthawk owned his own rig, a big black Kenworth to which was attached a fifty-foot trailer bearing the logo of a national transportation company. It was parked in the barn, which had been converted into a garage cum workshop. From all appearances, he also did all his own work on the truck.

"This seems a mighty strange place for an independent trucker," Garrett remarked. "How many big loads go out of this town?"

"He's got a regular hauling job with a big trucking firm. They hire owner-operators all the time."

He gave her a sheepish grin. "I'd forgotten that. But it still seems like a mighty strange place to call home. He must drive a long way to pick up a load."

She turned to look fully at him. "You can question him about that if it seems significant."

"Maybe I will, Counselor. Let's see what else turns up first."

The sheriff searched the truck first but found nothing of significance there. "Looks like he cleaned it up getting ready for another haul," Nate remarked. "Hell, the rug in the cab has even been vacuumed."

The compartments in the cab yielded nothing of interest, either.

The house, a single-story ranch, had the sterile look of a hotel room.

"Man doesn't spend a whole lot of time here," Garrett remarked quietly to her.

The only things that gave evidence of occupancy in the main part of the house were a rinsed-out coffee mug and spoon in the kitchen sink, some cereal and coffee in the cupboard, and cold cuts in the fridge. Not much. There were no family photos in the living room, no sign of personality or habitation. The back of Sandy's neck began to prickle uneasily, and more than once she glanced at Garrett to find him looking doubtfully at her.

"He's not here much," she whispered to him as deputies checked beneath the sofa cushions and chairs, and behind the curtains.

"Yeah." Still looking doubtful, he kept his attention on the searching deputies.

Sandy found she had wrapped her arms around herself, a sure sign of uneasiness. This didn't look good, she thought. A home shouldn't be sterile, not even when it was only occupied for a couple of days a month. Had she been a complete fool? Was the man simply an accomplished liar?

"I don't like this," Nate said finally, looking Sandy right in the eye. She didn't reply.

They moved down the hall, finding two bedrooms that didn't contain any furnishings. Even the closets were empty. The next room appeared to be his bedroom, with a neatly made iron bedstead that looked old enough to be a relic from the last century, complete with nicks and dings. The dresser was small, four drawers on wooden legs. A deputy searched it minutely while Nate and Sandy watched. Little there but clean underwear and neatly folded T-shirts.

In the very bottom drawer, however, they came across a photo album, one of the old-fashioned kind with black pages and little black corner-holders that had to be glued in place. Black-and-white photos covered every page, and many were tucked in between pages.

"Family photos," Nate said, as they flipped through the album.

For an instant Sandy considered objecting, because it was highly unlikely that they were going to find a little girl's underwear tucked into the pages of a family photo album. Strictly speaking, there was no need for the deputies to even look. But she held her tongue, because they could legitimately argue that a tiny pair of underpants could be tucked almost anywhere, and a photo album would be a likely hiding place. Chances were a judge would uphold the deputies on that one.

At least they tucked the album back safely before they continued their search. In fact, the entire search was respectful of Nighthawk's property. Everything that was disturbed was returned to its original condition.

Next came what appeared to be a combination of hobby room and office. A huge sand table dominated the room. It had been carefully contoured into hills and valleys, and miniature trees dotted it. What really caught Sandy's attention, though, were the exquisitely crafted and painted tin soldiers that had been positioned on it.

"He's a war-gamer," Garrett remarked. "A really serious one, to judge by this. Almost nobody bothers with sand tables anymore."

"Looks like Austerlitz," Deputy Beauregard remarked. "Those are French and Austrian uniforms from the early part of the nineteenth century."

Nate cocked an eye at him. "You a war-gamer, too?"

Beau shrugged. "I read a lot of military history."

"Boss!"

They all turned in response to the excited exclamation from Ed Dewhurst, who had just opened a rolltop desk.

"Boss, come look!"

Sandy was right beside Nate as they hurried across the room. Her only thought was, *Please don't let it be Lisa Dunbar's missing panties*.

It wasn't. But it was almost as bad. Lying on the desk in plain sight was a color photo of a little girl, maybe two or three years old. She stood in a big metal washtub, and she was completely nude.

Chapter 4

Garrett and Sandy were nearly silent on the drive back to town. Nate had taken the photo of the little girl as evidence, and while it didn't prove a thing, it was damning nonetheless. Sandy's stomach felt queasy even as she tried to put an innocent explanation on it. She could hardly bring herself to look at Garrett, who must have been wondering what he had gotten himself into. She was afraid he was going to tell her that he couldn't continue helping her.

That thought upset her far more than it should have. After all, she could find another private investigator somewhere. But she wanted to work with Garrett, not with some stranger from Cheyenne or Laramie or wherever. The strength of her desire warned her that more than professional considerations were involved. She wanted the excuse to be near him, to see him, to talk with him. It was a purely selfish desire, the likes of which she couldn't remember having since high school.

Oh, it was ridiculous, she scolded herself. Absolutely ridiculous. She had more important things to occupy her time than her attraction to a man who would be leaving the

county in a few weeks. But she couldn't help stealing sur-
reptitious looks at him and wishing he weren't leaving.
Wishing he would turn those intensely blue eyes on her with
something more than friendliness.

But she had wished that before, and nothing had come of
it. All the lessons life had taught her still hadn't squashed the
girlish hope that somewhere there was a Prince Charming
for her, a man who could make each day a joy. A man who
could make her feel that she was important and needed. A
man who could make her feel loved and cherished. A man
who could grant all those foolish, girlish dreams that her
marriage had demolished with such careless precision.

Unwittingly she sighed, then realized it when Garrett
glanced her way. He was frowning, she saw, and she could
almost imagine him forming the words to tell her that he'd
changed his mind about working on this case. Instead,
astonishing her, he said, "I think you'd better ask Nighthawk about that photo. It doesn't look good."

"No, it doesn't." In fact, sitting there and thinking about
Prince Charming had been a great way to avoid thinking
about that very thing. She wasn't ordinarily the kind of
person who refused to look facts in the eye, but this fact was
more than a little unpalatable. The thought that she might
have been completely mistaken in her judgment of Nighthawk undermined what little self-confidence she'd been able
to amass in the years since her divorce. If she could be this
wrong about Nighthawk, then she couldn't trust her judgment about anyone.

Scary thought indeed.

"It could be purely innocent," she said finally.

"Given the reason he's been arrested, that's a little hard
to believe just now."

"I know." She hated to admit it, but she was too honest
to do otherwise. As an attorney she could see all too clearly
the difficulties such a photo would raise if presented to a
jury, and how hard it would be to overcome the doubts it
would plant. If that picture was innocent, they had to prove

it in such a way that it would never come before a jury as evidence.

Sam Haversham would undoubtedly try to get it admitted under Rule 402, claiming relevance because it showed a tendency toward pedophilia on the part of Nighthawk. Unless Nighthawk had a good story to explain the picture, she would have to argue from Rule 403 that the photo would excite prejudice in the jury. Somehow she didn't think she would win that one.

She sighed again and looked at Garrett, wondering what he was thinking. Here they were, confined by the cold day to this small space in the cab of his Explorer, and yet she felt utterly isolated. Which was stupid. She hardly knew this man, after all, but he seemed so far away right now....

He turned suddenly and glanced at her. "You have to be in court this afternoon, right?"

She nodded. "For Nighthawk's arraignment and bail hearing."

"Word of this is going to get out, Sandy. Nate's not going to be able to keep the lid on it much longer."

"I figure it'll get out this afternoon. Somebody at the courthouse will undoubtedly spill the beans, probably right into Kent Reed's lap."

"Kent Reed?"

"Publisher and editor of the *Conard County Sentinel*."

"Ah, the media."

Sandy was surprised to feel a smile tug her lips. "Yes, the media. Only I don't think Kent sees himself that way. He's not a caped crusader, merely somebody who likes to tell a story. Before Gutenberg, he would have been a troubadour, I think."

"I'm surprised he can afford to keep a paper going in a community this size."

"I don't imagine it's easy. He used to publish three times a week, but now he's down to once."

"So how long does that give us before the story is the talk of every household in the county?"

Us. His choice of word left her feeling weak with relief. *Us.* "So you're not quitting?"

"Quitting?" He glanced at her again and smiled slightly. "No. I figure he's guilty as sin, but the evidence will show that. All I'll be doing is looking for evidence. If it proves him innocent, well..." He shrugged one shoulder. "Wouldn't be the first time I've been wrong."

"Nor I." With an effort, she suppressed another sigh and looked out the window at the passing snowy countryside. "Well, if Kent publishes the story based on information he gets today, I would imagine it'll be on the front page tomorrow."

"That doesn't give us very long."

The muscle in his cheek was working, as if he were clenching and unclenching his jaw. "It's been nagging at me that whenever the news gets out, Nighthawk won't be the only person who could become a target."

She felt the skin on the back of her neck crawl. "I don't think..." The sentence trailed off as she realized that she *did* think it was possible that some person might actually choose her as a target if they couldn't get to Nighthawk because he was in jail. It sure wouldn't be the first time an attorney was threatened for defending an unpopular client.

"I didn't think that had occurred to you," Garrett said. "I've been in law enforcement a long time, Sandy, and I've seen plenty of lawyers threatened by people who hold them responsible. Take a case I saw just recently, where a prosecutor was sent a bomb because he didn't get some guy convicted in a rape case. Then there was the defense attorney who got shot at for getting an accused murderer off. Funny thing was, in that case the guy *was* innocent. We found the real perpetrator just three days after the acquittal. Problem is, too many people think that just because someone is charged, he's necessarily guilty."

"I've been saying that!"

"And I've been hearing you. You're right. Innocent people *do* get charged and tried. But guilt and innocence isn't the issue so much as what people perceive to be the failure

of the criminal justice system. Your neighbors are probably
going to see you as some slick lawyer who's going to try to
get a crud off on some technicality or other."

"They know better than that! I've lived here almost my
whole life!"

"And now you're defending a man who's accused of
raping a child. Sandy, they're going to believe Nighthawk is
guilty, and they're going to believe that you're somehow
standing in the way of justice. Oh, most of them will realize that isn't the case, but all you need is one nut. Just *one*."

She averted her face, looking blindly out at the snowy
countryside. She didn't want to think any of the people she
knew were capable of such things, but she couldn't deny the
possibility.

Garrett was right—faith in the criminal justice system had
never been lower. People were inclined to believe that anyone who was arrested was guilty. What they failed to remember was that, in many cases of acquittal, a jury—made
up of people just like themselves—hadn't been convinced of
the guilt of the accused. And when a defendant got off on a
so-called technicality, it was because the error was so serious that it had prevented an impartial trial. Those "technicalities" were the very things that prevented innocent
citizens from being beaten into confessing crimes they
hadn't committed, that protected ordinary people from being tried and convicted on the basis of lies or past behavior.
In reality, those "technicalities" protected the innocent
more often than they protected the criminal.

Most criminals didn't get off, despite popular opinion
after several highly publicized cases, such as one where the
defendants had actually been videotaped in action. Most
criminals who were caught were convicted.

But that was neither here nor there. The people of this
county had a great deal of faith in Nathan Tate, and if he
had arrested Nighthawk, then a good eighty or ninety percent of the people were going to believe that Nighthawk was
guilty. Which came right back to the necessity of finding the
real culprit. In this case, a verdict of not guilty wouldn't be

sufficient. Not when people believed that where there was smoke there was fire. Not when public outrage would demand that someone pay for this heinous crime.

And if people believed that Sandy might keep Nighthawk from paying, then they could well make her the scapegoat.

Garrett sat in the back of the courtroom, waiting for Judge Williams to make her appearance. Sandy was at the defense table, sitting with crossed legs and talking to Sam Haversham, who was resting one hip on the table and idly swinging his foot. It was apparent that however much those two might go toe-to-toe in the courtroom, there was a great deal of liking and mutual respect between them. That spoke well of them both, Garrett thought.

The courtroom was busier than usual this afternoon. Across the hall, the municipal court was, as always, busy with traffic court and small claims actions. Here, matters tended to proceed at a slower and quieter pace, as he'd noticed during his few weeks in the county. Crimes tended to be rather minor as a rule, most cases being more like Les Walker's burglary trial. Rarely was there more than a small handful of people present, most of them older folks.

But today it was different. Word had gotten out somehow; there wasn't a doubt in Garrett's mind. There were too many people for an ordinary arraignment and bail hearing. These folks had heard that something big was happening. So much for Nate's desire to keep things quiet for a little while.

The side door opened, and two deputies escorted a handcuffed and leg-shackled Craig Nighthawk to the defense table. The man's eyes burned, Garrett noted. Those dark eyes swept the courtroom with a kind of angry disdain. It was the look of a man who'd had his worst suspicions confirmed.

Garrett watched him with a policeman's eyes, wondering if the man was really guilty. Before he'd seen the photograph of the little girl, he would have said Nighthawk was probably innocent. The man had been too calm the night of the search; nothing about him had struck Garrett as being the behavior of a guilty man. And most guilty people telegraphed their nervousness and lying somehow. But not all. Not all. And that left the question of whether Craig Nighthawk was simply an incredibly good liar and a nerveless criminal. Though they were rare, they existed.

"All rise."

Judge Williams took her seat at the bench, and the hearing proceeded. The charges were read; Nighthawk was questioned as to whether he understood them. Sam Haversham argued against bail, pointing out that Nighthawk's ties to the community were very slender. It was Sandy who broke the ritual and sent an audible ripple of shock racing through the courtroom.

"The defendant waives bail, Your Honor."

The judge waited a few moments for the murmuring to die down before she spoke, this time directly to Nighthawk.

"Mr. Nighthawk, do you understand that waiving bail means you will remain in jail during the pretrial and trial periods?"

Nighthawk didn't even glance at Sandy. "Yes, Your Honor. I do."

"Is there a reason you prefer to waive bail?"

"It appears that I will be safer in jail than at home until this is settled."

Judge Williams looked down at the bench for a few moments, then returned her attention to Nighthawk. "Unfortunately, Mr. Nighthawk, I'm inclined to agree with you. This court accepts your waiver of bail. Defendant will remain in custody until such time as the charges against him are decided."

The courtroom emptied almost immediately, substantiating Garrett's suspicion that the people had come only because they had heard about the case. Another arraignment was scheduled to follow, but as it wasn't Sandy's case, she was free to leave. Garrett joined her, walking with her out into the cold, clear late afternoon.

"People know," he said.

"So it seems. It was bound to get out."

"Yeah." His breath created clouds of ice crystals, which sparkled in the slanting, almost golden, sunlight. "Sandy, I'm probably being overly protective, but I don't think you ought to go anywhere alone until this is settled."

She stopped walking and turned to face him. Most of the crowd from the courthouse had dispersed, and they were the only ones walking down Front Street. The homes lining either side of the street presented opaque windows and closed doors, creating a sense of privacy. Even the snow added to a sudden sense of isolation as it muffled all sound.

"I can't hide, Garrett," she said. "I can't allow myself to become a prisoner of fear. I learned that a long time ago."

He looked down at her, admiring her fine eyes, wide and clear and straightforward, and wanted to ask her how she had learned that lesson. Instinct warned him that it was not something she would be willing to discuss with a near stranger. "I'm not suggesting you become a prisoner of fear. Just asking that you be cautious. Instead of walking between the courthouse and your office this way, maybe you ought to take your car. Don't go out alone after dark. Just that simple kind of stuff."

For an instant she hesitated visibly. Then she shrugged and resumed walking. "For a woman, danger doesn't exist only on the streets, Garrett. It just as often exists in the home and among friends."

He stared at her back for a moment before he took a couple of quick steps and caught up with her. "What's that supposed to mean? I'm aware of domestic violence, but that's not the issue here. I'm worried about what one of your neighbors might take a notion to do if he starts to think you might get Nighthawk off."

"And I'm telling you that I refuse to live my life in fear. If I did that, I'd have to hide in a windowless, doorless room and never talk to anyone again!"

Her words struck him. Something about the words she'd chosen told him that she had faced fear, real fear, and conquered it. That she had measured in very real terms exactly what the cost would be of letting it control her.

His entire perception of her shifted sharply. For whatever reason, it had never occurred to him that she might have known serious hardship and fear. It gave him a better idea of just how much courage she really had and raised his estimation of her even higher.

It also made him even more concerned for her. Such courage was founded in innate strength, but it could also be very fragile precisely because it had once been so severely tested. There was simply no way to know in advance.

"I'm probably worrying too much," he admitted. "It's part of being a cop, to expect the worst of people."

They turned onto the sidewalk leading up to her office and climbed the steps onto the porch. "That's okay." She glanced up at him with a faint smile. "It's nice that you care. I just don't think folks around here are like that. They may get angry at me during the course of this case, but I honestly don't think anyone would attempt violence."

Violence, he thought as he escorted her inside, was not always necessary to create terror. Terror could be as intimidating as any actual threat of violence, and it could be just as psychologically damaging. It wouldn't take much for someone around here to scare Sandy half to death.

But he kept that thought to himself.

"Someone needs to open a Chinese restaurant here," Sandy told the empty room. The lack of Cantonese and Szechuan fare was about her only complaint about Conard County. Tonight, sitting on her living room floor surrounded by copies of all the prosecutor's files on the Nighthawk case, she was faced with a choice of canned chow mein or frozen pizza. Neither one tempted her.

She loved to cook, but cooking for one was a pain in the neck, and shopping for one was just about as bad. As near as she could tell, frozen foods were designed for one, but everything else was designed for three or more. It became tiresome to have to buy enough food for three and then repackage it . . . and then go to all the trouble to prepare a single stuffed pork chop. If she got the urge for lasagna, she made the smallest one she could manage, froze the left-overs in individual portions... and wound up eating lasagna for the next eight weeks.

Hence, frozen dinners, canned chow mein and French-bread pizza. Faced with that selection, she once again postponed dinner, even though her stomach was growling. The only other alternative was to go to Maude's, and she hated to dine out alone—even though she'd had plenty of practice at it. Besides, the night had turned blustery, and even in her cozy living room, with the curtains drawn, she could hear the rattle of snow blowing against the windowpanes.

The physician's report on Lisa Dunbar was uncomfortably graphic, even though it was couched in medical terminology: vaginal lacerations and contusions; bruises around her neck as if her assailant had choked her; assorted other cuts and bruises indicating that she had struggled and been struck; a mild concussion consistent with shaking.... Sandy felt her gorge rise, and along with it fury at a man who could do such things to a small child.

There was no doubt Lisa had been brutally raped, but whether physical evidence—vaginal swabs and nail scrapings—would yield any conclusive evidence about the identity of her attacker remained to be seen.

Which left a lot of circumstantial evidence. The girl's clothes had been found hastily buried on Nighthawk's property, the girl herself had been found along a stream bank just across the road from Nighthawk's property, and a photograph of a nude toddler had been found in Nighthawk's house. Other than that, there was a vague description of a man with a dark, "mashed" face and long black hair.

And not one other thing. What they had right now shouldn't be enough to convict. If genetic testing wasn't conclusive, then the jury shouldn't return a verdict of guilty. But the jury probably would, anyway. Sandy felt it in her gut, and knew that if she were on the jury and was presented with this crime and this evidence, it would be damn hard to maintain a reasonable doubt. An act of this nature cried out for retribution and punishment. She would need a lot more than Craig Nighthawk's protestations and a lack of definitive evidence to get him acquitted.

And now, in the privacy of her own mind, she could admit that, after finding the photo, *she* needed more than that, too. She didn't want to spend the rest of her life wondering if she had gotten a guilty man off merely for lack of evidence.

She wasn't sure she could live with that. The man who had hurt Lisa Dunbar deserved to go to prison for what he had done. But more than that, he had to go to prison to protect other little girls. It was a sad fact that people who committed crimes of this type rarely committed them only once. The man who had raped Lisa was a threat to every little girl he would ever meet. That couldn't be allowed.

So this time, lawyer or not, she needed more than a reasonable doubt. This time she needed proof. She needed to be sure that the real criminal was found and convicted. Her intuition told her that Nighthawk was telling the truth, and for that reason she would take the case. But beyond that, she couldn't allow intuition to guide her. This time she had to *know*.

After having lived for many years in the belief that it was not innocence that needed proving, but guilt, she found it strange to be taking the opposite position on this case. It was uncomfortable to realize that the principles she had always espoused were not enough this time. That she, like most of the rest of the world, needed definitive proof of innocence.

If Nighthawk wasn't guilty, then they had to find out who was. Discovering the real rapist was essential for so many reasons.

And if anyone could discover who'd really done it, she suspected Garrett Hancock could.

With a mental shake, she tried to drag her thoughts back to the file folder in her lap, but her stomach growled, and her mind wanted to wander down byways that involved Garrett. The man was taking up too much of her time, invading her thoughts at the most unexpected moments and making her want to moon over him the way she hadn't mooned over any man since her marriage.

Shaking her head again, she forced herself to start reading the paper in front of her. It was the physician's record of his interview with Lisa Dunbar, reporting the questions he had asked about her injuries and her responses.

"Was it a man who did this to you, Lisa?"
Child nods.
"A grown-up?"
Nod in response.
"Did he put something inside you here?"
"Hurt me!"
"Yes, I can see you're hurt, Lisa. It must have hurt very badly."

Just then the doorbell rang. Sandy hesitated, thinking that whoever it was could just go away. It had to be a salesman, because any of her friends would have called first. On the other hand . . .

Sighing, she put the folder aside and struggled to her feet, wincing as her legs protested a little from being folded up under her for so long. "Use a chair next time, Keller," she muttered to herself as she headed for the stairs. "That's what they invented desks for!"

For convenience' sake, her office and home were in the same house, with her office downstairs and her living quarters upstairs. Moving the kitchen upstairs had been the most expensive part of the transition, but it had given her a truly cozy apartment.

But it also meant that she had to descend the stairs into the darkened office to answer the doorbell, and even though she flipped on the stair light, she found herself strangely uneasy. All Garrett's talk about people getting angry at her, she thought, it must be working on her subconsciously, although she quite seriously believed she had nothing to fear from her neighbors, other than a few harsh words.

Rationalizing her uneasiness didn't keep her from peeking around the edge of the curtain that covered the window beside the door. A relieved breath escaped her when she recognized Garrett. What was he doing here?

It took her only a moment to throw the dead bolt and fling the door open. "Garrett! What's wrong?"

"Not a damn thing," he said with a wry half smile. "I went to Maude's for dinner and realized I didn't feel like eating alone. So..." He held up a big brown bag. "I talked her into making us some roast beef sandwiches and a salad. Please tell me you didn't already eat dinner?"

A laugh escaped her as the wind swept icy snow up from the yard and tossed it against her face. "Come inside before we both freeze!"

Garrett followed her upstairs. "So, you haven't eaten, have you?"

"No, I haven't. I was just trying to figure out which canned or frozen concoction I could stomach tonight. I'm famished!"

"Well, there aren't a whole lot of fast-food places around here to add to your options. I considered the drive-in for hamburgers, but then I decided Maude could do better than that. Wait till you see these sandwiches."

The sandwiches were as great as he'd said; Maude had spared nothing in their construction. Garrett's presence made her cozy apartment seem even cozier, and she began to enjoy the icy rattle of snow at the windows and the whistle of the wind around the corners of the house. It was a great night to be indoors.

"So what's that all over the living room floor?" Garrett asked while they ate.

"All the information the prosecutor has on the Nighthawk case."

"Can I look at it?"

"Sure." She felt a pang of disappointment that he was going to get absorbed in the files. It would have been nice to spend an evening just chatting and getting to know him. As soon as she had the thought, she warned herself to cut it out.

There was no room in her life for a footloose Texas Ranger. Besides, he would want sex, and she was no good at sex. Not since she'd been raped, for sure. She always got panicky and . . .

"What do you think of the case?" he was asking her. "Strong? Weak?"

"Weak. Very weak. Everything is so circumstantial without a positive ID. If Lisa pointed her finger, or if the physical evidence points to Nighthawk, then we've got serious trouble. But as it stands . . ." She shook her head. "It really shouldn't be enough to convict him."

"But you're afraid he might get convicted, anyway."

"Yes. I am. Juries are an unpredictable element in any trial. That's why the jury system is probably the best method ever devised for deciding guilt, because their decisions can be tempered with mercy. Unfortunately, they can also swing the other way, so I'm going to recommend that Nighthawk waive a trial by jury. I really think a bench trial would be a better choice for him, given the type of case and the weakness of the current evidence. However, I think Sam is going to insist on a jury."

"Can he?"

She blinked, surprised by the question, and then remembered that not everyone had her acquaintance with the inner workings of these things. A policeman probably wouldn't know about such maneuverings, since his part in them would be limited to being told when to appear to provide his testimony. "Yes, he can. The constitution guarantees a trial by jury only to the accused, but the Supreme Court has upheld the prosecution's right to insist on a jury trial. Given the emotions that are bound to surround this case and the weakness of the evidence as it stands now, Sam's best hope for a conviction is a jury. A judge would dismiss the whole thing at this point."

"Well, I'm sure they're going to come up with a lot more evidence before matters get that far."

"Probably. But I'm sure hoping *we'll* come up with some to exonerate him."

He had been just about to take another bite of his sandwich, but he paused and looked at her. "This is getting to you, isn't it?"

Reluctantly she nodded. "You've heard me spout off about the defense attorney's role in guaranteeing a fair trial under the constitution and the law, and how it's not my job to determine guilt or innocence, but only to make sure the verdict is reached based on legally admissible and legally sufficient evidence."

One corner of his mouth edged upward. "I've heard you."

"Well, I believe that. I really do. I kind of hang on to that like a floating log in the middle of a river, because most of the people I defend are as guilty as sin and I know it. But I have a job to do, a responsibility to uphold, and I can't afford to have nightmares about getting a guilty person off. But this time...damn it, this time I'm scared to death of the consequences if we don't get the guilty person behind bars. I have to *know* the truth!"

He nodded slowly and put his sandwich down. "Are you beginning to think Nighthawk might be guilty?"

Her head jerked a little, as if the question in some way astonished her. "No. Actually no, I still feel in my gut that he didn't do it. But that doesn't solve my quandary. My gut could be wrong, and I know it. That's the first problem. The other is, what if we don't catch the right guy? What if this happens to some other little girl because we tried to nail the wrong man ... or because we *do* nail the wrong man?"

"Yeah. I've been kind of worrying that around myself. I know Nate Tate thinks he has the right man. But ... well, I might have thought so, too, except that you're so sure he didn't do it, and there wasn't anything at his house except that one photo, so I'm wondering, too. By the way, did you ask him about that picture?"

"Of the little girl? Not yet. I only got to see him for that little bit of time in the courtroom, because they had an appointment to collect some tissue samples from him. I'll see him in the morning, and that's soon enough, I guess."

"I'd like to come with you, if you don't mind. I need a chance to talk with him."

"Sure. I don't think he'll object. I told him I was hiring you. Is there something specific you need to ask him?"

Garrett shook his head. "I just want a chance to watch his face and listen to his voice when he responds about the photo."

"A lie detector test?"

He smiled broadly at that. "Sort of. I'm sure you know just how much can be revealed by the subtle way a person reacts to things that make him feel uncomfortable."

She knew; that kind of perception was indispensable in the courtroom. Both the jury and witnesses had to be continuously monitored for those subtle shifts of eyes and posture that could betray everything from boredom to disbelief, emotional distress to lying. "Well, I'll have to ask him, of course, but I honestly don't think he'll mind talking to you."

Later they sat together on the living room floor and pored over the files. The doctor's report on Lisa was every bit as distressing to read as Sandy had anticipated, but she forced herself to wade through it even though her mind rebelled. And despite her distress, one thing was tragically clear: nothing Lisa had said in any way definitively identified her assailant. At this rate, whoever had committed the crime might very well walk free.

"It's not a whole hell of a lot," Garrett said as he set the last of the files aside.

"Enough to uphold the charge, but not enough to convict."

"A jury might convict, anyway."

"They might. It would probably get overturned on appeal, though. But we're far from through gathering evidence. I'm hoping against hope that the genetic testing proves unequivocally that Nighthawk didn't do it. That would settle it fast. But..." She chewed her lip and looked away.

"But you want the bad guy caught and put behind bars. Yeah. Me, too."

"I keep getting afraid that maybe people will stop looking for the truth because they think they have the right man in custody. That the real rapist will hurt another little girl. And that an innocent man will rot in jail."

"That's a concern in every serious case," Garrett replied, speaking slowly. "Most of the time the obvious suspect *is* the right one, but there are always cases where the immediately obvious isn't the correct choice. It's an investigator's nightmare. I don't think the Sheriff's Department will limit the scope of its investigation simply because they've made an arrest."

"That's the ideal, of course. The reality is that we see what we expect to see and are blind to anything that doesn't fit our preconceptions."

The crow's feet at the corners of Garrett's eyes deepened as he smiled. "Are you concerned that I might be blind?"

Her cheeks burned faintly for the first time in more years than she wanted to remember. Good grief, the man could make her blush! "I could be blind myself, Garrett. I keep wondering if I'm refusing to see something that's right under my nose, and it's driving me crazy."

"I don't think you're refusing to see anything. The evidence as it stands now isn't conclusive. As an investigator, I'd feel I'd hardly begun, and I imagine Nate feels pretty much the same. But it *is* enough evidence for an arrest and a charge. If the case doesn't get any stronger, then I imagine the charge will be dropped."

"I'm not so sure about that," she admitted glumly. "Public pressure to convict somebody may force the issue. It wouldn't be the first time."

"Now, that's borrowing trouble!" But he spoke gently, not scornfully, and edged closer to her.

Their shoulders brushed, and in a heartbeat Sandy found herself acutely aware of him as a man. He didn't wear cologne, so she was able to smell the soap in his clothes and on his skin, and underlying that, a delicious masculine aroma. In the most absurd way, she wished she could just close her eyes and inhale him.

But her eyes had to remain open, and because they did, they wandered over the parts of him she could see without being obvious. His legs, clad in starchy-looking jeans, stretched out before him on the floor, long, hard and lean. Cowboy boots, something he was apparently never without, disappeared under the jeans, so she couldn't judge the shape of his calves. But she *could* judge his thighs, and what she saw made her mouth go dry.

Garrett Hancock might be an urban cop, but he rode horses and rode them often. She recognized a cowboy's legs when she saw them; she'd grown up among cowboys, after all. Powerful legs, accustomed to tightening around a horse or standing in the stirrups.

Gads, when had she developed a thing for men's legs? When she'd looked in the past, she'd discovered a weakness for male posteriors. This was a new one.

A tremulous little sigh escaped her, and she forced herself to look away. No point thinking about it. She'd put the rape long behind her, but its aftermath—a husband who held her somehow responsible for the attack and a tendency to freeze up during sex—had convinced her that she was better off avoiding sexual entanglements. And for all these years she *had* kept clear of involvement. It wasn't that she never yearned for the warmth and strength of a man; it was that she didn't know if she could withstand another rejection in such a vulnerable state. Far better to keep her guard up. Far better not to sigh over powerful legs encased in sexy denim.

And denim *was* sexy, she thought with an inward smile. She wasn't sure what about it struck her that way, but it beat gray flannel hands-down any day of the week. Her fingers were just about itching to reach out and run over Garrett's thigh. The thought almost made her blush again.

That was when she became aware that Garrett was watching her, and something in his expression told her that his thoughts were wandering in the same direction.

The realization nearly stole her breath. When was the last time anyone had desired her? She couldn't even remember.

But suddenly a pair of blue eyes were trained on her with an intensity that left her almost light-headed. They wandered over her face slowly, leaving her feeling almost as if he were touching her gently. Her lips parted helplessly, just a little, in unconscious invitation. At once his eyes wandered to her mouth, resting there almost softly before moving on.

Please, Garrett. Please. She couldn't have spoken the words out loud—she couldn't have spoken just then to save her life—but when he drew a quick, sharp breath, she knew the plea was written on her face. For an instant she hung suspended in breathless anticipation, sure that he would kiss her.

But then his eyes drifted downward, slipping lazily across her sweater in a way that seemed to paint fire on her breasts. The caress of his gaze was almost as exciting as a physical touch, and when his eyelids began to droop and *his* lips parted, she felt a clenching thrill of arousal unlike any she had ever before known. This man unmistakably found her attractive.

But though his eyes wandered over her in an incredibly seductive manner, leaving her breathless and weak, he never touched her. She would not have believed it possible to be seduced by the way a man looked at her, but Garrett had done it effortlessly.

And when, slowly, so slowly, his eyes lifted once again to hers, she could tell by his faint smile that he was aware of it. But he didn't give her a chance to resent his knowledge. Instead he spoke in a husky voice that sent warm shivers running along her spine. "You're a beautiful woman, Sandra Keller. Beautiful."

She could have arched like a cat being petted. His words made her *feel* beautiful, and his smile seemed to reach deep within her to pluck a golden chord.

But much to her disappointment, he didn't kiss her. Didn't even touch her in the smallest of ways. Instead he sat up a little straighter and reached for one of the manila folders strewn about the floor.

"I guess we need to start thinking up a plan of operation," he said. "This investigation has to start somewhere."

For a moment so fleeting she felt it only as a pang, she nearly wept. And then she straightened her own shoulders and focused on the task at hand.

No man had ever really wanted her. No reason to think a miracle would happen at this late date.

Chapter 5

He squeezed the tennis ball until the cords in his arm stood out. The effort didn't help his mood any.

Sitting in his room at the Lazy Rest Motel, Garrett watched green neon blink outside his window as he did the exercises a sport physician had prescribed for him. Unbeknownst to anyone but himself, Garrett was fighting for his future. The accident had left him with nerve damage in his right arm, damage that kept his grip weak and his arm unsteady when he raised it. Fact was, he wouldn't dare fire a gun the way his arm was now, and if he couldn't fire a gun, he couldn't remain in law enforcement. They would give him a medical retirement the instant they heard about it.

So he had to be sure they didn't hear about it until he had no alternatives left. Holding the tennis ball in his right hand, he squeezed it again and again, working toward greater strength. The sport doctor he had seen felt there was a slim chance that he could encourage nerve regeneration by working out. It certainly couldn't harm him. So, slim though the chance was, Garrett exercised his arm religiously.

It seemed to be getting stronger, he thought as he watched his fingers tighten around the green tennis ball, then relax. It looked as if they were compressing the ball more than they had a couple of weeks ago. In his suitcase was a small device for measuring grip strength. He could take an objective accurate measurement right this very moment.

But he didn't. At the end of his convalescent leave, there would be an inevitable reckoning when he tried to go back to work. He would have to pass a rigorous physical before his return to duty, and that would be soon enough to know if his efforts amounted to anything. Right now he didn't want to risk discouragement, because it might make him feel that he was wasting his time. These exercises were the only thing he could do to help himself, so he was going to do them and leave the results in the hands of the Almighty.

At least the physicians who had cared for him in the hospital hadn't told his bosses that he would never be fit for duty again. They'd told Garrett it wasn't likely that he would ever recover full use of his arm, but they'd been vague with his bosses, saying that only time would tell.

But he didn't have a whole lot of time. In just a very few weeks, he might be taking his last shot at the job that was his whole life.

But he didn't want to think about that right now. Right now, about all he could think about was one sexy-as-sin attorney and the mess she was dragging him into. Just the way she had reacted when he looked at her had been enough to arouse him, and it had been extremely difficult to resist the offer implied by her gently parted lips.

But he knew himself far too well. When he fell, he fell hard and held nothing of himself in reserve. And when he was jilted, the pain was almost more than he could endure. It wasn't a risk he was prepared to take again, not after two bad experiences. Time had taught him not to open himself up and give himself so quickly, but whether he fell fast or slow, the cost of rejection would be devastating.

So he refused to fall. And he suspected that Sandy was no more in the market for a serious relationship than he was.

She had evidently managed to remain unattached for quite some time now, according to what Micah had been able to tell him. Sandy had divorced nearly twenty years ago and avoided entanglements ever since.

And that was another good reason for him to keep a safe distance. The woman plainly wasn't interested in involvement with *anyone*. Hell, she probably had as many good reasons as he did, and if he had half a brain he wouldn't be thinking about her. Nothing but pain lay along that path.

He squeezed the ball again and watched his hand tremble. An oath sprang to his lips, but he swallowed it. Swearing wasn't going to help matters, nor was getting frustrated and angry... although he was sorely tempted. Life had handed him the short end of the stick yet again, and while he ordinarily found self-pity disgusting, tonight he was tempted to indulge in just a little of it.

But he wouldn't. Self-pity was a waste of time and energy and never made anything any better. Instead he forced himself to think about the Nighthawk case.

After he had a chance to talk to Nighthawk tomorrow, he would be in a better position to know whether the man was an accomplished liar or an innocent victim. It wasn't that Garrett didn't trust Sandy's judgment, but he had a lot more experience with skillful liars than she could possibly have. It wasn't as if she dealt with criminals on a daily basis; he had. Most people were lousy liars, saying too much, being too quick with explanations... in general betraying themselves by revealing that they were aware they had something to explain or conceal.

But every so often a skillful liar came along, one who never volunteered anything, who never betrayed prior knowledge. A liar who could look you straight in the eye and feign both shock and innocence in exactly the right way. He'd questioned more than a few of them and had learned to detect them more often then not. Which was not to say he was never wrong, because of course he was, sometimes. But he would feel a whole lot better if tomorrow he reached the same conclusion as Sandy about Nighthawk's innocence.

Thinking about Sandy again. He exhaled a quiet breath of amused frustration and wished he still smoked. Wished he could reach for a cigarette and forget the warm heaviness that pooled in his groin when he thought of that woman.

And what a woman! Tonight he'd been frank in his perusal of her, letting his eyes fill themselves as they chose, and he had realized that every time he looked at her he wanted her even more. Insanity. Sheer insanity. It could be nothing but a mistake for both of them.

But she did have lovely curves, and that silk blouse she had been wearing had kind of slid over them in the slinkiest damn fashion every time she moved. He wouldn't be the least surprised, he realized, to discover that beneath that silk she had been wearing equally enticing lingerie. She looked like a satin-and-silk woman, despite the no-nonsense wool suits she wore. Heck, those high heels of hers gave her away. She was a woman who liked to feel feminine. If not, she would have worn flats of some kind. He would have staked his last dime on it.

But she wore those nice three-inch heels with her suits, a startling contrast to the half eyeglasses she peered at the jury over. He would be willing to bet that somewhere in her closet there was a pair of red heels. And maybe a red suit for special occasions. She sure would look nice in it.

And this was getting him nowhere. Damn it, why couldn't life be easy? Why couldn't he simply suggest they explore the attraction and then say adios once the fires had cooled?

Because he wasn't that kind of bastard. Because she wasn't that kind of woman. Because somebody would get hurt.

So he squeezed the tennis ball until the veins on his arm stood out and tried to think of all the questions he would ask Nighthawk tomorrow, if he had the chance.

If he had the chance. There were few enough of those in life. And Sandra Keller was a chance he wasn't going to take.

* * *

There was nothing like a man for ruining your sleep, Sandy thought irritably as she drove to the sheriff's office for her appointment with Nighthawk. Garrett was supposed to meet her there at eight, and she hoped he looked as exhausted as she felt. It would be nice to know his sleep had been as disturbed as hers.

Oh, this was ridiculous! At her age, to have been kept awake by yearnings she had buried a long time ago. To have lain in bed like a college girl, hugging her pillow and remembering every look, every word, every nuance. Remembering the way he had looked at her. The way his eyes had touched her with such intimacy.

With such approval.

Another errant thrill ran straight to her womb, causing her to clench deep inside. Approval. When you came right down to it, the approval Garrett's face had reflected was as sexy as anything she had ever seen. As a woman, she needed to know that she appealed to a man, to know that it was *her* he wanted and not just a convenient body. And it had been so very long since anyone had looked at her that way, as if they liked every line of her.

At her age!

Another thrill, softer this time, trickled through her. She couldn't afford this. She didn't have time for this, and she'd never been the type for a brief fling...although the notion was certainly appealing right now. If she could be sure she wouldn't get emotionally wounded, she might have a terrible time talking herself out of this attraction. But she knew better. Nothing but pain could come of a few weeks with Garrett Hancock.

Besides, she would actually have to test herself as a lover, and that was something she had steadfastly refused to do for a *long* time. After all these years, the pain of failure had faded, and it would be easy to forget what she already knew—just how deeply wounding it was to have a man look at her with pity. Or disgust. Or any of the other things a man thought when he found out that a woman was a lousy, inhibited and possibly frigid lover.

But even if Garrett didn't let her see those things, she would know she had failed when he didn't want her again. And she *would* fail. She had *always* failed.

And this was definitely not the time to be thinking of these things. Actually, there was no good time to think about her failure as a woman, a deep-rooted pain she had lived with for a long, long time. Better just not to think about it at all.

The sheriff's office was already bustling when she stepped in the front door. Shifts had changed, and the men who had been on graveyard were busy filling out reports. Nate Tate's voice drifted from his office at the back and was answered by Micah Parish's. Velma Jansen, the dispatcher, nodded from behind her console.

"Hancock's waiting for you upstairs, Sandy," she said.

"Thanks, Velma." So he was already here. The notion unsettled her for some reason. Silly to have hoped she would have a few more minutes to herself, a couple of minutes to prepare inwardly. Well, he was up there waiting, and there wasn't a darn thing she could do about it.

Upstairs, she found Garrett in conversation with the jailer. He looked over at her with the kind of smile one stranger gives another, and a brief nod. Irritation scorched her cheeks, ridiculous though it was. After the way he had looked at her last night, how dare he look at her now as if he'd never seen her before.

But, of course, he regretted the moments of intimacy they had shared, brief and fleeting though those moments had been. For just a few moments they'd both lowered their guards, and now they were both uncomfortable with what they had revealed. It was a silly way for two adults to act, and she knew it even as she gave him a distant smile and turned to follow the guard to the conference room.

"I have to make sure that Nighthawk is willing to talk to you," she reminded Garrett as she turned away.

"I know. I'll be right here."

Snow melting from the roof had formed an incredible fringe of icicles right outside the window of the conference room. One of them reached from the top of the four-foot barred window nearly to the sill and was so clear that the slanting morning sunlight made it glisten like a diamond. Beyond the window, the courthouse square was still quiet, buried beneath its blanket of snow. Only a flock of sparrows were to be seen, hopping around the base of the feeder the high school shop class had built and still maintained.

Behind her, the heavy steel door opened. She turned and summoned a smile for Craig Nighthawk. He looked like hell, she thought. He apparently hadn't slept, either.

"Good morning, Mr. Nighthawk."

He nodded briefly and waited for her to settle at the table before he sat facing her.

"Do you need anything?" she asked him. "Cigarettes...books...?"

He started to give a sharp, impatient negative shake of his head, then caught himself. "Sorry. I'm kind of irritable this morning."

"Trouble sleeping?"

"Yeah. Cages don't fit me. But that's not your problem. A book would be nice. Science fiction, maybe."

"Great. I'll get you A. L. Tierney's newest. She's almost your neighbor, but I guess you know that."

"No."

"Oh. Well, she's Amanda Laird. She and her husband run a sheep ranch not too far from you."

He nodded slowly, his eyes never wavering. "I met them once."

"Are you close to anybody at all around here?"

"Not really. I'm on the road most of the time. Just nodding acquaintances around here."

She wanted to sigh, but that wouldn't do any good, so she suppressed it. "Garrett Hancock is outside. He's the investigator I hired. Do you mind if he sits in with us? Anything you say in his presence will still be protected by privilege."

"I don't have a damn thing to hide, Ms. Keller." Impatience edged his voice. "Bring him in."

Nighthawk stood when Garrett entered the room. The men shook hands, and there was no mistaking the measuring way they looked at one another. Garrett stood in the corner, leaning his shoulder casually against the wall and folding his arms as he listened attentively.

"Why did you decide to move to Conard County, Mr. Nighthawk?"

"Because it reminds me of home, but it's prettier. Because the price was right on the ranch."

Sandy cocked her head attentively and waited. As she expected, after a moment, he continued.

"I was raised on the rez—reservation—in North Dakota. Once I managed to get away, I sure as hell didn't want to go back. But this is my part of the country. I like the wide-open spaces. The solitude. I heard about this place at a truck stop east of Des Moines, if you can believe it. This other guy and I got to talking about how we'd like to retire someday, and when I mentioned I wanted a ranch in the Dakotas or Wyoming, he sent me out this way to talk to a shipper who was trying to unload his parents' spread. Simple as that."

"Unusual choice for a bachelor," Garrett remarked.

Nighthawk looked up at him. "I was married once. Been there, done that, as they say. No desire to be a fool a second time, Hancock. I figured that once I could afford some cattle, I could get my sister's family down here to run the place while I'm away. I'd like her kids to have a better chance than I ever did."

Sandy felt an uneasy prickling at the base of her skull. He wanted to bring his sister's family here. Kids. Surely... She wouldn't even let herself complete the thought. It was too terrible. "There was a photo on your desk, Mr. Nighthawk. A photo of a little girl in a washtub."

He nodded. "My niece."

"The sheriff has taken it as evidence."

"Evidence?" He sat up straight. "Evidence! What the hell for?"

"She's . . . not wearing any clothes."

"Oh, for God—" He broke off, jumping up from the table so quickly that the chair slid across the slick tile floor and hit the wall. "Damn it!" He strode to the window and stood there holding the bars as he stared out at the brilliant day. "Damn it. Filthy minds!"

"Tell me about it," Sandy said gently after a moment.

"That's my sister Paula's daughter. Paula sent the photo in a letter I got the day before I was arrested."

"Where is the letter?"

He gave a quick jerk of his head, as if he were trying to shake off an annoying mosquito. "I tossed it."

"Why?"

His tone grew impatient. "I don't keep stuff like that. Why would I?"

Sandy considered that, never taking her eyes from his back. "It's a summertime photo." She was careful not to be accusatory, but it was a point that had to be made.

Nighthawk whirled around. "Actually, it was taken just a couple of weeks ago. They don't have indoor plumbing! Paula has to bathe the kids in a washtub, usually inside in front of the stove, but the weather was nice that day, so she decided to keep the mess outside. A friend took the picture, and she thought it was so cute she sent it to me. And if you don't believe me, ask *her!*"

"I have to ask these questions, Mr. Nighthawk. If I don't, someone else will, most likely in court. Okay, it's your niece, and your sister sent the photo. If you'll give me her number, I'll call and verify it, and maybe we can get the photo excluded from evidence as being irrelevant. Needless to say, if a jury gets a look at that, it will probably prejudice them."

He swore harshly. "Do you realize what a sick society this has become? A picture of a two-year-old splashing in a washtub is going to *prejudice* a jury? My God, it's unbelievable! It's a damn witch hunt! There was a time when people thought pictures like that one of my niece were *innocent!* What the hell has happened?"

"What has happened," Sandy said quietly, "is that little girls like Lisa Dunbar are being sexually assaulted. A five-year-old girl, Mr. Nighthawk. When that happens, people get very upset. And a picture like the one of your niece can appear very suspicious. So give me your sister's phone number. Once I verify this, I'm sure the photo will be removed from evidence."

He looked away. "My sister doesn't have a phone. You'll have to send her a letter and ask her to call you. Or get somebody to go out on the rez and question her."

Sandy nodded. "Okay. Give me her address, or some kind of information on how to find her, and I'll see what I can do. If I write, do you think she can get to a phone easily? She can call collect, so it won't cost her anything."

He shrugged. "It might be a week or more before she picks up her mail. She only goes to the post office every couple of weeks, because I'm the only one who writes to her."

Sandy glanced at Garrett. This didn't sound good. They didn't have all the time in the world to collect information and get ready for trial. "Then I'll see about getting somebody to hunt her up and get her to a phone. Any suggestions?"

"Tribal police would be your best bet, I guess. They'd probably get to her quickest."

"That's what we'll do, then." Sandy shoved the pen and pad across the table. "Give me her full name and address, please."

"Do I have to get her involved? I don't even want her to know this is happening!"

"I'm sorry, Mr. Nighthawk. Truly I am. But consider what's at stake here. You can't afford to leave any stone unturned, because if you get convicted, you're going to spend a long time in prison. And then, for the rest of your life, you'll have a record as a sex offender. Weigh that against getting your sister involved just this little bit."

He resisted a little longer, but finally nodded. Seated once again at the table, he wrote down the information Sandy had requested. "Can you . . . ask them to break it to her as gently as possible?"

"I'll do what I can. I promise."

He shoved the pad and pen back across the table to her and shook his head. "God! I can't believe all this is happening because of an innocent photo of my niece."

That question led Sandy directly to another topic she needed to discuss with him. "That's not all they have, Mr. Nighthawk. They arrested you because the girl's clothes were buried on your property and because you appear to fit the girl's description."

His head jerked as if he'd been struck. "I didn't—I never— Damn! It must be a frame!"

Garrett spoke. "Who would have a reason to want to frame you?"

Again an almost helpless look from dark, anguished eyes. "I don't know. I don't know! All I know is that I didn't do it!"

Sandy waited a moment before continuing. "Appearances right now aren't so good. From the description I had from the prosecutor, the clothes were found on your property, approximately one hundred and fifty yards behind your house."

"*Behind* it? But that's farther from the road!"

"Exactly. Somebody had to go right by your house to get there."

"I would have heard a car." Nighthawk's eyes moved from her to Garrett and then back again. "If anyone had driven up, I would have heard them. It's not the kind of sound I could ignore, not out there."

"So," Garrett said slowly, "you're suggesting a scenario in which somebody walks up your driveway and past your house in the dead of a dark cold night to bury clothes a hundred and fifty yards behind your house. Somebody who's just dumped a little girl on a creek bank across the road from your place. On a creek some two hundred yards from the road. So this person leaves the child, hikes back up to the road, then up your driveway and past your house. Do you know how *unlikely* that sounds?''

"Unlikely or not, that has to be what happened, because I damn well know *I* didn't do it!''

"Then maybe you'd better start trying to figure out who might want to go to so much trouble to make you look guilty.''

"Is that it?'' Nighthawk demanded. "Unless I can figure out who's done it, I'm going to get screwed?''

"There's still the physical evidence,'' Sandy said quickly. "Genetic tests may show beyond a doubt that it wasn't you.''

"Of course they—'' He broke off sharply as her choice of words struck him. "Are you saying there's a chance they might not prove I'm innocent?''

"They can be inconclusive, yes.''

"How can that be? No two people are exactly alike.''

"That's true, and a complete genetic code for a single individual is unique to that individual. Even more unique than a fingerprint, I hear. I've been reading up on it, as you can probably tell.'' She gave Nighthawk a small smile. "However, the lab can't test for a one-to-one comparison, because there are just so many genes, so the method is to pick a half-dozen alleles ... Well, suffice it to say they make a comparison of a number of points on the chromosome. The test is highly accurate, although in your case I could probably demolish the importance of a match in court—''

"You won't have to demolish it,'' he interrupted tautly. "It won't be my DNA.''

"I don't expect it will be.'' She shook her head slightly and smothered a sigh. "What I'm trying to do is prepare you for the possibility that genetic testing may not prove anything at all, least of all that you're innocent. In the first place, the tests won't work if the sample is contaminated or damaged in some way. Then, of course, there's the possibility that they might not have found any DNA samples at all other than the victim's because the rapist wore a condom ... or that if they did, there might not be a sufficient quantity to permit both the initial test and the confirmatory test. FBI procedures require that the test be duplicated before they'll call it a match. That protects *you*, of course, although it may not feel like it if they say the sample is insufficient."

He absorbed the information stoically, staring steadily at her from dark eyes. When he spoke, his voice was strained. "I was counting on genetic tests to clear me."

"They may well do that. I'm certainly hoping they will. But while we wait for the results, we need to keep working on the case. Trial is set for nine weeks from now, and there isn't a whole lot of time to waste. And maybe, if we're lucky and turn up something really definitive, we can settle this without going to trial."

But what, she wondered later, could they possibly turn up that would accomplish that? The real rapist? If that were going to be easy, the sheriff would already have done it.

Garrett followed her back to her office and took a seat facing her across her desk. He gave Nina an absent smile when she asked if he wanted coffee, then looked at Sandy.

"Well?" she asked.

"It's a picture of his niece but his sister is hard to get a hold of? He just happened to have thrown the letter away?" Garrett shook his head. "Too slick. Bet they can't find the sister at all."

"You think he was *lying?*" Sandy couldn't believe it. Everything about Nighthawk's demeanor and responses had seemed honest and open to her. "Garrett, not everyone in this country has a telephone, and life on the reservation is hard. So many of the Indian population are dirt-poor! If someone doesn't have indoor plumbing, they're hardly likely to have a phone!"

"I realize that. I'm not saying it's impossible. It's just too damn convenient, that's all."

"It's convenient only if he's guilty and that photo is some kind of kiddie porn."

"Exactly."

"You think he's guilty, then?" Her head almost felt as if it were spinning, because her belief in Nighthawk's innocence had been reinforced by this morning's conference. How could Garrett have received such a different impression?

"I'm reserving judgment," he answered. "I'm *not* convinced he's innocent. But then, I'm not exactly convinced he's guilty, either. Just keep in mind that this sister story is a little too convenient. Don't be surprised if the tribal police say they can't find her."

Rising, Garrett thrust his hands into the pockets of his jeans and began pacing to and fro before her desk. "The entire thing is difficult to believe. First off, I honestly can't imagine the perp risking discovery by burying the clothes so far from where he left the little girl and on somebody else's property...unless the property is his own. Otherwise he risks being seen and identified by the occupants of the house."

"In the middle of the night? Come on, Garrett!"

"Well, tell me that it makes any sense to bury the stuff there instead of somewhere far away where it would never be found!"

"Exactly! Nighthawk doesn't strike me as the kind of fool who'd bury the evidence in his own backyard."

"You'd be surprised what fools criminals can be. Take the guy who told the cops he hadn't meant to rob the store, that he had really meant to rob the place next door. My point is that it's far more likely, in my experience, that the criminal would bury the clothes someplace on his own property, thinking it was far enough away from where he left the girl, than that he'd go creeping through strange country in the dead of night and risk discovery by an irate householder, just so he could bury them on somebody else's place. And if he's going to go creeping around the countryside in the dead of night, it would make a hell of a lot more sense for him to drive ten, twenty, even thirty miles away before burying the stuff."

Much as she didn't like to admit it, Sandy was beginning to see the logic in his argument, and it didn't look good for Nighthawk. "Somebody *could* be trying to frame him."

"It's possible. But considering that he claims not to know anyone around here, I wouldn't bet my hat on it."

Neither would she, when she considered that Lisa Dunbar had probably not been a simple target of opportunity, given the isolated place where she had been snatched. No, someone had been stalking her, and if someone had been stalking her, it had to be someone from around here. Someone would have noticed a stranger.

The phone rang sharply, and she looked at Garrett. "Excuse me."

"Go ahead." He crossed to the window and stood staring out at the snowy street.

She picked up the receiver and heard Sam Haversham on the other end. "Sandy, word of Lisa Dunbar's rape is getting around."

Sandy sighed, but before she could reply, Sam continued.

"Anyway, somebody heard about it and showed up at the sheriff's this morning. It seems he saw Craig Nighthawk talking to Lisa Dunbar outside Soop's Supermarket last month."

Sandy's stomach sank with a sickening thud as her hand tightened around the receiver.

"We need to take his deposition," Sam said. "The sooner the better. Can you get over here sometime this morning?"

Stunned, feeling as if she had to force herself to move, Sandy drew her calendar across the desk and looked at it. "Uh...yeah." She'd been planning to spend this morning drawing up the wills for Mel and Doris Dahl, but that could wait. "I'm free until three." When she had a consult on a deed dispute.

"How soon can you come over?"

"Right now."

"I'll have Nate shuttle the guy over here, then. See you in about twenty?"

"That'll do."

After she hung up, she turned her head slowly to look at Garrett. He had turned to face her.

"What's up?" he asked.

"It seems Nighthawk knew Lisa Dunbar after all. He was seen with her about a month ago."

He stiffened, and she realized that the news had shocked him as much as it had her. He didn't want to think he was working for a rapist who was an accomplished liar any more than she did. Her stomach lurched again, a sickening feeling.

"Sam's going to depose him," she said, forcing herself to speak through a dry mouth. "I need to go over there right now."

"I'll ride shotgun."

She hardly heard him. Once before she had been this mistaken in a man. Then it had been her husband. This time it was a client. Damn, how could she be such a fool?

Dudley Willis was one of the community's more respected members. Sam Haversham couldn't have asked for a more credible nail to drive into Nighthawk's coffin. The Willis family had been in the county almost as long as the Conard family and had been one of the great powers until financial reverses had cost them most of their cattle empire just after the Second World War.

The empire might be gone, but Dudley Willis continued the tradition of community service. He was an active scoutmaster, a pillar of his church and he ran several of the biggest charitable fund-raisers in the county. Everyone knew Dudley Willis, and no one would question his word.

When she saw him, she suddenly experienced the uncharacteristic wish that she could just crawl into a pair of powerful arms and hide. Preferably Garrett's arms. Not that it would do any good. Nighthawk was hung, she found herself thinking. Whether or not he had raped the Dunbar girl, he was hung, because two and two made four even when the answer was really five...and Dudley was the second "two."

"I couldn't believe it this morning when I heard from Kent Reed that the little Dunbar girl had been raped, and that Craig Nighthawk had done it."

Sandy felt again the unpleasant lurching in her stomach. It was difficult for her to believe Kent Reed had revealed the little girl's name to anyone. She had always thought him far more responsible than that. Since it wasn't the point of this interrogation, however, she remained silent on the subject.

"The first thing that flashed into my mind when I heard about it was Nighthawk showing the little girl the cab of his truck."

"You saw him do that?" Haversham asked him.

Willis nodded. "Right in front of Sooper's. Ben Dunbar and I got to talking in the checkout line about that robbery over at the Watering Hole the night before. Anyhow, we came outside, and there's little Lisa sitting up in the cab of the truck. It was parked right out front of the store. Only place to park it, I guess."

Sandy scribbled on her notepad: *? Lisa outside w/o supervision?*

Sam asked another question. "What was your initial impression when you saw her sitting in the truck's cab?"

Willis didn't even hesitate. "I felt kind of uneasy. Well, it's these times we live in. You see kids with adults who aren't their parents, and you start wondering what's going on."

"So you know the Dunbars pretty well?"

Willis nodded. "Pretty well. From church and school activities. My daughter is in Debbie Dunbar's class."

"Johnna is your thirteen-year-old, correct?"

"That's right."

"So it was your daughter Debbie was with when she didn't come home on the bus Monday evening with Lisa?"

Sandy thought Willis stiffened a little, as if sensing an accusation, then relaxed. "I don't know," he said. "My ex-wife is remarried and lives in town. The kids live with her. I guess Debbie could have been there. Do you want me to find out?"

Sam shook his head. "Never mind. I'm just trying to get events clear in my mind. Okay, you and Ben Dunbar came out of Sooper's and found Lisa sitting in the cab of Craig Nighthawk's truck. Was Nighthawk in the cab with her?"

"No."

"Where was he?"

"Standing on the truck step."

"So he was off the ground, standing on the step. And what was he doing?"

Willis shrugged. "Talking to her, I guess. I don't know."

"What was his demeanor?"

"How do you mean?"

"Did anything about him seem . . . unusual?"

Willis thought about it a moment. "No, not really. He was just standing there."

"What about Lisa? How did she strike you?"

"I'm not sure." He sighed. "I was alarmed to see her in the cab of his truck. Whether that was because of the way she was behaving or just instinctive . . . well, I can't say for certain."

Sam looked at Sandy. "Do you have any questions?"

"Yes, I do. Okay, Mr. Willis, you felt alarmed when you saw Lisa Dunbar in Craig Nighthawk's truck. Do you know Craig Nighthawk?"

"No, I don't."

"So your alarm didn't come from anything you know about him?"

"No."

"If you don't know him, how could you be sure it was him standing beside the truck?"

"I've seen him around." He shook his head quickly. "He lives right up the road from me, Ms. Keller. When he first bought his place, I stopped in to invite him to the church. Other than that, I just see him around sometimes."

"Didn't he buy his property from your aunt, Hattie Maguire?"

"Yeah." Willis made a disgusted sound. "I asked her to hang on to it a little longer, until I could buy it, but she needed the money. Ah, well. I offered to buy it from Nighthawk last year, but he isn't interested in selling."

"So you *do* know him?"

"To nod to. What's this got to do with anything?"

"I'm just trying to determine how you could be so sure it was Mr. Nighthawk you saw with Lisa."

"Well, ask Ben, then. He recognized Nighthawk right off, too."

"How did *he* react?"

"He was upset. He shouted out, 'Lisa, you come down from there right this minute!' Nighthawk reached right up and lifted the girl down to the ground."

"Did you see him touch her at any other time?"

Willis hesitated briefly. "No. Just when he lifted her down."

"The little girl didn't seem disturbed in any way?"

"Well, I can't say exactly. I mean, it happened fast, and she was sure upset once her father shouted at her. Maybe she was upset before he shouted. I couldn't tell you."

Little by little Sandy pinned him down to exact descriptions of what people were wearing, and how long he and Dunbar had chatted at the register, so that by inference they could judge how long Lisa had been unattended. With each detail that was added, she was in a better position to determine his truthfulness. More importantly, by drawing out details, she could prevent him from speaking in sweeping generalities when he testified. Generalities tended to leave juries able to draw sweeping conclusions that were not necessarily accurate.

By the time she finished questioning Willis, she was convinced the episode was innocent...and utterly damning, given that the little girl had been raped. And even though the episode had been innocent, could the same be said about the motive behind it?

God, this case was an attorney's nightmare! At this rate, whatever the outcome, she was probably always going to wonder if justice had been done.

What if Nighthawk went to prison and he was innocent? And far, far worse, what if Nighthawk were guilty and acquitted, and went free to rape again?

Chapter 6

"Well, you're in for it now, Sandy," Nina said the instant Sandy stepped into her office.

For an instant, just a fleeting instant, Sandy had an overwhelming urge to throw something. She had never once in her life thrown a thing—other than a snowball or a softball—but right now she wanted to pitch something and hear the satisfying sound of shattering glass. It never rains but it pours, she reminded herself, quoting her mother's favorite adage. She'd taken on this damn case, and now she was just going to have to endure the doubts and concerns that went with it . . . and still handle all of life's usual complications. That was, well, life.

The thought leavened her mood just a little and made it possible for her to turn attentively to Nina. "What's up?" she asked. Being "in for it now" could mean almost anything, from a new case to trouble with the central heating system.

"The hate calls have started."

Sandy stared at her blankly for a moment, almost as if her secretary had spoken Greek. "Hate calls?"

"I don't know what else to call them. I've had three calls this morning from people—men, actually—who want to know if you've lost your mind to be defending a child molester. Only they weren't quite so polite about it. And, frankly, I don't want to answer any more of those calls!"

"You mean they used foul language?"

"I mean they were foul, vile and threatening! And whether you like it or not, I called Nate Tate and told him I'd had three threatening calls—"

"Nina, you didn't!"

"I did!" Nina folded her arms beneath her breasts and scowled at her. "And Garrett said—"

"You didn't tell Garrett!" She couldn't say why that upset her so much, but it did. It was almost as if something dirty had touched her, and she didn't want anyone to see it. "Nina, don't get so upset about it! Anonymous callers—good grief, they haven't got the guts to do anything or they'd say it to my face."

"Right. And cows fly. Don't be stupid, Sandy. People are mad enough that you're defending Nighthawk to pick up the phone and make threats. Someone could get mad enough to actually try to do something about it. You can't afford to take the risk!"

"And I suppose Nate told you there wasn't a damn thing he could do about it."

"Actually, he suggested we call the phone company and have them put a tap on the line so they can trace the calls and give those folks hell."

"Calls like this go with the territory, Nina. Have you forgotten some of the nasty calls we got when I defended the toxic waste dumpers?"

"These were different." Nina shook her head sharply. "Very different, Sandy. These calls scared me."

Much as she wanted to, Sandy couldn't ignore her secretary's assertion. Nina *had* laughed off the calls during the toxic waste trial, and some of them had been pretty vulgar. That these calls had been different enough to frighten her...

Absently she crossed the front office to look out on the quiet street that fronted her house. The leafless tree limbs reached to the gray sky. The snow was melting away, leaving patches of brown grass and dark earth visible. Winter was always so pretty when it first arrived and always so ugly as it slipped away. The ground had already started to thaw before this last snowfall, and now, stepping off the pavement, one was apt to sink into several inches of mud.

She was trying not to think the unthinkable. Her neighbors, she had always believed, were essentially good and law-abiding people. She couldn't imagine any one of them failing to understand the legal system to the extent that they somehow transferred the blame from the perpetrator to the attorney.

Yet she knew a lot of people did that. The justice system was often blamed, as if it were somehow responsible for the crimes people committed. It was as if the mere fact that justice were being meted out fairly, impartially and legally somehow rubbed the taint of the crime onto the system that dealt with it.

Not fair, certainly, nor even logical, but certainly it was human. It was also something she could understand. Recent highly publicized trials had created a public impression that guilty people always walked on technicalities, and that juries were capricious and out of touch with reality. Nothing could be farther from the truth.

But that perception often made lawyers appear to be the enemy, as much as any criminal. And that perception had led to a number of violent attacks on members of the legal profession.

Yes, it could happen. The question was, did she think it could happen here in Conard County?

She shivered, feeling suddenly cold despite the warmth of the office. She knew what men were capable of. It was not mere speculation for her, because a long time ago a man with no motive other than his own need to inflict pain and fear had leapt out of the darkness of a winter night and raped her in the snow not a hundred yards from her office.

She had long since put the trauma behind her. It flickered into her mind only rarely now, when some event or circumstance made her suddenly uneasy. What she had never been able to forget was that a total stranger had come out of the night to hurt her.

Eventually she had overcome her lingering fears, had put the assault behind her and learned to live without the constant companionship of fear.

Until this very instant, she had believed that she had put it all behind her. Until right now, when she quite suddenly realized that she didn't feel safe. Other people lived in the blind belief that such things couldn't happen to them. Sandy Keller knew better, because it *had* happened.

She couldn't ignore the possibility, much as she longed to. One of her neighbors had raped a five-year-old girl. Could she really delude herself into believing that others couldn't possibly be capable of violence against her because they felt so morally outraged by her defense of the accused rapist?

She turned and looked at Nina, who was still watching her. "All right. Call the phone company and get a tap put on the line."

Nina expelled a relieved breath. "Good! Nate says we both need to be more careful for a while, too. Not go anywhere alone, especially after dark. Make sure windows and doors are locked—that kind of thing."

Sandy chewed her lower lip briefly, a characteristic gesture when she was unsure how to say something. "Nina...Nina, if you're uneasy, you don't have to come to the office until this case is over. I hadn't thought... Look, I don't want you to be here alone while I'm at court and dealing with other things."

Nina put her hands on her hips. "And just who's going to handle the phone, the appointments and typing the briefs? Sandy, you can't function without a secretary! You couldn't possibly get ready for court without me, never mind all the other stuff on your desk!"

"Well, I'm damned if I'm going to think of you spending hours here all alone and scared because of phone calls and maybe other stuff."

"They're not threatening *me*, Sandy."

"If somebody's crazy enough to take the law into his own hands, can you be sure you won't be caught in the cross fire?"

"Well, you can't get along without me, so that settles it!"

"No, it doesn't. Look, you can take the laptop home with you and work there. At least you won't be all alone, because Dex will be right nearby in his shop." Dex was Nina's husband, an electrician who ran a shop out of his home. These days Dex stayed in his office running the show while younger men did the footwork for him.

"I don't know...."

"Look, you can come in here several times a day when I'm here. We can catch up then, and you can ferry disks back and forth as necessary. I just don't want you to be here all alone if you're frightened!"

Nina wasn't inclined to back down any more than Sandy was, and that amused Sandy just a little. They could advise each other to be careful but were loath to take the advice themselves.

"I don't want you to be alone here, either," Nina said finally. "You're in far more danger than I am, and you're alone a lot more."

"That's my problem. I'll deal with it. What I don't want to do is put you in a dangerous position. I chose to take this case, after all, but you didn't. No reason you should suffer for it."

For a moment it appeared Nina was going to argue, but finally she compressed her lips and nodded. "Okay. Have it your way."

In her own office, Sandy settled down at her computer and logged on to a national law data-base system to read court decisions involving cases with issues similar to Nighthawk's.

The law was not carved in stone but was constantly growing and changing as new cases were tried, new rulings handed down. Yes, there were laws against rape, but the way a rape case was tried, what kind of evidence could be admitted, what factors could be used in jury selection... those were changing all the time.

The first case she called up was a recent one dealing with the admission of DNA analysis in a rape case. The Wyoming Supreme Court not only agreed with the admissibility of DNA matching as evidence but had decided that the statistical evaluation of the evidence was also admissible.

Ordinarily no statistical claims could be admitted in a trial, because regardless of what statistics claimed, they were not relevant to a particular case. Or to put it another way, just because a third of all women were abused by their spouses, that did not mean that a particular woman had been abused by her husband.

In this instance, though, the court felt that failure to admit statistical evidence would deny a jury the information to evaluate the relative importance of the DNA matching process.

And that gave her some ammunition, should the DNA point to Craig Nighthawk. If statistics could be admitted, then they could be used to undermine the importance of a DNA match, especially in the case of a Native American, where the likelihood of matching the wrong person was a thousand times higher than it was for a Caucasian.

Some people would call that a technicality and get mad at her for using it, but the simple fact was that DNA evidence was not infallible. There *was* a chance the wrong person could match, especially in the case of a Native American suspect, because Indians tended to marry among themselves, and the gene pool was small to begin with. That increased the likelihood that the markers used in DNA testing might match the wrong person. No chicanery was involved in making sure the jury understood that possibility, just as there was no chicanery involved in proving that a witness lied. They were the same thing, a matter of making sure the jury understood the real value of the evidence and testimony being presented.

But the DNA test would exonerate Craig Nighthawk. It had to. If there was enough genetic evidence collected, then it would prove beyond a reasonable doubt that Nighthawk was *not* a match. That much, DNA samples could do.

And despite all evidence to the contrary, she was still convinced that Nighthawk hadn't committed the crime.

But that testimony from Dudley Willis this morning was going to make it appear that he had. It was circumstantial evidence of the worst kind: the victim had been seen in the company of the accused. Sam was going to call Ben Dunbar in to give a deposition about the incident, too, but she had no reason to believe Dunbar's statement would be materially different from Willis's. Two men had seen the victim sitting in the cab of the accused perpetrator's truck a couple of weeks before the rape. Who was going to believe there wasn't a connection?

Why hadn't Lisa Dunbar's father remembered the incident right away? Why had Willis been the first person to show up in the sheriff's office with the story? Had Dunbar somehow failed to hear who had been arrested in his daughter's case? Had he just forgotten the entire thing? Could such an event have seemed so insignificant to a little girl's father that he didn't even remember it? How likely was that?

Her head was still spinning with unanswered questions when she logged off the data base and realized that she had a client due in fifteen minutes.

But the client didn't show.

"I don't understand it," Nina said. "I called to confirm the appointment yesterday, and they said they'd be here."

"Maybe something came up." But she didn't think so. No, she had an edgy, fluttery feeling in the pit of her stomach that said her clients had decided not to keep the appointment because she was defending Nighthawk.

"They said they're going to find another attorney," Nina told her twenty minutes later, after calling the people to find out what was wrong. "Because you're defending a child molester."

Something inside Sandy seemed to snap. She rose swiftly from her desk, slamming a law book shut with an emphatic gesture. "Why the hell are we bothering with a trial? Nobody's heard a smidgen of evidence, but they're already convinced the man is guilty! Why don't they just hang him right now?"

Garrett's voice reached her from the outer office. "Wouldn't surprise me if some folks are talking about that very thing right now." Two seconds later he filled the door of her office. "It's started, has it?"

Nina forestalled her. "You better believe it. I'm going to call the rest of the day's appointments and see how many more are planning not to show up."

"Let's not exaggerate this, Nina," Sandy said quietly.

"I'm not exaggerating anything! You have a right to know if people are going to show up or not. It's just common courtesy!"

"Let her call, Sandy," Garrett said. "If you find out you don't have any appointments this afternoon, you can come with me."

Her heart seemed to skip a beat at the thought of spending an afternoon with Garrett, but almost before it rose in her, she repressed the feeling of excitement. He wanted to discuss the case, that was all. Probably wanted to ask her about the deposition this morning.

Then, in a moment of uncomfortable clarity, she faced her initial reaction and what it meant ... and the emotional danger it put her in. She couldn't afford to care one way or another whether this man wanted to spend time with her. Not only could she not afford it, she absolutely didn't *want* to care. Caring had been a cage in which she had nearly suffocated once before, and she had promised herself that she would never again let any man put her in such a position.

But some integral part of her didn't want to listen to reason. It wanted to kick up its heels and fall madly, wildly in love, and damn the consequences. Some unfulfilled part of her yearned for all the promises that had never been met, hungered for the dreams that had never come true. She knew better—life had certainly taught her that those dreams were just dreams, never to be matched by reality—but some part of her apparently couldn't quite relinquish the longing.

"Go ahead and call," she told Nina, managing a small smile. "I know when I'm outnumbered."

Turning away from Garrett, she reached for one of the books on her desk, meaning to put it back in the floor-to-ceiling bookcase that covered the wall behind her desk.

As suddenly as if someone had flipped a switch, she found herself remembering something her mother had said a couple of years ago, after reading a romance novel. "I could never write one of these," her mom had said. "I'm too old and I was married too long to even remember what it felt like to fall in love."

At the time Sandy hadn't paid much attention to the statement, primarily because she couldn't remember, either, and had no desire to. Now here she was, facing those scary, uncertain feelings again and trying to turn her back on them. Sad, she thought abruptly. It was so damn sad. Sad that her mother couldn't remember those feelings, and sad that she herself only wanted to avoid them.

"Are you okay?"

Garrett's concerned voice right behind her made her aware that she had sighed. "I'm fine, Garrett. Just disgusted, I guess."

"Hardly surprising. It never fails to amaze me how rarely most people bother to think things through. Most of the folks who'll be giving you hell about this case would agree in principle that a man's innocent until proven guilty. Most of 'em would agree that everyone is entitled to a defense attorney, and that a miscarriage of justice can't be tolerated. Funny how fast they forget all that when somebody's arrested for a terrible crime. Unfortunately, this kind of crap goes with the territory, Counselor."

"I know that." She turned her head so she could glance at him over her shoulder. "I know, but it doesn't make it any less disgusting. The whole point of the system is to make sure that innocent people don't get sent to prison, but that's what everyone seems to forget the instant someone gets arrested."

"I think we're all guilty of that."

Sandy expelled a soft breath, letting go of some of the tension. "Even me, and I'm an attorney." A quiet, rueful laugh escaped her, and she faced Garrett. "I imagine you want to hear about the deposition this morning."

"What I want to hear about it are your impressions. I can read the actual statement when you get a copy. Are you going to interview the girl herself? What about members of her family?"

"Sam's going to have the father come in tomorrow to give a statement. We're both kind of curious as to why he hasn't told us about finding his daughter in Nighthawk's truck."

"Me, too." He frowned faintly and rubbed his chin absently. The skin of his forefinger rasped against the darkening stubble of his beard. "I'm also wondering why Nighthawk didn't mention the incident."

"Believe me, I intend to question him about that."

Garrett shook his head. "I'm beginning to wonder about a lot of things. When you stack it all up, my feeling is that Nighthawk isn't being real helpful. Why didn't he mention that the girl had been in his truck?"

"Maybe he doesn't know that was the little girl who was raped."

"That's possible, I guess, but it makes him look even more suspicious. Who in their right mind puts strange little girls into their trucks?"

"I have to agree it wasn't the brightest move in the world, but you can't hang a man for stupidity."

"Oh yes, you can! Work in law enforcement for a little while, Counselor. You'd be amazed how many people get into serious trouble over *stupidity*." His startling blue eyes seemed almost to glare at her, but his mouth framed a slight smile.

Well, she thought, maybe he was genuinely exasperated at the way things were happening. She knew she was. Every time she turned around she seemed to be discovering something that boded no good for her client. Inevitably she was being nagged by doubts about his innocence.

And while that shouldn't matter—couldn't matter—to a defense attorney, in this instance it mattered one hell of a lot to her. She had taken this case with the blind conviction that the man was innocent. The sorry fact was, if she had believed him guilty, even all her principles couldn't have forced her to take the case.

Apparently her principles weren't as steadfast as she'd always believed, and that realization was as unsettling as an earthquake. The ground on which she had so firmly stood for so long had shifted, leaving her feeling disoriented.

"Damn," she whispered softly. "Damn."

"Sandy?" Garrett's expression had lost its unnerving intensity and now reflected concern. "What's wrong?"

She shook her head, not wanting to discuss it. "This case is just making me uneasy."

"I can sure understand that. I wish I had something positive to offer, but I'm having trouble finding anything."

"What do you mean?"

"Well, I was kind of nosing around this morning, trying to find out if anyone around here knows Nighthawk."

"And no one does."

"Not quite." One corner of his mouth lifted just a hair. "Dirk Bayard at Bayard's Garage knows him. Nighthawk goes in there from time to time to order parts, and they apparently shoot the breeze."

"Did he have anything useful to say?"

"Only that Nighthawk seems decent enough, and Bayard would never in a million years believe Nighthawk could hurt a kid."

It was kind of a relief not to be the only person on the planet who thought Nighthawk couldn't have done it. Not that that helped a darn thing. A man's opinion was a long way from evidence. "Nothing else?"

"Afraid not. I'll keep poking around, Sandy. Nighthawk said he didn't know anyone around here, but it turns out he did regular business with Bayard, and Bayard knows him. There are probably other people who know him the same way. Maybe somebody can shed some light on things."

"But why didn't he mention Bayard when I asked who he knew around here?" Another troubling omission.

"Maybe," Garrett said, "he's just unassuming."

"What do you mean?"

"I mean that maybe he doesn't think Dirk Bayard would remember him, because Bayard does business with so many people. Maybe it never entered Nighthawk's head that Bayard would consider him to be an acquaintance."

"Possible, I guess, but it seems to me that someone facing what Nighthawk's facing would be clutching at any straw, not dismissing things that don't seem important."

"Maybe that's how you'd handle it, but Nighthawk's a different person with a different outlook. Maybe you need to jog him a little bit and get him to thinking."

"I'm sure going to try."

"So are you going to get to question the little girl?"

Sandy shrugged. "As soon as the doctor says it's okay. The sooner the better, actually. As time goes on, her memory won't be as good."

"I don't envy you."

"Me either." She gave him a crooked smile. "I have this nightmare of her testifying on the stand and me having to cross-examine her. Lord, I don't want to have to do that."

"*Can* she be allowed to testify? I thought kids weren't brought into the courtroom in these cases."

"They can be, and the Wyoming Supreme Court has already declared that a five-year-old was a competent witness in a similar case. All that's necessary is for Judge Williams to determine that Lisa Dunbar is competent to testify."

After a moment Garrett shook his head doubtfully. "Is there any way you can prevent that?"

"I'm sure going to try to. The simple fact is, if Lisa takes the stand, I'm going to *have* to cross-examine her. That's my constitutional duty. I *have* to verify the accuracy of anything she says. And regardless of the truth of her testimony, the jury is going to see me as a nasty old witch giving the poor little girl a hard time, and that hostility will be transferred to my client. So when all is said and done, I'd be very happy to have the judge declare Lisa incompetent."

Nina tapped on the door and poked her head in. "Sorry, Sandy. You've got the rest of the day off. Two more cancellations, one over the Nighthawk case, the other not saying why. And the third appointment rescheduled for tomorrow. Car broke down."

"Thanks, Nina. That's not too bad." She managed a smile. "I still have one client left."

Nina sniffed. "They may change their minds by tomorrow!"

The corners of Garrett's eyes creased as he looked down at her. "Great. Now you're mine for the rest of the day."

All her concerns about the case faded as sparklers of excitement ignited within her. "All yours? For what?"

"I want to go out to Willis Road and take a look at the crime scene. Nate gave me the go-ahead."

The flares of excitement winked out as suddenly as they'd burst into life and left her feeling crabby. It was a disappointing plummet.

"You'd better change into jeans and boots," Garrett said. "It'll be pretty muddy out there."

The afternoon sun shone brilliantly in a cloudless blue sky. The warmth of the sun's rays had melted the snow in patches, leaving bare ground and brown growth visible like islands in a shrinking sea. The air was still chilly, though, a stimulating contrast to the heat of the sun.

Because Garrett drove, Sandy was able to relax in the seat and soak up the delightful sunlight through the windows. She had forgotten how good it felt to just let the sun beat down on her and drive all the tension away.

In fact, it suddenly disconcerted her to realize how long it had been since she had simply taken the time to relax. How long it had been since her last vacation. She'd grown so accustomed to working all the time to support herself and Gerard, that she had forgotten how to do much else. And now finances weren't even an adequate excuse. Actually, she had no excuse whatsoever not to take an occasional vacation.

Except that how much fun could a vacation be all by oneself? Maybe she needed to look up that all-women's travel group one of her acquaintances had mentioned. Or maybe she ought to just poll some of her friends. There were probably a few of them who would love to take a vacation away from their families.

That thought almost made her smile. For all that she often felt a little lonely, she knew plenty of her friends envied her independent life-style. Funny how different positions could create such a different perspective.

They turned a corner, and her cheeks felt bereft when shadow replaced the sun. Opening her eyes, she turned and looked at Garrett. "What do you hope to find out here?"

"Nothing, really. I just want a chance to look things over and get them fixed in my mind. Sometimes you can get an inkling of what the perp was thinking by following his footsteps."

He pulled over suddenly and braked, leaving the engine running. "Aspen Meadows Ranch," he announced, pointing at the open gate and cattle guard. "The Dunbar girl was dropped off right here by the school bus. I called ahead, and they said it's okay to drive up the road to the house and check things out."

He put the Explorer in gear and turned onto the rutted private ranch road. "She had to be snatched somewhere along here. It seems to me that if the car had been waiting within sight of the gate, the bus driver would have mentioned seeing it. Hell, he probably would have asked the girl if she knew who was in the car."

"Probably. You can be sure I'll ask him about it, though."

"I figure he drove far enough up the road that he couldn't be seen from the bus when it pulled up, and certainly far enough up so that nobody could see him snatch the kid. We need to find out if he was wearing a mask when he kidnapped her, or if she ever saw his face."

"There's a lot we need to find out as soon as she can talk to us," Sandy agreed. "She may well remember a lot of little details, particularly from earlier, before he started hurting her, that could help clarify things considerably."

"We can hope." He glanced in the rearview mirror. "Okay, from here you can barely see the top of the gate. Let's see how much farther before you can see the ranch house, and that'll give us a pretty good idea of where he must have snatched her."

"Why would he care if anyone could see from the house? If it was a planned kidnapping, he'd know that no one would be there."

"Would he? How could he be absolutely certain? How would Nighthawk, for instance, know the schedule June Dunbar follows that gets her home after six? Or that Ben Dunbar would be working in town that day? I hear his job is part-time and intermittent, according to when the feed store wants him to help with deliveries."

"I didn't know that." She turned a little in the seat so she could see him better and was surprised when he flashed her a smile.

"That's why you hired a detective. Okay, Ben Dunbar ranches, but they're not exactly making ends meet out here, so June works year-round as a dental hygienist, and during the winter months Ben takes whatever work the feed store offers. There was no way for somebody to be *sure* he wouldn't be home that day...except maybe a good friend or someone at the feed store."

"Neither of which fits Craig Nighthawk."

"Exactly."

They hadn't driven too much farther up the road before Garrett braked again. "There's the roof of the house. If I were planning to snatch a kid, I wouldn't want to be this close to the house when I did it." After turning the vehicle, he set the hand brake and looked at Sandy. "I'm going to walk back toward the highway and see if I can spot anything along the side of the driveway here that might tell us something. "You follow behind me in the car."

He walked down the middle of the narrow track, scanning from side to side. The snow hadn't helped a whole lot, but now that it was melting back from the edges of the drive, there was a slim chance he might discover something, though he wasn't holding his breath.

Bringing Sandy along had been a spur-of-the-moment idea when he had realized her clients were deserting ship. Better to keep her distracted than let her spend the afternoon brooding about what those canceled appointments meant. She had faced the possibility of this happening when she decided to take the case, but this was one of those life events that tended to feel a whole lot different when it actually happened than she'd expected it to.

She was bound to feel hurt by what was happening. No way to escape it. These folks weren't strangers to her, the way they might well be in a big city. Nope, these folks were her neighbors. She probably knew damn near every one of them, and this had to hurt like hell.

And it was going to hurt a whole lot worse. He kinda figured those canceled appointments were like the sweeping arc of stratus clouds on the leading edge of a hurricane. Once this case became a topic of local discussion, she was probably going to hear a lot of not-so-nice stuff to her face.

The thought made him clench his fists. One of his biggest failings was the way he felt protective of folks he considered to be his friends. The way he felt protective of women, in particular. Lots of women didn't much appreciate that anymore, and he'd been told more than once that they could take care of themselves. On the other hand, there had been some who'd tried to take advantage of that weakness of his by inventing troubles and asking for his help. Good thing he'd learned to harden his heart long ago, or it would have been busted a whole passel of times instead of only twice.

But he felt extremely protective of Sandy Keller. So protective that he'd had to battle an urge to ask Nina for the names of the fools who'd canceled their appointments so he could go have a talk with them about the constitution of these United States and all the civil liberties people held so dear... until they applied to someone else.

But he'd stomped down on the urge. Instinct told him that Sandy wouldn't have appreciated it at all, and he had the sense to see he would only have made her look like some kind of a fool by his interference. No, she had to handle this herself so she wouldn't look weak.

Well, she had to give the *appearance* of handling it herself. Sure enough, if he could find unobtrusive ways to help her through this, he would.

Of course, it would probably be better if he just stayed clear. He knew better than to get involved, but Sandy Keller would have been one easy woman for him to get involved with. Something about her had him thinking about slippers before the fire and other nonsense to do with long, lazy evenings and the company of a loving woman.

Dreams he'd given up on years and years ago.

Funny how a woman could resurrect wants and needs that were buried and ought to be dead. Real funny. So damn funny that he didn't feel at all like laughing.

From time to time he heard her rev the engine, slip into gear and catch up with him. He was as aware of her eyes on him as he would have been if someone had been stalking him. And maybe it wasn't so different, considering that he'd seen his own wanting reflected in her eyes last night when he'd looked at her from head to foot.

He'd known how bold his look had been, but he hadn't been able to stop himself. There was a peculiar kind of hunger in him for her, and it worried him considerably. It wasn't the simple sexual hunger a man often felt for an attractive woman—a hunger he'd felt countless times over the years. Nope. This was a hunger for scarier things, and alarm bells were going off inside both his head and his heart.

Just then he noticed a tire track off to one side, a scar in the muddy ground. It could have been almost anything, one ranch vehicle pulling aside to let another one pass, the mailman, or someone stopped because they'd taken a wrong turn. He moved in for a closer look anyway and saw small footprints right next to the track. Footprints that might have been made by a five-year-old girl coming home from school in her boots.

He straightened and motioned Sandy to pull up alongside.

"I may have found a tire track belonging to the kidnapper. Hand me the cellular phone, will you? It's under the console cover between the seats."

The connection was pretty good—not surprising, since there was a repeater just outside of town. Nate Tate promised to send a deputy immediately to make a cast and asked if Garrett would please wait there to protect the track until the deputy arrived.

"Not that anything's likely to happen to it," Nate said, "but why take a chance?"

"No problem," Garrett assured him.

When Sandy had hung up the phone and closed the console, he motioned her to slide over so he could get in behind the wheel.

"Chilly out there," he remarked, rubbing his hands together briskly.

"How come you never married, Garrett?"

The question came at him sideways, utterly unexpected from Sandy Keller. Astonished, he turned his head so he could look straight at her and found her blushing violently.

"I'm sorry," she said quickly. "I don't know where that question came from. Just an attorney's insatiable curiosity about people, I guess."

But he knew where the question had come from. Women started wondering about things like that when they were interested in a man. His heart took an unwelcome leap of delight even as his stomach sank with a dread he knew all too well.

Damn it, he couldn't afford to get involved! It always wound up hurting too damn much. And from the horrified expression on her face, he would guess that Sandy Keller was no more eager to get involved than he was. Nothing but pain could come out of this if they weren't careful. Nothing but god-awful pain.

"I got jilted twice," he heard himself say. And that was when he knew he was in serious trouble.

Chapter 7

"Jilted? Twice?"

He had her attention now, he realized, and there was no way he could refuse to answer, not when he'd brought it up himself. Nope, he was just going to have to bite the bullet on this one and tell the gruesome tale.

The strange thing, though, was how difficult he suddenly found it to discuss something he'd honestly believed he'd come to terms with. It was as if the hurt he'd felt so long ago had never really gone away. Or maybe it just wasn't easy to admit to someone else that he didn't measure up. That he'd been rejected.

Stupid, he told himself. How could it hurt to admit that a couple of women had left him because of his job? It wasn't as if they'd rejected *him*.

"Back when I was twenty-seven, I was engaged to a wonderful woman named Janine. She was what I thought I wanted back then. You know, the Donna Reed kind of thing. She wanted to stay home and raise kids and bake cookies. About a week before the wedding, I was involved in a shoot-out with some drug dealers. Didn't get a scratch on me, and it's not very often most cops even get into a shooting match. Hell, I've known plenty of cops who've gone their entire careers and never had to fire their guns except on the range.''

''I suppose you told her that.'' Sandy could easily hear him making that argument to Janine.

''Of course I did.'' He felt almost embarrassed now to realize the degree of passion that had entered his voice, embarrassed to realize that he still felt it necessary to defend his career as he once had to Janine. It was apparent even to himself that this scar wasn't as faded as he'd been telling himself. In fact, it sounded suspiciously fresh, to judge by the degree of emotion in his voice. He cleared his throat and tried to sound detached.

''It happens, of course. I couldn't promise her that I'd never get shot at again, or that I'd never get killed. The fact is, though, that I don't do the kinds of work that are most dangerous to the average cop—traffic stops and domestic disturbances. And I'm not involved in any undercover work, so my job is probably safer than some.'' But not so safe that he didn't need to carry a gun. Not so safe that he could promise he would always come home in one piece. Not so safe that the tremor in his hand was of no concern. No, he had to be able to use that gun.

''Then there was Wanda,'' he continued. ''I was a little older and a hell of a lot more cautious then. I'd given up on the Donna Reed idea. I wanted a woman who could stand on her own two feet and not be scared to death that I might not come home. Scared that she might be left with kids to clothe and feed by herself. Wanda didn't especially want kids, but what attracted me to her was that she had a good career in a telecommunications firm.'' He shook his head a little ruefully, remembering.

''What happened?''

''Well, Wanda believed that you put in your forty hours and a couple extra if you really needed to, and then you came home and forgot about it until the next business day. Unfortunately, I'm not like that.''

"Me either."

He flashed her a smile. "You probably understand what I mean when I say I'm a Texas Ranger twenty-four hours a day. When the job needs it, I don't quit except to sleep. Now, I reckon that's not necessarily something to brag about. Some folks would call it obsessive, I guess, but that's the way I am. I don't blame Wanda for getting fed up with it, though. A little while after I met her, I got assigned to a really tough case and . . . well, it started to take all my time. I lost count of the dates I had to break, or the weekends I worked. She finally had enough." He shrugged. "I guess any woman would."

"Was that unusual for you, or typical?"

"Unusual. Oh, the occasional case comes along that just devours every minute of every day, but most of 'em work out a little better than that. I work a lot of evenings and weekends, but not *all* of them. She saw the worst of it, wham, bang. Can't really blame her for backing out."

"Well, you saw what I was doing when you dropped by last night. Up to my ears in work. Gerry—my ex—used to be annoyed by that, but I always felt he was being unfair, because he used to bring work home from the office, too. We were employed by the same legal firm, and I don't understand why he could never comprehend that I had just as much work to do as he did."

Garrett tilted his head. "Simple to explain. Your work wasn't as important because you're a woman," he said wryly.

Sandy's eyes widened a little. She'd figured that out herself a long time ago, but she had never expected a man to understand it. Everything in her ex-husband's attitude had devalued her simply because she was a woman. He would praise her cooking but never her legal briefs. He bragged about the clean house she kept but never about her trial work. The effect had been subtle but ultimately devastating: she had lost confidence in her abilities as a lawyer. His refusal to even acknowledge that her work was as important as his had been undermining in a very indirect way. Just his insistence that her work could wait while she cooked a meal or ironed his shirt had evinced a priority that demeaned her efforts.

Except for his comments about her sexuality, his attitude had been one of simple male superiority and so much a part of the times that it had taken her years to realize what was happening to her. To this day she didn't blame Gerry. Lord, no! The man's attitudes had been bred in him since birth, part and parcel of his society. And she had accepted them because she had been raised with the same attitudes. Only when she came to realize that he was wounding her did she develop the anger necessary to fight for her personhood.

The anger had resulted in the death of her marriage and her own resurrection as a competent, capable, *independent* woman. A woman who didn't *need* a man. But a woman who wanted one, anyway.

She glanced at Garrett, but he was looking out over the sun-drenched, snow-dappled countryside. Apparently he didn't expect an answer to his remark, which was just as well, because she really couldn't think of any casual response. The issue was too emotionally loaded for her.

"Right about here," he remarked lazily, "I could think I'm in West Texas. As long as I don't turn a little and see the mountains."

She gave a quiet laugh. "Getting homesick, Ranger?"

He turned to smile at her. "Reckon I am, a little. I think you'd like San Antonio, Sandy. One of these days you'll have to come visit and let me show you around."

"I'd like that." And she would, she realized. She would like it a whole lot. If she could ever make herself take a vacation.

Garrett straightened a little and peered through the windshield. "Somebody's coming. Hope it's a deputy. I'd like to get on out to Willis Road."

Nate had sent two deputies, and after chatting a few minutes with Garrett, they sent him and Sandy on their way.

Since they had left town, clouds had begun to appear over the western mountains. As they drove toward Willis Road, the sun sank low enough in the west that the heavy gray clouds swallowed it.

"More snow?" Garrett asked as gloom seemed to suffuse the world.

"Looks that way."

"Isn't that unusual?"

"To have this much snow at this time of year? Unusual, but not unheard of."

"I wish the light were better. Well, we might as well check things out anyway. If it snows again, there's no telling how long before it'll melt enough."

He parked the Explorer on the shoulder of Willis Road. Looking out across the range toward the creek where Lisa Dunbar had been found by Nate Tate, Sandy was glad she'd worn her winter boots. It looked muddy and unwelcoming.

With the disappearance of the sun behind the clouds, the omnipresent wind had strengthened and taken on an icy edge. Sandy snapped her parka all the way to her chin and tugged on a stocking cap and gloves. Garrett wore a shearling jacket and leather gloves, but only a cowboy hat. She guessed his ears were going to get really cold.

"All right," he said. "I'm going to assume the guy assaulted her somewhere else and brought her here to dump her. As I remember, it was pretty damn cold that night. Cold enough that he probably took her somewhere that was heated. Then he needed to get rid of her. Common sense says he takes her somewhere away from his place."

"Not right across the road, you mean?"

Garrett looked down at her. "You'd think so, but not necessarily. Was there any reason to think that the searchers would look for her out here? We're seven or eight miles from where she was snatched. He probably figured that before anyone looked here she would have died of exposure."

Sandy repressed a shudder. If she lived to be as old as Methuselah, some of the things of which people were capable would never cease to horrify her. "Except for her book bag, you mean."

"That's right. That's what moved the search in this direction. How did the sheriff find out about that?"

"Someone called the office and reported that a little girl's book bag, full of school books, had been seen alongside the road here."

"Where?"

"I'm not sure, exactly. The report didn't say. You'd need to ask Nate to point out the place to you."

"So somebody called and said they'd *seen* it? Not that they'd found it?"

Sandy shook her head. "Weird, isn't it? No, somebody called, said they'd seen a kid's book bag alongside the road, that they hadn't touched it because they'd heard about the Dunbar girl being missing, and then before Velma—she's the dispatcher—could get their name or anything, they hung up."

"Pretty much everybody knew the kid had turned up missing, huh?"

"You bet. The Dunbars have been here a long time, and lots of folks know them. When the sheriff formed search parties, it was inevitable that word would spread like wildfire. I figure nearly everyone must have heard about it by midnight. Certainly by the next morning, when they got to work."

"So that part of it isn't suspicious."

"Not in *this* county."

"What time did that call come in to the sheriff?"

Sandy racked her brain. "Mmm, maybe around eight in the morning. I can check the report for the exact time. It's in my briefcase in the car."

"Don't bother. We can check the time later. The call is suspicious, though."

Sandy tilted her head back a little so that she could look directly at him. "Why?"

"Well . . . it sounds to me like it might have been the perp calling."

She put her hands on her hips. "Why in the world would he do that?"

"Couple of reasons, maybe. It's not unheard of for the perp to suddenly get a conscience. Could be he put her out there but didn't want her to die. Could be he started to get really uneasy about it and changed his mind about letting her die. Could be he figured she was already dead, and he wanted her to be found before the search extended too far and turned up something he didn't want to turn up. Or maybe he was thumbing his nose at the sheriff. Or...maybe he was trying to point the finger at somebody else."

"You mean Nighthawk?"

"Could well be."

"Good grief." She turned and looked over the wintry countryside, shivering a little as the wind snaked into the collar of her jacket.

"The book bag keeps bothering me," he continued. "It's unlikely that little Lisa was in a condition to think of shoving it out of the car like Hansel and Gretel leaving bread crumbs behind. Not at that point, right before he dumped her. I also don't think it's likely it just fell out of his vehicle when he pulled her out. You said it contained schoolbooks. No way he wouldn't have heard it fall out, even in the dark."

"You think he left it by the road deliberately?"

"You might say the thought keeps crossing my mind." He turned a slow circle, taking in the gentle rolling of the land here. There were a lot of dips and gullies to hide things. "Without that book bag, they might not have found that girl's remains for years."

Sandy nodded, unable to find words to describe how it was making her feel to listen to him list possibilities that could only be coldly calculating. The thought that anyone could have considered such matters—could have treated such a little girl's survival in such terms—utterly horrified her.

"Come on. Let's walk down to the creek."

She grabbed a notebook and pen, and stuffed them into a deep pocket. Experience had long since taught her to be prepared to take notes at any time.

The remaining snow wasn't very deep, and before long they started trying to walk in it in preference to the soggy and often slippery ground where the snow had melted away. The ground had become a web work of shallow gullies carved by spring runoff. None was much more than a foot or so deep, but they made the walk treacherous.

"Why would he have carried her all this way?" Sandy demanded breathlessly at one point. "I seriously doubt she walked."

"She couldn't be all that heavy, a little five-year-old. He probably wrapped her in a blanket and slung her over his shoulder. It's only about five hundred yards, and you have to remember, he wanted to conceal her. If he put her too close to the road, there was always a chance she might make enough noise to be heard. Or might wander back to the road. We need to ask her if she *did* wander around after he left her. She might not even have been abandoned on the creek bank."

The creek itself was swollen and muddy with early spring runoff. The water was icy and raced swiftly between its banks.

"In a few more weeks this'll be a real torrent," Sandy remarked. "I imagine all the gullies will be full of running water."

"Most likely." Garrett squatted and pointed downstream a little way. "That must be the cottonwood copse where Nate found her."

Sandy nodded. The only other visible trees were quite a distance upstream. "That's what he described in the report."

"And it's right across from Nighthawk's place, like he said. Come on, let's hike down that way along the bank. I figure he had to have dumped her just before dawn."

"Why?"

"Well, it couldn't have been too long before that or she probably would have frozen to death."

"She came damn near it, from what the doctor said."

"I imagine so. Anyway, he would have wanted to dump her and get out before it got light, so nobody would see him. The easiest way to navigate would be to follow one of the gullies to the stream, then follow the stream to the trees."

"Why would he even think it necessary to take her to the trees?"

"Because that way she wouldn't be spotted from overhead by an air search."

Sandy shivered again, not from cold. Garrett was thinking like the perpetrator, and the efficiency with which he did it was chilling. She was, she realized, getting a glimpse into the criminal mind. There was no doubt that thinking this way helped him to be a better investigator, but it unsettled her nonetheless to have this look into what must be a sick mind. "God," she whispered softly.

"Horrible, isn't it?" he agreed levelly. "Our perp is no idiot. He did an awful lot of thinking about this."

"Which means?"

"Not a whole hell of a lot. Yet. Okay. He kept the kid all night. And that means nobody would wonder about his whereabouts if he didn't show up for a while."

"That means someone who's single." Like Nighthawk.

"Not necessarily." He took a few more cautious steps along the slippery bank and gave her a hand to steady her. "From what the kid said about his face being 'mashed,' I figure he was wearing some kind of mask."

"That's what Nate figures."

"There aren't many masks he would have found comfortable to wear for twelve hours, which is approximately how long he had her. That means he must have had a place to stash her so he could get out of the mask for a while. He might not have done anything at all until hours after the kidnapping."

"So he could have been home until the wife and kiddies fell asleep, and then left to rape Lisa? Good God!"

"Awful, isn't it? But yeah. It could have happened that way. All he'd need is some place to keep the kid until he was ready."

The thought that the rapist might have calmly gone home to a wife and children left Sandy feeling ill in a way that was impossible to describe. Bad enough to think the perpetrator might have been some slug living alone in a solitary world, but far, far worse to think of him raising his own children. She shivered, slipping a little on the muddy creek bank.

Ordinarily she found the rushing sound of water soothing, but all of a sudden it seemed to be an isolating cocoon, cutting out the sounds of the larger world, making her feel as if she were moving through a separate world. She found herself wondering what it must have been like for a little girl in the icy predawn air after a night of terror. Dropped out here to die. Only saved, perhaps, by a belated twinge of conscience. Or by a simple, inexplicable accident that had left her book bag by the roadside.

"You know," Garrett said suddenly, "the best proof of Nighthawk's innocence is that damn book bag."

"Why?"

"Because if he buried her belongings out behind his house, wouldn't he have buried the book bag, too? The more I think about it, the more convinced I become that somebody left that bag out there on purpose."

To point a finger at Nighthawk. He left the implication unspoken, but it hung in the air like the leaden clouds above. The wind blew a little harder, seeming to push her forward as it swept between the creek banks. Like a giant hand on her back.

Why would someone want to frame Nighthawk? Had a little girl been raped because someone bore a grudge against him? No, no one could be capable of such a thing. The girl would have been abducted regardless. Framing Nighthawk was simply a way for the rapist to protect himself.

And all of this had been planned. The earmarks were unmistakable. Someone had, like a repulsive spider spinning a web, plotted and planned every move in this heinous crime. She couldn't have said why, but she would have found it all a lot less revolting if it had been an act committed on the spur of the moment.

"All this premeditation," she said to Garrett as they worked their way toward the copse of leafless cottonwoods, "doesn't fit with the idea that he had an attack of conscience after he dumped her."

"Sure it does." He stopped walking and turned to face her. "The truth of it is, the perp gets high on the adrenaline. He gets higher and higher through all the planning and through the commission of the act. Sexual excitement propels him, too, as often as not. And what happens in the aftermath, Sandy? Surely you remember what happens when the sexual compulsion is satisfied."

"Afraid not." She didn't know why she let those words pass her lips. She had guarded her secret for years and years, and now, standing beside an icy stream on a cold, wintry day in the middle nowhere, she let the truth come out.

Garrett grew suddenly still in a way that told her he had not missed the significance of the words. His brilliant blue eyes bored into hers, seeking answers. But he didn't ask. Thank God, he didn't ask. He left her secrets alone.

"Sexual compulsion is a powerful motivator. It's pretty good at silencing conscience and fear, actually, which is why so many kids get into trouble. Our perp has a thing for kids that's probably been goading him for years. Given that no other child molestation appears to have happened around here, I'd say he's either very new to the area or he's been controlling the urge for a long time.

"Let's go with the latter, since I don't think Nighthawk did it. So this guy has been repressing some very, very powerful urges for a long time. And suddenly they start to get the better of him, propelling him to satisfy them. Probably when he started planning this, he told himself he'd never carry it out. Told himself he was just fantasizing, but that he'd never do this thing.

"Only as he got more and more into it, it began to seem more and more possible. More and more likely he could pull it off and never be detected. And as he thought more and more about it, the compulsion to do it kept growing. Until finally it was controlling him rather than the other way around. It seemed so easy to do it, and it was just about impossible to stop.

"So he does it. Satisfies the compulsion. It loses its driving grip on him, and his brain begins to kick in again, just a little. Fear sets in. He ditches the girl and leaves a trail pointing to someone else, the way he'd planned it. Then he gets home...and the adrenaline quits. Without the high, he's scared, alone, facing reality, possibly for the first time in weeks. And then he thinks about that little girl lying out there on an icy creek bank and his conscience starts to work on him. No one'll ever find him, he tells himself. He pointed the finger at somebody else. But does the little girl have to die?"

Sandy drew a shaky breath. "So he picks up the phone, calls the sheriff's office, and tells them about the book bag."

"That's about it."

Something in the way his gaze slid away from hers told her that he was withholding something. "What's the rest of it, Garrett? What aren't you saying?"

He turned a little, so that she was looking at his profile, and kicked a loose stone into the rushing water. "Just that what this guy did goes beyond pedophilia. It's not a mere sexual quirk but something more. That's apparent by the fact that he abducted her, kept her for approximately twelve hours and left her to die. I've investigated more than one case of this nature, unfortunately. Usually the perp goes through a strong period of remorse and shame, but then the compulsion starts to take root again. As a rule, they do it again. And the next time is worse. He needs more to get the same high."

He looked over his shoulder at her. "This guy will move again, Sandy. I can't say when. There's no way to predict his schedule based on one incident. But the chances are good he'll work himself up to it again fairly soon. It just gets easier and easier for him each time. He's done it once, and now he'll do it again."

She nodded. "That possibility has been scaring me to death. We've got to get the right man behind bars."

A small boulder, left there long ago by a rushing torrent or a glacier, rested half in and half out of the water. It looked dry, and Sandy sat on it, electrically aware when Garrett settled beside her. She stared back up the stream coursing so hurriedly between its high banks, a swiftly moving muddy torrent from the clean white snow on the mountains.

This case had moved far beyond a matter of providing a defense as required by the constitution. It had become a matter of saving an innocent man and finding a vicious serial rapist before another child could be hurt. Sandy had never met Lisa Dunbar, but that didn't matter. She was a mother, and she'd had a five-year-old, and the thought of *any* child experiencing any part of what Lisa Dunbar had...

She shook her head, wiping the horrible thought away. It made her want to kill, when she really thought about it. A person who could do such things to a child was unfit to live.

The sheriff thought he had the right man. So until she and Garrett could prove otherwise, they would be the only people on earth trying to find the real perpetrator. The real rapist. The man who had to be stopped before he did it again.

And she knew Garrett was right. She hadn't made a study of it, but over the years she'd read here and there enough to know that people who committed this sort of crime never committed only one. Instead they would do it again and again in an ever-escalating spiral of violence, each act coming sooner after the last. If the rapist in this case had indeed just committed his first crime, then they might have weeks or even months before the next attempt. But if this wasn't his first...

She shivered again. The rock felt cold beneath her, almost icy even through her jeans. She shouldn't sit here long, she thought absently. She would quickly lose body heat through contact with the rock.

But she didn't move. It might be cold as all get-out, but she could feel Garrett's arm just brushing against hers, and she didn't want to lose that contact, even with the layers of clothing between them.

Some deeply buried place in her seemed to be opening, reminding her of things so long forgotten. How long had it been, for example, since a man had placed his arms around her shoulders? Oh, so long! She ached now for just that simple contact. That feeling that someone on this planet truly wanted to be close to her. How badly she needed to be hugged.

Before she could deny the yearning, Garrett seemed to read her mind. What was more, he didn't even try to be casual about it. He turned, looking fully at her, waiting until she turned tentatively to look back at him. When he had her full attention, he draped his arm over her shoulders and tucked her up against his side.

Her breath locked in her throat as she tilted her head back farther and looked up into his amazing blue eyes. Such a wonderful blue, she thought hazily, as her whole world seemed to narrow to this man, this moment.

He was going to kiss her. A flare of panic erupted within her, then faded, as a warm, needy feeling filled her. It had been so long, and Garrett was such a unique man, that this risk didn't seem too terrifying. A kiss. Just a kiss. How much harm could come from a simple kiss?

She let her eyelids flutter closed as his head bowed toward hers. This much trust she could give him. This much she had in her. It was, she told herself again, just a kiss. Nothing to fear.

That was her last coherent thought. Garrett's lips touched hers with warmth and tenderness, a gentle questing that demanded nothing and offered so much. Soft little kisses, sprinkled against her mouth with hardly more pressure than a warm raindrop, that made her soften internally, driving everything else from her mind before a tide of yearning.

The darkening afternoon spun away; the cold was forgotten. Nothing existed except Garrett and the blossoming hunger within her. Her head fell back, inviting a deeper invasion, and Garrett's tongue joined his lips in caressing her. Soft, sweeping strokes that made her mouth tingle, a tingling that seemed to spread through her in the wake of the softening warmth and arouse forgotten needs.

What could be the harm in a simple kiss? Now she knew. If he had wanted to sweep her beneath him and take her on that cold boulder, she would have let him. Awareness of her danger struck her like a bolt of lightning. In an instant she stiffened and pulled back, arousal and warmth lost in the frigid awareness of her inadequacy.

As soon as she stiffened, Garrett released her. She feared he would question her, would demand to know what was wrong. Instead he dropped a quick kiss on her forehead and slid off the boulder.

Turning, he offered her a smile and a hand. "We'd better hustle, or night is going to catch us before we're done."

Her legs felt like rubber as she followed him along the bank toward the cottonwood grove. Looking up, she saw that the clouds were scudding swiftly and seemed to be almost low enough to touch. If they didn't have snow, they were sure going to have some rain.

It was easier to think about the weather, about the case, than it was to think about what had just happened, so she pondered the cold spring, the slippery bank and the mind of a man who could abandon an injured child out here on a cold, dark night.

The distraction would work for a while. It always did. But later, when she was trying to fall asleep, she was going to have to deal with that kiss somehow. Deal with her reaction to it. She felt as if everything inside her had somehow been shaken free and was now drifting, rearranging itself, taking on a new and different configuration.

But she couldn't deal with that right now. That would have to wait. She didn't dare confront her confused feelings until she was safely private.

* * *

It was extremely unlikely that they would discover any new evidence among the trees where Lisa Dunbar had been found. Even in the slowly failing light, they could tell that the ground had been pretty well trampled.

"Crime-scene unit went over this with a fine tooth comb," Garrett remarked. Yellow streamers of plastic tape strung from tree to tree, still demarcated the area. Garrett didn't even bother to cross the line, just circled the area, looking at it from all angles. Leafless tree branches above nearly obscured the sky, they were so thick.

"A hell of a place to dump the kid," he said. "He sure didn't want her to be found. Let's walk up to the road now."

From here the terrain wasn't too difficult. Not impossible to cross at night, though it would require some care, Sandy thought. The hay had been mowed before winter set in, and the brown stalks were just thick enough to have concealed the passage of someone on foot. He had picked his ground well.

Garrett spoke. "So he made his way down to the stream with the kid. Probably had her wrapped in a blanket. Came back this way with the blanket, went to his vehicle, which could have been anywhere along this road at that time of night. I doubt anybody would drive along here before dawn, but even if they did, they probably wouldn't pay any attention to a vehicle pulled to one side unless there was something unusual about it. If he parked right at the end of Nighthawk's drive, nobody would notice at all."

"Probably not."

"So he gets back to the road, gets the girl's clothes from his trunk or wherever and then hikes up Nighthawk's driveway and buries the stuff behind the house."

By the time they had walked up the driveway and then the hundred and fifty yards to where more yellow tape was strung from stakes around a hole in the ground, Sandy was convinced of one thing: every step had been deliberate.

Nighthawk would have buried the clothes near Lisa, not on his own property. Not behind his house.

"Somebody is framing him," she said.

Garrett nodded slowly. "I reckon," he said.

"But who? And why?"

"Well, darlin', at this point I'd kind of guess somebody has an ax to grind. And I think we need to ask Nighthawk again about anyone who might have a grudge. Although, often enough, people really *don't* know someone is mad at them."

Darlin'. The absent endearment stuck with her as they drove back to town. He hadn't meant anything by it, she told herself. It had just slipped out and he didn't even realize he'd said it. Some people called *everyone* darling or honey.

Except that Garrett didn't seem to. At least, she'd never heard him do it before. But then, how well did she really know him?

Twilight had descended just about the time they reached the pit in Nighthawk's backyard, but it didn't linger long as the clouds swallowed the last of the light. The wind strengthened, each gust of its cold breath causing the Explorer to shudder, forcing Garrett to constantly correct for it.

It was not snow that began to fall, finally, but heavy drops of windswept rain that rattled against the windows of the car.

"It's damned inhospitable tonight," Garrett remarked as he slowed down and leaned forward a little to better see the wet road.

It even *sounded* cold, Sandy thought. Turning in her seat, she looked at Garrett and spoke before she could change her mind. "Why don't you stay and have dinner with me?"

He shot her a sharp glance, then nodded. "I'd like that. Thanks."

Only as they neared her house did she realize how that invitation might have sounded to him, coming as it did after their kiss earlier.

A blizzard of panic instantly filled her with ice. What if he took her invitation to dinner as an invitation to make love? Oh, God, what had she done?

Her stomach began to flutter nervously, and her brain scurried around frantically, trying to find an excuse to change her mind that wouldn't sound rude but also wouldn't reveal her panic. She didn't want him to know how scared she was of making love. She didn't want *anyone* to ever know that.

Nor did she want to face her fear. It wasn't fear because she had been raped, though that had been a brutal experience that had left an aftermath of problems for her to deal with. What scared her was not that Garrett might hurt her, but that he might humiliate her, as Gerry had done so many times.

That Garrett would discover she was frigid and would come away dissatisfied and scornful. That, even if he said nothing to humiliate her at all, her failure as a woman would still lie exposed to the glaring light of someone else's knowledge.

Her inability to respond to her husband after the rape had scared her as no mere rape could have. What if she tried to make love with Garrett and the old ghosts reared their heads, and she froze? What if, as had happened so often with Gerry in the immediate aftermath of the rape, she closed her eyes, felt a man's hands on her body and panicked? What if revulsion filled her and caused her to twist away as if Garrett were the attacker?

But that had only happened for a brief time after the attack. What had happened thereafter had been the direct result of Gerry's response to her panic and revulsion. She quite simply froze up inside. Withdrew to someplace safe in her own mind and refused to let any of it touch her, so that when he began to say those vile things about her frigidity, they wouldn't be able to touch her where it hurt.

And the root of the problem was that deep inside she believed Gerry had been justified. Throughout their marriage she had been sexually inhibited, but after the rape... well, what had been a perfectly normal reaction to the assault had been turned by Gerry's condemnation into something considerably worse.

It had, however, resulted in her facing what a farce her marriage had become. His lack of support for her after the attack had forced her to look hard and long at all the other ways he had failed to support her. All the ways he had undermined her.

And leaving Gerry had unquestionably been one of the smartest moves she had ever made. Little by little she had pieced herself back together, had nurtured her own confidence and strength... and had unquestionably raised a better son as a result. She had never, and would never, regret the divorce.

But there was a part of her that had never healed. A part that she had chosen to bury, rather than deal with all the painful scar tissue. A part of her that she was being forced to look straight in the eye as Garrett helped her down from the Explorer, as they entered her house and climbed the stairs to her apartment above the office.

Like a frightened horse, she had a wild urge to bolt. If she just turned and ran out into the rain-lashed night, Garrett would take the hint and never trouble her again.

But was that what she really wanted?

At the head of the stairs, on the landing, he took the key from her trembling hand and slipped it into the lock that kept her apartment inviolate during the day when the lower part of the house was open for business. She heard the thump as the dead bolt slid back, the creak of hinges as the door swung open. Garrett reached across her and felt for the light switch.

Oh, God, she thought, her heart hammering wildly, what now?

Light flooded the landing, and Garrett looked down at her. There was barely a breath of air between them, making her certain he must be able to hear her heart hammer.

He smiled, the corners of his blue eyes crinkling attractively. "Can I see your file on the case after dinner?"

It was as if he had pulled a plug; all the tension seeped out of her, leaving her almost weak. "Sure," she said. "After dinner."

Dinner and work. That was all. Relief should have made her giddy. Instead, all it did was disappoint her.

Chapter 8

For dinner she made a stir-fry and had the unique experience of being assisted in the kitchen by a man who actually knew how to slice vegetables.

"Now, that's a female chauvinist attitude," he teased her when she commented. "I've been living alone a long time, darlin'. It was either learn to cook or spend my whole paycheck in restaurants."

"I take it you don't like that old staple, the fast-food hamburger?"

"If I'm going to eat a burger, it has to be all beef, thick, cooked rare and smothered in onions and Swiss cheese."

"Picky, picky."

After dinner they sprawled on the floor with the file again, just as they had last night. Tonight, though, Garrett was particularly looking for the record of the phone call to the sheriff about the little girl's book bag being seen along Willis Road.

"Here it is," he said. "'Male caller at 8:33 a.m. Said he'd seen what looked like a kid's book bag while driving to work. Said he hadn't touched it, but wondered if it might belong to that little girl who was missing. Disconnected abruptly without identifying himself and didn't call back.'"

Garrett, who was sitting on the floor, closed the file and leaned back against the couch. "I don't like the sound of it. Something fishy as hell about that call. How many people live out along Willis Road?"

"I'm not sure. I could find out."

"In the morning. We'll check it out in the morning." He tilted his head back and turned it so he could look at her. She was curled up with her feet tucked under her, leaning against the couch at the opposite end. Avoidance, he thought. Something had made her as skittish as a doe about the time she'd asked him to have dinner with her.

At first her distancing had struck him as strange, but now, as he thought it over and put it together with her abrupt pulling away when he had kissed her, he had to conclude that she was afraid of the sexual attraction between them.

Well, he couldn't blame her for that. If he had a grain of the common sense he'd always prided himself on, he would get up right now and get out of here before he followed through on a growing desire to wrap his arms around her and hold her close. Because once he got her close—if she let him—he might not be able to keep it casual.

He might not be able to let go.

Looking away, he pretended fascination with the toes of his socks. Problem was, or so he tried to tell himself, that as he got older, he got a whole lot more discriminating about women. In practical terms that meant it had been many months since he'd held a woman, and one hell of lot longer since he'd made love to one. That was the price of pickiness. And that meant that when he met a woman like Sandy Keller, a woman who appealed to his head and heart as much as his body, he was damn near a pushover.

Time to get out of here, before he did something they would both regret. Refusing himself an opportunity to change his mind, he rose to his feet in a single swift movement. Sandy looked startled, then quickly unfolded herself and stood. "Leaving?" she asked.

But he couldn't make himself. Silly as it was, he couldn't make himself reach for his boots and get the hell out of there. Instead he reached for Sandy. His arms stretched out toward her, open, his palms turned upward a little, beseeching. If she had stiffened, if she had run, if she had made the least movement or sound of rejection, he would have turned and left.

But she didn't. She licked her lips nervously, looking from his arms to his face, probably never realizing how much he read in her expression. Like a mistreated child, she both yearned for the offered affection and was terrified of it.

If he had any doubts of the wisdom of escaping, that should have settled it. Whatever had happened to this lady, he was hardly likely to be able to fix it. Maybe he couldn't even deal with it. How could he possibly know? And if he *mis*handled it, he might make her problems worse. He didn't dare risk it.

Which was precisely why he stepped toward her and, ignoring her fear and uncertainty, swept her into a bear hug that hauled her flush to his body. Ah, hell, he thought dismally, and squeezed her even closer. She felt so damn good. A bundle of feminine softness, complete with the faint, enticing fragrance of woman.

"It's okay," he heard himself say huskily, though he hadn't the vaguest idea what needed to be okay. Nor did he have the dimmest idea of what he might be promising. "It's okay," he said again.

He felt a shudder rip through her. If her hands had tried to push him away, he would have let go instantly. Instead they clutched at him, crushing the front of his shirt in a death grip. She was scared to death, but the lady didn't want to be somewhere else.

In which case... Taking a huge chance, he tilted her head upward with the gentle pressure of one finger. Her eyes were closed tightly—too tightly—but she didn't try to pull her head away.

So he kissed her. Kissed her and hoped to hell he wasn't making a huge mistake. He would hate it if Sandy got angry with him or wouldn't have anything more to do with him. For an instant she grew really stiff against him, but then nothing else seemed to matter, for her lips parted beneath his, and there was no mistaking the way her head fell back in timeless surrender.

The woman softened for him. There was no greater aphrodisiac in the world than realizing that a woman wanted him, and this one did. She was scared, maybe even terrified, but she wanted this kiss as much as he did. Taking care not to scare her, he touched her lips gently with his tongue, then slipped it inside tentatively, alert for any sign of fright or rejection.

None came. A little more boldly, his tongue foraged in her warm silky depths, and he found himself wishing his whole aching body could slip into her just like his tongue. In this woman's depths he would be able to forget everything else, would be able to put aside all his problems and worries for a little.

Even as he had the thought, he felt guilty. She wasn't an anodyne to his problems, and he had absolutely no right to even think of using her in such a fashion. She was a woman with feelings and needs every bit as important as his own, and she deserved to be treated as such.

But even the fleeting attack of guilt couldn't make him let go. Couldn't make him stop kissing her. His need for her warmth and closeness was almost desperate.

But not desperate enough to make him forget that she was frightened. Her breasts, belly and thighs were pressed snugly to him, but before they could make him forget his good sense, he lifted his head and tucked her against his shoulder.

"You're a beautiful, sexy woman, Sandra Keller. I'd better get out of here before I get carried away." He didn't mind admitting what she made him feel. What he hoped was that she might confide in him about her fears.

But she didn't. A soft, regretful sigh escaped her, and slowly she pulled away. Reluctantly he let her.

Two minutes later he was standing outside next to his Explorer, with icy rain slapping his cheeks. It was a dark, cold night, and he didn't think he'd ever felt so alone.

"Ninety-nine...one hundred." He let the tennis ball go and watched it bounce across the dingy motel carpet. No question but that he was about ready to chew the furniture. The wind howled noisily around the corner of his room, the rain rattling loudly against the window, beginning to sound very much like heavy sleet. Everyone in Conard County except him had probably gone to sleep hours ago.

He resisted the urge to get out his pistol and see if he could hold it steadily yet. No point in even attempting it. He might heal. It was entirely possible that he would regain full use of his arm. But there was no way he could gauge improvement, and no way that simple improvement would be enough to get him back on duty. That arm had to work flawlessly, and he still had plenty of time before he had to face that. In the meantime, there was absolutely no point in riding a roller coaster of emotion from day to day as he tried to tell if he was improving.

But it was close to driving him crazy, this wondering. With a disgusted sigh, he flopped back onto the bed and tried not to think about his hazy future. Tried, too, not to think about a certain lady lawyer who was preoccupying far too much of his thoughts lately.

Only a damn fool would get involved under these circumstances. She was as skittish as a woman could get, obviously afraid, probably a mess from her marriage. He was leaving shortly, and anyway, he might not even have a job at this rate. How could he even consider getting involved?

And involved was what he was going to get if he spent too much time with Sandy Keller. Something about her kept tugging at him in the most uncomfortable way, despite the fact that she seemed to be as determined as he to remain uninvolved.

Ready to growl, he looked at his watch and decided that *this* time his sister was going to have to put up with being awakened, the way she'd roused him so many times when Bobby had gotten drunk and abusive.

Damn! His hand paused over the phone, hovering, as he remembered his sister's seemingly endless marriage. How many times had he begged her to leave, offered her a safe haven, promised to protect her from that crud? But like so many victims, Ginny had been sure Bobby meant it when he wept and swore he wouldn't do it again. Believed it when he blamed her for his rages, saying he wouldn't have hit her if only she hadn't done some little thing like make the mashed potatoes too creamy. Believed that if only she were a better wife he wouldn't hit her at all.

"Hell!" The word escaped him, briefly filling the silence and emptiness of the motel room. It was always hard from the outside looking in to understand why anybody put up with that crap. Hard to fathom why anybody would take that treatment for so long. Some took it for a lifetime. His sister hadn't, largely because she'd had alternatives.

He'd been rousted out of bed in the middle of the night a lot of times in his life. For one thing, it went with his job. Then there had been Ginny. How many times had he picked up the phone and heard her frightened, weepy voice begging him to come and get her and the kids because Bobby had been drinking again? How many times had he begged her to file charges and then listened to her insist that she'd banged her face on a door or fallen down? Or worse, had insisted that Bobby hadn't meant to hit her, and no, she wasn't going to send him to jail over a few little bruises. Besides, it had been *her* fault because . . . because . . . because. The stony silence when he had persisted.

Finally one night Bobby had beaten her so badly that Garrett had to take her to the hospital. That night Garrett had returned to the house with a city police officer, who arrested Bobby for assault with intent to kill. Because that time Garrett had arrived in time to see some of it with his own two eyes.

The years since had been good, watching Ginny put herself back together with the aid of counselors, watching the fear gradually fade from her eyes and the eyes of the children.

And, of course, there was the memory of the fear in Bobby's eyes when Garrett had told him in no uncertain terms that if he ever came near Ginny or the kids again, Garrett would shoot him.

It really wouldn't be very nice to disturb Ginny's sleep with a phone call. What would he say to her, anyway? Hi, I'm fine, and I'm trying like mad not to get involved with a lady who wouldn't want me, anyway? Ginny would immediately want to know all about Sandy, then would badger him to go for it and remind him that he would spend the rest of his life alone if he didn't at least make an attempt.

He found himself grinning at the ceiling, realizing that he didn't even need to call Ginny, because he'd already had the entire conversation. But he lifted the receiver and dialed her number, anyway. It had been a week or more, and he got to worrying about his little sister.

"Garrett!" She sounded sleepy but pleased, and brushed away his apology for calling so late. "I woke you up more times than I can count. Are you okay?"

"I'm fine, Ginny. Fine. Just got to hankerin' for the sound of your voice. How are you and the rug rats doing?"

"We're doing just fine."

But there was a very faint hesitation when she answered, just enough to alert him that she was worrying about something. He would let it ride a bit, see if she brought it up herself. If she didn't, he would pin her down. It wouldn't be the first time.

"Bobby, Jr., is collecting bugs for a school project. Did I tell you about that? Well, I opened the microwave last night to put the broccoli in, and there was a jar full of bugs. Garrett, I swear! He doesn't want to kill them the way the teacher told him to, because it takes too long and he doesn't like hurting them. So he microwaved them!"

Garrett couldn't have stopped the laughter that rolled out of him. "Makes sense to me."

"Well, not to me! It makes my skin crawl to think of him putting those filthy things in there, where I cook food! Even if they were in a jar." A quiet chuckle escaped her. "Actually, it reminded me of you, and I can't for the life of me say why."

"A jar of bugs reminded you of me?" He tried to sound offended but didn't quite succeed.

"No, silly, not the bugs. No, it was the way Bobby, Jr., handled the situation. Creative problem solving, to say the least."

She went on to tell him a few amusing tales about her two younger children, but he didn't hear a thing that could have caused her any concern at all. Finally he asked her point-blank what was worrying her.

For a few moments silence hummed between them on the line. Finally she spoke in a subdued voice. "The parole board sent me a letter."

"And?"

"It seems Bobby's going to get out of prison next month. It's mandatory, they said."

Garrett swore, knowing how that news had to make her feel. "Listen, Ginny. I promise I'll be home before then. You won't have to deal with this alone."

"Isn't there some way they can make him stay in jail?"

"I'm afraid not. If they said it's mandatory, then he's got enough time served and enough good time to get out, and there's nothing anyone can do about it. It's the law."

"Well." She managed a shaky laugh. "He's stupid, but not stupid enough to try to come after me."

"No, I don't think he is. He knows I'll kill him if anything happens to you, so I expect he'll stay far away. But it doesn't matter, anyway, because I'll be there. I promise." Right, Hancock. As if you can keep another person absolutely safe twenty-four hours a day. Besides, the last time he had looked, there hadn't been a big yellow *S* on his chest. "I'll get back there soon, and we'll deal with it, Ginny. I swear. He's not gonna hurt you or the kids ever again."

Thanks to that little piece of news, they never got around to discussing him, which was just fine, because sure as shootin' he would have mentioned Sandy. Then it would have been the third degree for sure.

Later, wishing for a cigarette, he worked the tennis ball over some more and listened to the cold rattle of sleet against the window panes. The problem, he told himself, was that you couldn't always tell who was going to be a repeat offender. Spouse abusers and child abusers tended to keep right on doing it, no matter how many times you put them away. Problem was, they were prosecuted under the same assault laws that applied to knocking somebody down on the street because they drove into the side of your car. Consequently, the "good time" calendar and mandatory parole were applied evenly across the board, regardless of whether a person was liable to commit the same crime again.

It was an unhappy fact that, no matter what he'd told her, his sister was in considerable danger from her ex-husband. If Bobby Taylor felt Ginny was responsible for his incarceration, he might well take a mind to teach her a lesson. Or to get even. And there was no real way to know if he was that kind of person. The only thing anyone could know for sure was that, all too often, when somebody like Bobby Taylor got out of jail, he went after the person he perceived to be at the root of all his troubles: his ex-wife.

Well, he would worry about that when he got home and could actually do something about it. Until Bobby was released, there was no threat and absolutely no point in wondering if he would be what his sister needed when the time came.

He had enough demons on his plate right now, mainly wondering what he was going to do if he couldn't go back to work. He talked about it as if it didn't matter, but the fact was, early retirement was about as appealing as a case of cancer to him. Either one would gut him and kill him. But no point thinking about that right now, either. Some things could only be dealt with when you looked them right in the eye.

What he needed to be thinking about was the Nighthawk case. After tramping around out there earlier, he was convinced that Nighthawk was being framed. Simple as that. Oh, he could be wrong—that was always a possibility—but the way things looked now, he would bet the ranch on Nighthawk's innocence.

Which meant that the best way to exonerate Nighthawk was to figure out who was trying to frame him. Nighthawk didn't seem to think he had any enemies around here who would want to do that, but it wouldn't necessarily be someone who was mad at him. The little girl's father, for example, might be the perp. In fact, in far too many of these cases a relative was to blame. So just for argument's sake, say it *was* Dunbar who'd hurt the little girl. Why would he choose to frame Nighthawk, of all people?

Because Nighthawk had been seen with Lisa last month. Because someone else had seen the little girl in Nighthawk's truck and would remember it. Easy to frame the Indian. And that would explain why the initial report of the incident had come from what's his name—Willis—instead of Dunbar. If Dunbar were guilty, he wouldn't want to make himself obvious by bringing up the information first. But he might well have reminded Willis about it, jogging the man's memory, so to speak.

Perhaps the most frightening thing about the thoughts running through his head at the moment was their plausibility. Ben Dunbar the bad guy? Yeah. It made all too damn much sense.

And it made his stomach churn. There was nothing more horrible than a parent doing something like that to his own little kid.

In an instant, the night became a time of terror for Sandy. She'd been snuggled into her bed with quilts drawn to her chin, sleeping deeply, when something had startled her into wakefulness with a pounding heart.

The sense of threat was unmistakable. Ordinarily, when a sound woke her during the night, her mind registered it with a ready explanation that allowed her to turn over and go back to sleep. A tree limb brushing against the side of the house. The wind moaning around the corner. A car back-firing....

But this time she awoke with a definite sense of threat. She had heard something that was not a normal night sound, and her hammering heart demanded more air than she was getting.

Eyes wide open, she stared into the dark and listened so intently that her ears felt strained. Even when the night remained as silent as only the night could be at around four in the morning, she couldn't escape the sense that she had heard some*one* rather than some*thing*.

But there was no other sound, and after endless minutes of nerve-stretching fright and alertness, she began to relax. It had just been an odd sound from outside. Maybe some kid driving by in a car had shouted something and she'd mistaken it for a threat of some kind. Perhaps a cat had howled and her mind had registered it as a scream. Maybe she'd just been having a bad dream that had somehow commingled with a night sound to make something perfectly ordinary seem threatening.

Finally, facing the fact that she wasn't going to fall back to sleep soon, she sat up, tucked her feet into slippers and padded out to the kitchen to make tea.

The sky had cleared since bedtime, and moonlight fell through the uncurtained kitchen window, reflecting off icicles on the leafless tree just outside. The wind had died, leaving the night utterly calm.

Without turning on a light, she lit the burner beneath the teakettle and took a tea bag from the canister beside the stove. Moonlight, she thought, was so coldly beautiful.

Then she heard it again. Something was inside the house. Downstairs. She had heard it move.

She stopped breathing and reached over to turn the flame off beneath the kettle, wanting absolute silence from which to listen.

A mouse, she told herself. Some poor little field mouse must have come in from the cold and was—

Again. A sound so soft it was almost impossible to hear. As if... As if someone were climbing the stairs to her apartment.

For several heartbeats she was paralyzed, unable to move at all as her ears strained to listen but she could hear nothing except her own galloping heart. There was a dead bolt on the door between her apartment and the stairs, and it was a solid core wood door. It would take a little time for the intruder to break in.

That awareness released her from paralysis. Heedless of whether she made any sound, she scurried across the kitchen and grabbed for the wall phone. The sheriff was the first number on the autodialer, and she punched the button, listening to the familiar series of tones impatiently. Not even a machine could dial fast enough for her.

A sleepy-sounding Virgil Beauregard answered the phone.

"Beau, this is Sandy Keller. There's someone in my office downstairs, and it sounds like he's coming up here—"

"We're on our way, Sandy," Beau said abruptly, no longer sounding sleepy. "Keep the phone off the hook. I'm going to keep the line open, okay? Now, make sure the door is locked, then go hide in a closet."

But she couldn't bring herself to go hide in the closet. If the intruder managed to get through the door before the sheriff arrived, she didn't want to be trapped in a confined place with no escape route. After a moment's hesitation, she went to the cabinet beside the stove and pulled out a heavy cast-iron skillet. If anyone came through that door, she was going to be waiting right behind it.

But there was no further sound from the stairway—at least nothing that reached her through the closed door. From far away she could hear a siren and wondered if that could be the sheriff heading for her house.

But no, they would approach without sirens and probably without lights, so they wouldn't alert the prowler and cause him to run. Reaching behind her, she felt for the cord of the wall phone. The receiver was dangling almost to the floor, and she had to bend to find it. At last she tucked it to her ear.

"Beau?" she whispered.

"Aren't you hiding yet?" he growled. "There's a car pulling up two doors east of you. The officer is going to approach the house on foot. Now you go hide."

"No. I'm staying right here. If he tries to get through the door, I'm going to hit him over the head."

"Damn it, Sandy, this is no time to play hero!"

"I don't have the right build to be a hero," she managed to whisper shakily. Her mouth was so dry that her lips were sticking to her teeth, and her hand ached from holding the handle of the skillet. From below, she heard no sound at all.

"This is no time for humor, either," Beau grumbled. "Okay, the officer is approaching the house right now. This is the dangerous part, Sandy. No matter what you hear, keep that door locked until I tell you it's safe to come out. Hear?"

"I hear." God, if minutes could move any slower, they would encompass aeons. But even as she wished the officer outside would hurry, she felt concerned for him. It would have to be awful to walk into a dark building with no idea whether someone was in there, or if the intruder was armed. Closing her eyes, she said a little prayer that no one got hurt. "Who's the officer, Beau?"

"Ed Dewhurst."

Ed. She knew Ed pretty well, had dated him a couple of times after his first wife died and before he remarried. Now he had four kids, the eldest of whom was thirteen. Oh, Lord, don't let anything happen to him.

"He's at the front door, Sandy," Beau told her. "Someone definitely broke in. The glass has been knocked out so he could reach the doorknob."

"Tell Ed to be careful."

"Backup's on the way," Beau reassured her. "Should be there any second. He won't be alone."

There was still no sound from downstairs, but that could have been because she was hanging on to Beau's voice in her ear like a lifeline, so it was hard to listen for faint sounds from below.

But maybe the intruder had already left. The floors tended to creak up here when she walked, and it was audible downstairs. Or perhaps he had heard her call the police. She hadn't exactly been quiet about it.

Oh, how she wished she weren't alone right now! Thoughts of Garrett suddenly filled her with something that was almost despair. If she hadn't stiffened when he kissed her, maybe he would still be here. Maybe she wouldn't be alone.

She was so *tired* of being alone, locked in a prison of self-doubt about her womanhood. She didn't see how she could possibly escape it, though. Not when the only way out was for some man to make her feel sexually adequate, and that was unlikely to happen when she panicked every time anyone kissed her.

Nor was that entire subject something she wanted to be thinking about when something terrible could happen at any moment. At this point she didn't know which she wanted more—to hear something from downstairs or to hear nothing at all.

"They've finished checking around outside, Sandy," Beau said in her ear. "Ed's coming in now."

Probably the same way the thief had gotten in, she thought, through the door with the broken-out glass. But even though she strained to hear, there was still no sound from below. Ed must be as silent as a cat.

More minutes stretched tautly, and now Beau couldn't even give her a blow-by-blow, because Ed was busy checking out the house and was probably being silent. Sandy let the skillet dangle by her side and wondered if her fingers would ever uncramp.

And then, at last, Beau said, "Sandy? Ed's coming up the stairs now. You can let him in. No one's below."

"Thanks, Beau. Thanks."

"No problem. This is what we're here for."

Moments later Ed was smiling at her from the landing. "Whoever it was is gone, Sandy. Maybe you want to come down and tell us what's missing, though. He got into some stuff."

She pulled on a velour robe over her flannel nightgown and followed Ed downstairs. Light blazed everywhere—he'd evidently turned on every light in the place when he'd finished checking things out. Another deputy, whose name she didn't know, was standing near the front door.

"Somebody broke in through that door," Ed said. "Broke out the one pane so he could reach in and get hold of the knob. He broke into your secretary's desk and into a file cabinet in your office. Looking for money, I guess."

He'd found some, too, Sandy saw. The petty-cash box had been pried open and emptied of everything except receipts.

"There was definitely cash in there," she told Ed, "but exactly how much is something Nina will have to tell you. Couldn't have been more than a couple of hundred, but judging by the receipts, it was probably a good deal less."

Her office was another matter. Someone had broken into the locked file cabinet where she kept her case files. The top drawer had been pried open, probably with a crowbar, and files had been rifled. Her files from this year. Her stomach sank with a horrible sense of violation.

"He was probably just looking for money," Ed said, trying to be soothing. "What interest could anyone possibly have in your files?"

Plenty, thought Sandy grimly. Plenty. There was probably enough blackmail material in those files to fuel a crime wave. But she was reluctant to say so to Ed, reluctant to discuss such possibilities with someone who enjoyed gossip as much as anyone else in the county.

"We'll have to dust the files for prints," Ed told her. "Sorry, Sandy. It's going to be a mess."

For an instant she wanted to stamp her foot and protest all of this like a two-year-old. Not only had she been robbed, not only had the secrets of her neighbors been pawed through, but now the guardians of law and order were proposing to mess things up even more. She couldn't have said at that moment whether she objected more to the idea of black fingerprint powder all over everything or to the idea of police officers going through her confidential files. They wouldn't read anything... would they?

"You can't dust the files," she said flatly. "Anything else, but *not* the files."

"Look, Sandy—"

"No, *you* look, Ed! I realize you want to catch this jerk, but I can't have you going through my files. Those things are protected by attorney-client privilege. I can't let anyone else look at them. I won't allow it."

"But—"

"Absolutely not! Half the people in this county are my clients! How would *you* feel if you found out some cop had been dusting *your* file for fingerprints and maybe reading parts of your will and discovering you'd— Oh, never mind! This stuff is confidential, and confidential it remains."

Uncertain how to handle it, Ed called Nate. Twenty minutes later, looking slightly rumpled and with a pillow crease still visible on his cheek, Nate showed up.

"She's right," he told Ed. "Attorney-client privilege is protected by law. What's more, I don't feel like dealing with an irate Henry Freitag or a furious Steve Stephanopoulos if you guys come within five feet of their files here. As far as the files go, only Sandy touches them." He turned to her, almost glaring. "And you go through them and see if anything is missing."

For the first time since she'd been awakened, she felt things were genuinely under control. A crooked smile tugged her lips as she nodded to Nate. "You got it."

Nate spent the next half hour checking things out, too, and finally concluded it was the Walker kid. "It has his M.O. all over it," he told Sandy and Ed. "Even got through the front door exactly the same way. Damn it, Williams gives the kid a suspended sentence, and the next day he's out doing it again!''

Sandy wasn't so sure about that, but remembering Les Walker's sullen expression, she didn't see how she could argue.

"Did that kid know you had a cash box?'' Nate asked her.

She opened her mouth to say that all businesses kept a petty-cash box and everyone knew it, when she had a sudden memory of Les Walker delivering lunch from Maude's two days before he was arrested for the Mercantile break-in. And Nina taking the petty-cash box out of the bottom drawer of her desk.... "Yes, he knew."

"Well, that about settles it. Guess I need to have a long talk with that kid.''

Sandy turned back to her files, still not convinced—until five minutes later when she discovered that one file was indeed missing: Les Walker's.

By the time she climbed her stairs, dawn was beginning to lighten the eastern sky. From outside she heard the slam of the sheriff's car doors as Nate and his deputies drove away. This night was a lost cause, she thought. There wasn't a chance she could go back to sleep now.

Finally, risking it, she called Garrett at the motel and asked him if he wanted to join her at Maude's for breakfast. If she didn't talk to somebody, she was going to burst a gasket, or so she felt. And there wasn't anybody else she wanted to roust out of bed to have breakfast with. Or anybody else she wanted to talk this over with. Nina or any of her other girlfriends would all probably be seriously alarmed and start demanding she move out of her apartment above the office to someplace safer. She wasn't quite sure what that safer place might be. Heck, there wasn't a safer place in the country than right here.

Although at the moment it sure didn't feel like it.

"Give me twenty minutes, Sandy" was Garrett's response to her invitation. He didn't sound sleepy at all.

She had taken only one step from the phone when it rang, a jarring sound in the early morning quiet.

"I saw the cops outside your place, lawyer," said a muffled male voice. "Getting scared? You ought to. Maybe if somebody raped you, you wouldn't be so quick to defend the guy who hurt that kid."

With a loud click, he disconnected.

Sandy stared blankly at the kitchen wall, at first too stunned to even react. Cold waves began to wash through her, and her knees threatened to buckle. Then an electric jolt of anger strengthened her, and she slammed the phone back into the cradle. How dare he? How dare *anyone?*

When she arrived, Garrett was already at Maude's, sitting in the booth by the front window, stirring a steaming mug of coffee. The way he looked at her as she slid into the seat facing him warned her that he didn't at all think this was a casual invitation.

"What happened?" he asked as soon as Maude brought Sandy coffee and a menu.

"My office was broken into. Someone took whatever was left of the petty cash and broke into my filing cabinet. Les Walker's file is missing, and Nate thinks Walker did the break-in."

"Why? Just because his file is missing?"

"No, he said the M.O. is exactly like Walker, too. The way the window pane on the front door was broken out so he could reach inside and unlock it."

"That's hardly a unique way of breaking in." Garrett shook his head slightly. "I have all the respect in the world for Nate, and maybe y'all don't have a whole lot of burglars around here, but that's hardly enough to hang Walker on." He lifted his mug halfway to his mouth, then paused. "Something else is bugging you. You don't think it was Walker, either."

"No, I don't. There was no reason on earth for him to take his file. It's not like I had proof of his guilt or innocence stashed in there. But whoever it was took the money, too. And that *is* like Walker. Oh, I don't know." She shook her head impatiently. "I probably shouldn't even worry about it. It probably *was* Walker, and he probably took his file to thumb his nose at me. He never liked me."

"I gather the feeling was mutual."

She smiled wanly. "You could say that."

They ordered breakfast, Garrett going for a double stack of Maude's sourdough pancakes, sausage and eggs, and Sandy preferring just an English muffin. Then Garrett leaned back and looked out the window, drumming his fingers absently on the tabletop. He wanted a cigarette, Sandy thought. She wondered how he found the willpower to keep telling himself no.

"The break-in isn't all of it, Sandy," he said, surprising her. "What aren't you telling me?"

"When did you start reading minds?"

He gave her a wry smile. "After I became a cop and realized that most people weren't telling me everything. Something in the way your eyes moved, I guess. So what else happened?"

"Just a nasty phone call."

"At the office?"

"No, in my apartment. Right after I called you." She shrugged, as if it were nothing, but she could tell he wasn't buying it.

"What did he say?"

"How do you know it was a he?"

"Because it almost always is. What did he say?"

"Nothing, really. It was—" She broke off and looked away, fixing her gaze on the snowbank between the sidewalk and the street. It would be the last part of winter to vanish from Conard City. But thinking about snow couldn't help her right now, as she realized that the call had affected her far more than she had guessed. It shouldn't have been hard to repeat what had been said, but she found it incredibly difficult.

"Sandy?"

"He asked if I was getting scared. Said I ought to be."
She couldn't continue.

"And?"

"And what?"

Garrett sighed. "Damn it, Sandy, you don't expect me to
believe that you're this upset about a phone call simply because someone said you ought to be getting scared."

"That's enough, isn't it?"

"No." He leaned forward, locking her gaze to his. "He
threatened you in some way, didn't he?"

"Not exactly." She saw the impatience sweep over his
face, and somehow it made her blurt out the last of it. "He
said maybe if somebody raped me, I wouldn't be so quick
to defend Nighthawk."

Garrett swore. "That was a threat, and you know it! Did
he say anything else?"

"That was all. He hung up right away."

He reached across the table and covered her folded hands
with one of his. "You feel like ice." He squeezed gently but
didn't let go. "Why didn't you want to tell me that? Something all but locked the words in your throat."

It wasn't something she talked about. In fact, she didn't
think she'd mentioned it to anyone since returning to Conard City.

But now, without warning, she heard herself say, "A long
time ago, I *was* raped."

Chapter 9

Suddenly Garrett understood a lot of things about her that had vaguely puzzled him before. Her interest in him that was countered by her stiffening when he touched her. The fact that she had apparently avoided men for a long time.

"I'm sorry," he said quietly. "That must have been terrible for you."

"I think it was worse for my husband." She looked quickly away.

Uh-oh, he thought, tightening his grip on her hands to let her know he was still with her, even as the words dried up in his throat. Worse for her husband. That said a hell of a lot, none of which made him very happy.

"Why?" he asked after a few moments. "Why was it worse for him?" There were a lot of reasons why men withdrew from their wives after they were raped, everything from feeling the woman was somehow sullied or tainted by the rape to a fear that perhaps she had enjoyed it, even asked for it, to a simple concern that making love might reawaken the memory of the rape. Some men even became impotent. And none of that was very good for the woman who had been victimized by someone else and now found herself a pariah in her own bed.

The restaurant was beginning to fill up with local business people who wanted breakfast, and when Sandy glanced around at the growing crowd, he knew she wasn't going to answer him. Nor could he blame her; anyone could eavesdrop.

"I suppose," he said, "that your office is a mess right now."

"Slightly. Fingerprint powder all over the place."

"I'll come back with you and help clean it up." When she smiled at him, he knew he'd gotten over the rough spot. Later, he promised himself. Later he was going to get her to tell him all about it.

The newspaper broke the story of the rape that morning. Lisa Dunbar's name wasn't mentioned, but Craig Nighthawk's was, and so was Sandy's. By noon the answering machine had recorded more than thirty calls from people who were angry at Sandy for being Nighthawk's attorney.

There were no calls after that, and Sandy felt it wasn't nearly as bad as it could have been ... or as she had feared it might be. Of course, she didn't seem to have any clients left, but she figured that would change in a week or two when the furor died down a little. People would remember she was a neighbor, someone they had known all their lives. The reaction this morning was simply a way of expressing their revulsion at the crime.

"You're a lot calmer about it than most people would be," Garrett remarked.

"It'll get better." She had to believe that. What was the point of believing anything else? She had taken this case for valid reasons, and she wasn't going to allow herself to be intimidated into quitting. "Actually, this will give me more time to concentrate on the Nighthawk case, which will make me feel a whole lot better."

"An optimist, I see." He turned in a slow circle, looking around the office and reception area. They had cleaned up all the fingerprint powder and moved the files from the damaged cabinet into a new one. The place looked ready for business, but there was no business. The phone had stopped ringing, and the afternoon appointment book was empty.

"What say we get out of here for a while?" Garrett suggested. The last thing she needed, he felt, was to sit around here and brood about her evaporating practice and the nasty phone calls.

"Where to?" she asked. She was staring glumly at the telephone on her desk, as if waiting for it to ring with more bad news, and Garrett felt an uncomfortable tug in the vicinity of his breastbone. She would bounce back, he was sure, but he wanted to help her feel better faster.

"Well," he said slowly, "I can't ask you home to look at my etchings, because Texas is a little too far to go in a single afternoon."

"I could almost—" She broke off and looked up with a sudden smile as she realized what he'd just said.

He winked. "How's about we just get in the car and drive? The roads are pretty clear, and at the very least we can hit a restaurant in the next county for dinner. Just to add a little spice to life."

It actually added quite a bit of spice in her life, Sandy thought as they drove north toward the next county and what were supposed to be some of the best steaks in Wyoming. At least, that was what she'd heard, but she'd never wanted to make the trip by herself. Evidently someone had been telling Garrett about the place, too, because he was convinced it was worth driving more than a hundred and fifty miles.

"It's not so common these days," he told her, "but it wasn't so long ago folks in Austin didn't think anything of driving to Dallas for dinner... about three hours each way. I'd think folks in these parts are pretty much used to driving those kinds of distances, too."

"Most of us are, I guess. It's just not something I want to do alone."

"I can understand why," he said after the briefest hesitation. "It's a dangerous world for women. I talked to my sister last night."

The sudden change of topic came as a relief to Sandy, who'd been afraid he was going to question her about her rape. That would be her own fault, since she had brought it up herself, but it wasn't something she wanted to dig up. "How's she doing?"

"Pretty good. Kinda strikes me as ironic that just about the time she's getting herself back together and living a normal life, the parole board writes and tells her that her ex is getting out."

"Didn't she have a chance to protest?"

Garrett shook his head. "This is mandatory parole. No choice. So he'll be back on the street sometime next month. I've got to be back down there by then."

Disappointment filled Sandy as she faced how short a time Garrett had left here, but she forced it down. "Do you think he'd . . . come after her?"

Again he shook his head. "I wish I knew. There's just no way to predict something like that."

"Has he made any threats against her since he was sent up?"

"Not that I'm aware of. Oh, he said a few things to her right after the trial, but then he seemed to let it go. Impossible to tell if he was just blowing off steam or if he really meant any of it. Impossible to know if he still might feel that way."

"But some of them do."

"They sure do."

It was Sandy's turn to shake her head. "It's just terrible the way some men treat women. Just terrible."

"Terrible the way some women treat men, too," he said. "I've been called to more than one domestic disturbance where it was the woman beating up the guy."

She glanced at him with a wry smile. "Point taken. Terrible the way some people treat their spouses."

"Amen to that."

"How are you going to be able to watch over your sister, though? Does she live nearby?"

"I had her and the kids move in with me after she left Bobby. The house was sure big enough, and it was the best way to make her feel safe and help her get back on her feet. She's almost ready to graduate with a degree in math." He smiled to himself. "She was always a whiz with figures. Me, I can barely get my checkbook to balance."

"You and most of the rest of the world."

"Anyway, Ginny is supposed to graduate this December, and I want to see that she makes it. It'd be a damn shame if that idiot of an ex of hers got in the way."

"Does he know where to look for her?"

"I reckon. It sure wouldn't take him long to find out, anyway. It's not as if she tried to disappear. She still has friends near where she used to live, and I can be found in the phone book."

"Maybe you ought to move her somewhere else for a little while, to see if Bobby actually comes after her."

"I've been thinking about it," Garrett agreed. "But her friends know she's going to college, and there's no reason they'd keep that a secret."

"So he could track her to the campus."

"Yup." Garrett wanted to pound the steering wheel in frustration as he thought about all the possible complications arising from Bobby's release. If he sent Ginny up to live with his folks or their brother, she wouldn't be able to graduate in December. At this point in her education, she would lose a lot of ground if she transferred. "I'm going to have to think long and hard about this. There's got to be a way to keep her and the kids safe and not totally disrupt their lives."

"The kids? Would he hurt the *kids?*"

"He has before."

"My God." She knew about such things, of course. She didn't live in a make-believe world where everyone was nice and perfect, but child abuse struck her as the most heinous of crimes. "At least get the kids away from there for now,

Garrett. You can protect your sister pretty well, I'm sure, but it'd be easier without children to worry about."

He could protect his sister pretty well? The thought almost made him laugh bitterly. Yeah, right. With his damaged arm that couldn't lift a gun. Maybe he'd better say to hell with Ginny's education for a little while, and get her and the kids safely moved to someplace where Bobby couldn't find them. At least until he could be sure that Bobby didn't want to get even.

They pulled into the restaurant parking lot around six-thirty. The place looked full already, as if folks had come from miles around. Which they probably had, thought Sandy. The place must do a good steak.

The decor was an attractive rustic Western, and the music was quiet country. The barn-size structure had been divided up into smaller rooms, creating a pleasant feeling of coziness. A waitress gave them a private corner booth.

"This is really nice," Sandy told Garrett. Not until that moment had she realized just how much she had needed to get away. The slow uncoiling of tension was making her feel as if she were melting, particularly her neck and shoulders. Her head nearly drooped with relaxation. A glass of burgundy helped.

Garrett spoke. "Have you heard anything from the reservation about Nighthawk's sister?"

Sandy shook her head. "Nina called the tribal police. They said they'd locate her, but it might take a few days to get around to it. I guess they're understaffed, and this hardly qualifies as an emergency. I just need to get that photo yanked from evidence before trial, but that's nearly two months from now."

"How can you do that? I mean, even if it is a photo of his niece, why shouldn't the prosecution be able to present it? They *did* find it in his house."

"Rules of evidence. Probative value is outweighed by its prejudicial effect. Basically, it doesn't prove anything one way or the other, but it will probably prejudice the jury. That's enough reason to keep it out. A lot of evidence gets evaluated that way. On the other hand, if it turns out not to be his niece, it'll probably be admitted, even though pedophilia is not an indicator for the kind of crime that was committed against Lisa Dunbar. Most pedophiles, in fact, don't commit violent rape." She shrugged. "The court has to weigh that kind of thing all the time."

Garrett nodded, but it was apparent to Sandy that he hadn't really been listening. Why should he? He probably knew all this already, anyway. His blue eyes had taken on a faraway look, and he'd begun to draw patterns on his folded napkin with the edge of his fork handle.

"The perp thinks he's smart," he said abruptly. "And he isn't dumb. But he's not as smart as he thinks, either."

"What do you mean?"

"He left a false trail that points the finger at Nighthawk, but he did it so obviously that if you stop to think about it for a minute, you realize it stinks to high heaven. I'll bet Nate has started to wonder, too. I mean, you'd have to have the brains of a gnat to leave a book bag out on the road and bury the victim's clothes in your backyard if you really committed the crime. Now, I'm not going to say I've never seen a criminal that dumb, because I have. But Nighthawk isn't that kind of stupid. No way. So our perp is smart, but not smart enough. He frames Nighthawk, but does it in such an obvious way that I'm sure as hell not buying it."

Sandy nodded. Hadn't they discussed this same thing just yesterday? "Right. I know."

"Okay, so now we have an M.O. for the guy. When he does something, he points the finger elsewhere."

"You can't extrapolate from just one—" She broke off as understanding struck. She felt all the color drain from her face. "You're saying he broke into my office last night and tried to make it look as if Les Walker did it?"

Garrett nodded slowly. "I also figure he called you after the police left."

"Then he was watching...." She thought she was going to be sick. *Maybe if somebody raped you....* "But why,

Garrett? Why would he break in? Why would he want to scare me?''

"Maybe he just wanted to look at Nighthawk's file and see if you had any information that could get Nighthawk off so he could counteract it somehow."

"But I had all the information upstairs!"

"He wouldn't know that before he looked."

"But..." She shook her head. "It doesn't make sense. Oh, wanting to look at Nighthawk's file, I guess I can see. But the call?"

"Simple. He's already pointing the finger away from himself. So if he breaks in again to get the file, you'll think it's a would-be rapist."

"That's..." She trailed off again, thinking about it. In a perverted sort of way, it made sense. "He can't possibly be hoping to scare me off the case, can he? What good would that do? Another attorney would just take it."

"Another attorney who might not be quite as committed to getting Nighthawk off. Someone who doesn't believe Nighthawk is innocent. Someone who won't hire a private investigator to poke around looking for the real culprit."

Suddenly she didn't feel quite so relaxed. "What do you think he might do?"

What he was thinking was not something he wanted to share with her right now. Or any time, for that matter. "I need to think some more about it," he said. "There's really not a whole lot to go on." What he was beginning to fear was what might happen if the perp began to feel that Sandy was a threat to him. It was essential that Sandy be aware there might be danger—otherwise she might not be careful—but he didn't want to scare her half to death without something more to go on than an uneasy suspicion.

The truth was, after last night, he'd begun to feel seriously concerned for her. The man who had hurt Lisa Dunbar would not be interested in Sandy Keller in the same way, because she wasn't a child. But he was perfectly capable of harming or even killing someone he perceived as a threat. Trouble was, they didn't have a whole hell of a lot to go on.

"When are you going to question Lisa's father?" he asked.

"I'm going out to the ranch to see him in the morning. It won't be a deposition—Sam has that scheduled for Monday morning—but I want to just get a feel for the situation."

Garrett nodded. "So you're thinking along those lines, too."

Sandy's mouth drew tight, and she looked down at the napkin she was absently creasing. "He's the most obvious suspect if Nighthawk didn't do it." Which was about as sorry a comment as you could make.

"Yeah." Garrett leaned back as the waitress slipped a platter of prime rib in front of him. "And what about questioning the little girl?"

"Probably Monday. Sam said the doctor figures she'll probably be up to it by then. Apparently she's had some complications with infection that set back her recovery."

"It's going to be years before she recovers, if ever."

Sandy glanced away and down, hoping he couldn't read the knowledge in her face. *If ever* was about where she fit. Some scars never completely faded.

"Want to tell me about it?"

Garrett's voice, almost gentle, came quietly to her ears. No pressure, no insistence, in his tone, just a simple question. Reluctantly she dragged her eyes up from the napkin and met his gaze. What she saw was not ordinary curiosity but a look of understanding, as if he already knew what she would say. She drew a shaky breath.

"It was a long time ago," she said finally. "A long time ago. It doesn't matter anymore."

"Sure it does," he said quietly. "It affected you, and you dealt with it. The ways you dealt with it made you the person you are now. So it matters, Sandy. Even if it doesn't hurt anymore, it matters."

Her fingers closed into the palm of her hand and formed a fist. How could you tell someone about something like this? Where could you even begin?

"Did you know the assailant?"

As if he understood her dilemma, he asked a question. It was a policeman's question, but it was a starting point, and the phrasing of it somehow allowed her to gain a measure of detachment.

"No, I didn't know him. I had no idea who he was."

"Did they ever catch him?"

She shook her head. "No."

"If it's any consolation, they probably caught him later on another incident. These guys rarely act only once."

"I was hoping maybe he'd been hit by a trailer truck before he could hurt anyone else. Or trampled to death by an angry mob."

The corners of his mouth lifted, and his eyes crinkled. "That's always a possibility."

"Not a likelihood, though. No, I figure he'd raped a number of women before me, and he probably raped a few after me, and chances are he never got caught at all. Not as long as he kept picking women who didn't know him."

"Did he hurt you badly?" He waved a hand almost before he finished speaking. "Bad way to put it. I know he hurt you badly. I meant—"

"Did he break any bones or sever any major arteries?" She smiled mirthlessly. "It's okay, Garrett. No, I didn't need to be hospitalized. A few cuts, scrapes and bruises were the only injuries. He took me at knife point, but he didn't cut me. Which kind of surprised me, actually, because all the time it was happening, I was absolutely convinced he was going to slash my throat as soon as he was done with me."

Garrett didn't say anything, which was just as well. If he'd made a sound it would have given her the excuse she needed not to continue. His expression grew grim, almost remote, but his gaze never wavered.

"Well, he didn't," she continued. "He called me some vile names, hit me a few times, then left me. Then I was raped again. Oh, not really," she amended hastily, "but back then cops were pretty hard on rape victims. I'm sure you know the attitude I'm talking about."

"Yeah. I've seen it, though not as often anymore. They treat you like *you're* the criminal, as if it was your fault it happened."

She nodded. "And as if it never would have happened if I were a decent woman. Gerry kind of felt that way, too."

"Gerry?"

"My ex-husband. Oh, he wasn't a total clod. He understood that I'd been hurt and all that, but he was of the opinion that it never would have happened if I'd stayed home in an apron instead of going out to work."

"Your fault for venturing into a man's world."

"That about sums it up." She didn't intend to continue, but somehow she did. Part of her was appalled that she was even saying these things, and part of her was relieved to have it out. To let Garrett know the truth about her. "I, um, had some sexual problems after that."

"Hardly surprising. It would have been surprising if you hadn't."

"Well, Gerry never thought I was much of a lover, anyway, but after the rape I kind of...froze." She couldn't look at him. "I'm, um, frigid."

"And I suppose your ex lost no opportunity to tell you that." He swore. "Well, darlin', don't worry about it. You may be scared, but you're not frigid."

"You can't possibly—"

He interrupted ruthlessly. "I've kissed you, remember? You're as responsive as any woman I've ever held and more responsive than most. You're scared, all right, but scared and frigid are worlds apart." He suddenly flashed a smile. "But relax. I won't demand that you prove it."

It was as if a great big balloon of tension suddenly popped and drained all the nervousness and worry from her. It was a relief to have it out in the open. Now she didn't have to worry about any misunderstandings. Now she didn't have to wonder if something would happen and she would wind up being ashamed and embarrassed.

And now that he had made it clear that he wouldn't put her in that position, all she wanted was for him to do precisely that. She wanted him to reach out and draw her into those strong arms of his. To press her head onto his solid shoulder while he held her and told her it would be okay.

Silly, she thought, even as the yearning turned into a deep ache. Silly. A pair of strong arms couldn't hold reality at bay, and a murmured reassurance couldn't make everything all right. She was not all right and never would be, and she had long since given up wishing for the kind of love and passion that fairy tales were made of. They just didn't exist.

Maybe he was right that she wasn't frigid but just afraid. Hadn't she even once read in a medical book that frigidity was most often simply a lack of knowledge on the part of the couple rather than a real inability to respond? Yes, she'd read all that, even tried to convince herself that her problems had arisen from fear and inexperience, not from a real physical problem of some kind.

She even believed it. But that didn't counter the very real fear she felt. Not just the fear that had resulted from the rape—she honestly believed that had long ago faded away—but the fear she felt that her next lovemaking experience would be exactly the horror it had been with Gerry. All the technical explanations for what had happened, all the understanding of the physical and emotional dynamics of those last few episodes, couldn't soothe her fear that they would be repeated.

Nor could she tell Garrett what would need saying if a repetition were to be avoided. How could you tell a man you'd never been to bed with that your former lover had never troubled to arouse you sufficiently, that after you were raped, fear kept you from getting aroused at all, and that rather than be patient your husband had forced the issue, causing you severe pain?

She looked hastily down at her plate as she felt color stain her cheeks. How could you tell a man who had never been your lover that another man's voice spewing scorn and condemnation had drilled a hole in your brain, that you couldn't even think about making love without hearing all those horrible accusations and names?

How could you tell a man who had never been your lover that you wanted him to be as patient as a saint and make love to you despite all those hang-ups?

You couldn't, she admitted miserably. You couldn't say, "Garrett, give me all the time and patience I need, even if it takes all night, and help me to get over this." No, you could only hope that if you were foolish enough to make love with him that he wouldn't grow impatient and react in the same way your husband had. That you wouldn't hear those awful words spilling from the mouth of yet another man.

The rape hadn't scarred her nearly as much as her husband's reaction to it and its effects. How could she tell Garrett that?

So she remained silent on the subject and began to talk about other things.

Garrett let her. She would never guess how much he had seen flitting across her face, nor would he tell her. He had seen both her yearning and her fear, and felt he understood them. The question was whether he wanted to deal with them. It would be no simple task, he thought, to get around this woman's barriers. And there was no point in doing so unless he planned to stick around.

Which he absolutely did not intend to do.

The moonlight was bright, the sky so clear that the stars hardly twinkled. The roads were clear, but the grasslands and hills were still covered in snow, and the reflected moonglow turned the night coldly brilliant. Sandy had a quick, flashing memory of standing in the moonlight in her kitchen last night, trying to hear whoever was downstairs.

She shivered, wishing she didn't have to go home tonight. Wishing she wasn't going to spend the long dark hours sitting up wide-awake for fear the man who had made the phone call might come back. Wishing she could find an excuse to say, "Take me to Laramie, I want to spend the night there, where he can't find me." Wishing she didn't have to be alone.

"That was a great dinner," Garrett remarked. "Well worth the drive."

"It sure was." A three-hour trip home. It was likely to be after midnight by the time they pulled in. Could she invite him in for coffee without seeming to suggest something more? Hadn't he said he wouldn't demand that she prove she wasn't frigid? Surely that meant he had no desire to make love to her.

But if that was the case, why had he looked at her the way he had the other night? Why had he kissed her as if he didn't want to let go? She might be a mess sexually, but she had always been able to tell when a man was interested. But maybe her confession tonight had killed that. It would hardly be surprising.

Stifling a sigh, she kept her eyes fixed on the passing moon-drenched countryside. The mountains seemed to glow eerily in the cold blue light. And Thunder Mountain, the highest of them all, seemed actually to brood.

What would a mountain brood about? she wondered idly, remembering the fantasy stories she had once read with such appetite. Time would be on a completely different scale for a mountain. It couldn't possibly worry about such fleeting things as a kiss or a touch.

Or about having not been touched in so many years. It was something she never wanted to think about, because it did no good. All she could do was ache when she thought about how long it had been since someone last had held her, or hugged her with genuine affection. And when she *did* think about it, she wondered if the nerves of the skin of her back could actually hunger for the squeeze of an arm, the stroke of a loving hand. Because it sure felt like it sometimes.

Like right now. It wasn't even lovemaking she wanted so much as the loving touch of someone who cared. Someone who would hold her close and give her the blessing of human touch and caring. Such a little thing, something that most people took for granted. Something *she* had taken for granted until she had done without for so long.

If Garrett just wanted to put his arms around her and hold her for a few minutes, she would be grateful. She was that needy. She hated being so needy, hated the weakness that it signified, and yet she was honest enough to admit it was a natural need, one that every small child felt just as keenly. It wasn't a weakness, it was human.

She glanced over at Garrett. His face looked like a carved wooden mask in the pale glow of the dashboard light. What was he thinking? What did it matter? Even if he put his arms around her and held her, it would only be for just a few moments. He'd all but said in so many words that he wasn't interested in a long-term relationship, and a one-night stand would just about kill her.

Wishing for the moon, that was what she was doing. Just like a coyote on a long summer night, howling at the heavens. Or, as her grandmother had once told her, "If you're going to wish, you might as well wish for something impossible." Yup. That was exactly what she was doing, and that was why it would never come true.

Good grief, at her age she ought to know better. Prince Charming existed only in fairy tales. The reality of life could never measure up to a wish. Never.

But that couldn't keep her from yearning.

They arrived back in Conard City shortly after midnight. By that time Sandy was wishing she'd eaten more of her dinner than a nervous stomach had allowed. Well, she could rustle up something once she said good-night to Garrett.

He followed her up the stairs to the landing and waited while she unlocked her door. "I'll see you in the morning," he said. "I want to do some poking around, and I'll stop in before I head out."

"Okay." She tried to smile brightly, when in actuality she felt as if someone had just dropped a stone in her stomach. He had plans for tomorrow, and they didn't include her, apparently. Well, of course they didn't. But it disappointed her, anyway.

"Good night, then," he said, then turned and started down the stairs.

As if paralyzed, she stood where she was and watched him descend. She didn't want him to go, but the words that would have stopped him stuck in her throat.

Halfway down, he stopped. After a moment's hesitation he turned and started climbing back up to her.

"Garrett?" His name escaped her as little more than a husky whisper.

He didn't say a word, just climbed.

Instinctively, she inched backward, but something kept her from flying. Maybe it was the look of stony determination on his face or the brilliance of his blue eyes, but somehow she just couldn't run.

When he stood one step below her, he stopped. "Good night," he said, and before she could react, or even draw another breath, he hauled her into his arms and covered her mouth with his.

In that incredible instant, everything inside her turned warm and soft. Melting. She was melting like chocolate left in the warm sun, and at any moment she was sure she was going to puddle at his feet and slip slowly down the stairs.

His tongue found hers, and there was nothing playful in its touch. He meant business, and he wanted her to know it. She was at once terrified and exhilarated. Oh, God, she thought wildly, this man wanted her! How was she going to deal with that? How could she possibly cope?

Terror started to well inside her, threatening to swamp her. But just then he lifted his head, freeing her mouth.

Then his stomach growled, loudly and emphatically. Garrett swore.

And Sandy laughed as all the tension drained from her. It was impossible to be afraid of a man whose stomach was growling, and it was exactly the unromantic, humorous touch she needed to set her free.

"I think you ought to come in for a snack," she said, and giggled.

A slow, rueful smile dawned on his rugged face. "You'd never guess I finished a big meal less than four hours ago. I'm starving."

"Well, come on in. I bet I can make us some nachos."

He closed the door behind them, taking care to throw the dead bolt, and followed her into the tiny kitchen. "There's no way on earth a Wyoming lawyer can make a decent nacho."

"You wanna bet, Ranger?"

"It wouldn't be fair to pluck your feathers, little pigeon. Lord, you can't possibly find a decent jalapeño up here, never mind a decent corn chip. It wouldn't be gentlemanly to take your money."

In the end, however, he allowed as how he might have been the pigeon. They sat together at her table, laughing and talking as they hadn't been able to do all evening. Sandy wasn't sure exactly what had happened, but something had, removing the last barrier between them and leaving them as comfortable together as old, old friends.

Which was probably why she didn't try to avoid it when he turned from stacking the dishes on the counter and drew her into his arms. It probably explained how it was that she sank against him as he leaned back against the counter and quite naturally tipped back her head so that they could kiss.

This time it felt right to be in his arms, as if she were coming back to a familiar and cherished place. Amazing, she thought vaguely, how quickly one could become accustomed to something new.

But she wasn't interested in analyzing her reactions. All she wanted to do was revel in the experience. For the first time in years, she felt comfortable in the arms of a man. Felt safe and secure, rather than threatened and afraid. He made her feel that all she had to do was let him take care of her.

It was easy, so very easy, when he spread his legs to allow herself to be drawn between them until she was resting intimately against him. A shiver of fear passed through her and then was gone, soothed away by the gentle touch of his hands on her back.

"Ah, Sandy," he whispered as he lifted his mouth from hers and began to sprinkle soft, wet kisses all over her face. Those gentle little brushes of lips and tongue somehow relaxed her even more. It was as if some deep part of her, some place beneath conscious thought, judged that no one could touch with such tenderness if they meant any harm.

She softened even more, and Garrett drew her closer, allowing his hands to cross her back so his arms could hold her snugly. She felt so good against him. God, he wondered, had a woman ever felt so good in his arms as this one did?

He was sure, absolutely sure, that never in his life had he wanted to hold someone as much as he wanted to hold Sandy. Never had an embrace felt so satisfying to his soul as this one did.

And that should have scared him to death, because there was no hope for a long-term relationship with her. Their work and lives might as well have been at opposite sides of the country, and neither of them was likely to give up their way of life. He could only get hurt.

If she had wanted a man in her life, she probably could have had any of dozens. And even if she should suddenly change her mind, she wouldn't be able to take life with a Texas Ranger. A couple of women had already proved that beyond a shadow of a doubt.

If he would ever be a ranger again. That scared him as much as anything, that he might not heal fully enough to return to his job. And then what would he have to offer any woman? A disability check?

God!

Just then, just as he was summoning words to frame a good-night that wouldn't leave her feeling raw and used, she made a little whimper. Just the softest of sounds as she nestled even closer, reminding him of something warm settling into its safe burrow.

It was enough to deprive him of his common sense. The warning voice faded away in an upsurge of need, as if this woman had somehow unlocked everything he had kept buried for so long.

He wanted her. He would deal with the pain later. Right now he needed the warmth of her love and laughter the way a parched plant needed water. He could no more deny his need for her than he could have stopped breathing.

He widened his stance even more, half expecting a protest, but she merely snuggled even closer, like a contented kitten. Her lips were close and inviting, and he couldn't resist them. Kiss followed kiss as she grew softer and more pliant, leaning more and more into him until he couldn't stifle a groan.

The groan seemed to startle her, yanking her back from the haze of desire that had been enveloping them. The instant he felt her stiffen, he slackened his hold. It wasn't easy to let go when every cell in his body was screaming for him to hang on, but he managed to do it. The last thing on earth he wanted to do was frighten this woman.

A shaky sigh escaped her, and she started to back away. Nobility demanded that he let her go without a protest, but he didn't quite make it.

"Sandy?"

"I'm ... sorry, Garrett. Sorry."

"There's nothing to be sorry for, darlin'. Nothing. Did I scare you?"

She shook her head swiftly, backing away another few inches. "I'm sorry. It's just that ... just that ... Oh, I don't want to disappoint you!"

He liked her forthrightness. Liked the lack of coquetry in her answer. She wasn't trying to pretend that the past few minutes hadn't been exactly what they were. She wasn't hiding from the fact that he wanted to make love to her, and that she probably wanted very much the same thing. She was simply telling the truth, difficult as it was.

"You won't disappoint me, Sandy."

"Yes, I will!"

"No. You won't. You can't disappoint me, because I have no expectations of you. None whatsoever."

Chapter 10

For an instant her heart stopped beating as she wondered if she had completely misunderstood the direction their embrace had been taking. Had she made a fool of herself, leaping to a wrong conclusion? She would die of embarrassment.

But no, she hadn't been mistaken. Relief hit her in a soft wave as Garrett reached out and cupped her cheek in his hand.

"I won't be disappointed if you send me on my way," he said gently, "because I don't have a right to expect anything else from you. I won't be disappointed if you ask me to stay, because that would be more than I ever dared hope for. I won't be disappointed, because all I want is to be allowed to make love to you."

"But I'm . . . I can't . . . Garrett, I told you!"

"And I told you that I don't expect anything at all from you. I meant that. I don't expect you to perform. I don't expect you to react in any particular way. If I touch you and you freeze into a block of ice, it won't be a disappointment, Sandy. Not for me. I understand."

She shivered visibly, a great ripping wave of movement that passed through her from head to toe. Her worried eyes lifted to his, looking at once shy and scared. And there he saw her yearning as plainly as if she'd spoken it.

Moving carefully, he reached for her again and drew her close. "Just let me," he said, as he tucked her head onto his shoulder. "You don't have to say a word. Just let me. I won't promise to make this wonderful for you, because I'm not sure I can. All I can promise—the *only* thing—is that I won't be disappointed."

She didn't pull away, but she didn't say no, either. The slightest movement of her head against his shoulder seemed to be a nod, and he took it as consent. He would dearly have loved to sweep her off her feet, but he couldn't trust his arm that far yet, and he would hate like hell to have a tremor overtake him and be forced to lower her. Instead, he took her hand and guided her toward her bedroom.

She followed his urging without any hesitation.

This would be no passionate tumble on the living room couch or the thick pile of her pale gray carpeting. No, that kind of lovemaking, romantic though it could be, was too subject to inadvertent distraction, anything from bumping into something to falling off the couch. He couldn't risk that with Sandy. He wanted nothing to jar her from the soft, willing mood that had overtaken her, and the best way to keep that soft cocoon wrapped around her was in a soft bed beneath warm blankets.

He left the hall light on and the bedroom door open a few inches, giving them just barely enough light to see by. He didn't want her to feel shy or embarrassed about her body, but he wanted to be able to see her.

Standing beside the bed, he kissed her eyes closed and then began to undress her. She had donned a simple dress for dinner, a subdued navy blue jersey. One button fastened at her neck, and the zipper slipped easily down her back. She gave a soft gasp as he pulled it down to her hips, and he bent his head, kissing her deeply but gently, soothing her before he pulled the dress away.

His hands were shaking a little, but not from his injury. No, he was trembling with nerves and eagerness as he hadn't since he was a boy. He wanted this woman more than he had ever wanted any woman, including the two whom he had almost married. He couldn't put his finger on why, and he really didn't care. All he knew was that he thirsted for her and felt as if something in him would be wounded irretrievably if he couldn't get closer... and closer....

The jersey slipped to the floor with a soft whisper, leaving her in a navy blue slip. He let his hands wander over the smooth, creamy skin of her shoulders, along the fragile line of her lovely neck, and then lower to her breasts.

Gently he traced light circles around her breasts, taking his time, giving her a chance to get used to the familiarity. When her hands lifted and gripped his waist, he knew a moment's triumph. Frigid? No way! But he had to be careful and cautious, taking into account her bad experiences. Since most of her bad memories probably involved lying beneath a man, Garrett kept them both standing beside the bed. He wanted everything about tonight to be new for her.

Stepping back just a little, he ripped open the snaps of his shirt and tossed it aside. Her eyes fluttered open, and a slow, absolutely feline smile tugged at her mouth. He nearly grinned back with relief. She liked what she saw.

Not one to waste an advantage, he stepped closer and wrapped her in the warmth of his arms. Kiss followed kiss as he gave her time to grow used to being so close to him, time to grow familiar with the bare skin and soft hair of his chest. At first she felt stiff against him, but slowly she began to relax and rub her cheek against him, as if savoring his textures.

It was unconsciously sexual, and it nearly drove him out of his mind. He had to grit his teeth and draw a couple of deep breaths while he forced his raging hunger to subside. She had no idea, he thought. No idea just how sexy and responsive she really was. And he didn't know how to tell her without sounding as if he were making it up and just telling her what he thought she wanted to hear. She would never believe it. Not yet, anyway.

But those concerns began to drift away on a rising tide of sensations. Satiny tricot, soft warm skin, the faintest little murmurs as her pleasure began to grow and her fear to subside. Encouraged, he began to lift her slip, delighting in the way it slid over her skin with a quiet swishing sound. Everything else slipped away with it, leaving him conscious of nothing but his desire to love this woman and his concern for her fears.

When the slip fell away, her eyes fluttered open. He saw the flash of concern in them, but before it could take root, he wrapped her once again in his arms and drowned her in a rain of tender kisses. And once again she softened into him with a little sigh that told him that she wanted to be here with him, flickers of fear notwithstanding.

That touched him deep in places that had been cold and empty for so very long. He had refused to think about Sandy in more than superficial ways. They had both been looking the other way, pretending nothing was happening, that they were in control of their feelings . . . and now this. It was as if old barriers inside him were crumbling like a weak seawall before a storm tide. This was going to hurt. It was going to hurt like hell.

But he was damned if he could save himself.

Gentle touches drew her on, carrying her past instinctive fears and hesitations into the hazy land of love—a place she was beginning to realize she had never visited before. No one had ever touched her this way, as if the touching were a joy, as if giving were as important as receiving.

As if pleasuring her were important.

A soft shudder ran through her as she began to understand that she was being loved—not taken, but loved. Loved in a way she had always believed was the fantasy of novelists. This man actually cared about what she was feeling.

Slowly, slowly, she tilted her head back and looked up at him from passion-sleepy eyes. "Please . . ."

It was a breathless whisper, barely audible, but a gentle smile tugged up the corners of his mouth. "Yes, darlin'," he murmured huskily. "Yes, darlin'..."

Her bra slipped away, but all she felt was relief that another impediment was gone. When he bent and tugged her panty hose and panties down, she let her head fall back and gave herself up to feeling. It might come to nothing, but she didn't care. At the very least she needed this feeling of being loved and cared for, something she had always lacked. Passion was the least of it. Had he simply wanted to hug her and stroke her like a kitten, she would have been content. He was loving her in the way that mattered.

She felt cool, crisp sheets beneath her back, and briefly she felt the upsurge of fear, but then Garrett was beside her, warm and naked and oh, so very real.

But instead of feeling threatened by that, she felt protected. Probably because of the gentle way he drew her close and because of the touches that never stopped, touches that soothed and...

And excited. Oh, heavens, she felt the early blossoming of excitement at her center, and she hoped against hope that it wouldn't desert her, leaving her cold and frustrated and alone. But the slow, undemanding touches that flitted over her kept the glow alive and fanned the embers.

"You feel so good," Garrett whispered as he nibbled on her earlobe. "So good..."

The husky whisper in her ear sent runnels of excitement trickling along her nerve endings and awakening her in ways she had never imagined. How was it that she had never known it could feel so good to be touched? How had she missed this all her life?

But she could ask those questions tomorrow; right now all she wanted to do was gobble up the experiences Garrett was sharing with her.

And it *was* the most incredible sense of sharing. What before had always left her feeling lonely now made her feel a closeness she had despaired of ever knowing. Turning onto her side, she snuggled into his arms and kissed him, wanting to give him as much as he was giving her.

All fears of her own unresponsiveness fled before the caress of his hands on her flesh. Each touch set off little explosions that raced along her nerves to add to the pooling heat at her core. Gently, almost unconsciously, she began to rock her hips in response. Never in her life had she grown this aroused, and it was only just beginning.

For an instant she trembled on the edge of fear again, afraid that this would all vanish in a puff if some caress should jar her. But she pushed the fear aside, needing this experience enough to take the risk.

Garrett. For days now she had been responding to him in ways that had scared her, ways she had tried hard to ignore. Now he was touching her, his hand cradling her soft breast and pinching her aroused nipple in the most delicious way. If dreams could come true, then that was what was happening at this very instant.

Garrett's lips followed his hands, and she knew she had never felt anything as exquisite as his mouth on her breast, sucking gently, and later his teeth nipping softly.

Then his hand slipped between her legs. She arched in sheer delight, and a low moan escaped her, followed by a soft whimper that was almost a plea.

He chuckled gently and kissed her soundly on the mouth, while his fingers continued to dance maddeningly in her soft curls. Each touch was electric, filling her with fresh waves of excitement.

She ought to be doing something, ought to be reciprocating, but when she reached out blindly with her hands, he hushed her and whispered that she was just to relax and enjoy.

Higher and higher his fingers teased her, until she was seeing flares of colored light behind her eyelids and arching helplessly, her entire body reaching for more and yet more. What was happening to her was no longer a matter of conscious will but a helpless response that could not be denied.

She was caught on the arc of a welder's torch, burning... burning... burning....

"Let me," Garrett whispered. "Let me...." Gently he urged her legs apart and then completely deprived her of breath by slipping his finger into her.

She was his. As easily and simply as that, her last inhibition and uncertainty slipped away. It hardly mattered whether she climaxed or continued to feel aroused. What she needed and what he was giving her was this shattering, compelling intimacy. It nurtured some hungry place in her soul, and her heart cried out for more. *Come closer, Garrett. Closer.*

When he moved between her legs and entered her, there was no flashback to the rape, no memory of her misguided, unintentionally abusive husband. There was only now and the bell-like clarity of feelings never before experienced. There was only Garrett and the closeness of two human beings who cherished one another.

Because that was how he made her feel. And if she never again knew a moment like this, she was never going to forget what it felt like to be truly cherished.

"Fly with me, darlin'," he urged huskily. "Fly with me."

Amazingly, fantastically, she did just that.

He didn't say it. Sandy would have forgiven Garrett if he'd remarked that she wasn't frigid after all. If he had shown any justifiable signs of pride over what had just happened. But he didn't. Not even by the merest hint did he beat his breast in triumph.

Instead, all he did was cuddle her close and murmur, "Darlin', you're incredible."

The incredible thing was that she *felt* incredible. Absolutely, amazingly incredible. Fairy tales, fantasies and dreams *did* come true. She could have laughed with sheer joy.

The window at the head of the bed rattled as the wind kicked up. Unmistakably came the clatter of large rain drops against the glass. It sounded cold and miserable out there, and the sounds made it easier for her to slip her arms around Garrett's strong neck and murmur, "Please stay."

A rumble of laughter rose from deep in his chest and spilled into the darkened room. "You'd have to kick me out, Sandy. This bed is warm, you're warmer, and I'm not moving until I've made love to you again."

She liked the sound of that. She *loved* the sound of that. Some corner of her mind kept trying to nudge her back to reality, to remind her that Garrett would be leaving in a few short weeks, that she was going to get hurt because of her incautious behavior tonight, and that she would be a fool to give this man any part of her heart. But she didn't want to think about that right now. Tomorrow would be soon enough to deal with reality. Tonight she wanted to enjoy the fantasy of her Texas lawman lover as if it would be forever.

"I'm thirsty," Garrett murmured. "Can I bring you anything?"

"Just some water, please."

She envied him his lack of selfconsciousness as he slipped from beneath the sheet and padded out of the room. He left the door open a little wider, so that the hall light spilled across the bed. She was glad of the blankets that covered her to her chin, because she'd never been entirely comfortable with her body and was less so now that life had taken a bit of a toll—stretch marks, long since faded, from giving birth to her son, a waist that wasn't quite as youthfully thin as it once had been.

But even as she wished for a perfect body, she knew she was being silly. Garrett hadn't wanted a perfect body or he wouldn't have made love to her tonight. No, he'd wanted something else, and considering that there were far more likely prospects for a brief affair around here, she began to wonder what exactly he had seen in her.

There were no answers in the quiet night. No explanations for what seemed inexplicable. She had seen the desire in his eyes and had felt it in his body, and she could only believe that for some totally incomprehensible reason, he found her desirable. And that notion tickled her no end.

Garrett returned, closing the door enough so that only a small crack of light streamed into the room. As if he understood her uncertainty, she thought. Perhaps he did.

He handed her a glass of icy water. "I love how cold the water is here," he remarked as he sat on the bed beside her. "In Texas, it's usually about room temperature from the tap, but here it's practically refrigerated."

"I hadn't even thought about that."

"I also like that it isn't as heavily chlorinated. The stuff I get at my house, you can smell the chlorine when you turn on the tap."

"You trying to talk me out of visiting?" As soon as the words passed her lips, she regretted them. He would probably think she was trying to angle for an invitation, and she didn't want to make him feel that he was being put on the spot. Embarrassed, she tried to think of a way to salvage the moment.

But what he did was bend over her and brush a sweet kiss on her damp lips. "Anytime you want to visit, you just give me a shout. I'd love it. I'll even buy bottled water."

She couldn't help it; she giggled, as much from relief as from humor.

"Utopia spring water," he promised. "Real Texas water before the treatment plant got to it."

When she finished her water, they settled back against the pillows, Sandy's head cradled on Garrett's shoulder. Once, long ago, she had discovered how delightful this intimacy was, this lying together of a man and woman after lovemaking, with no more hesitations and games between them. That had been when she was first married, and she had long since forgotten how delightful it was.

But she was rediscovering it now. There was nothing to quite compare to the sense of freedom that followed lovemaking. No longer did anyone have to conceal their desires or pretend they weren't interested. No more hiding behind propriety. She was free to reach out and touch Garrett if she wanted to and not be concerned about being misunderstood. More importantly, she was no longer afraid.

"I can't believe," she murmured. "I can't believe how...what... Oh, Garrett, I've never felt what you made me feel!"

He turned on his side and hugged her close, squeezing her as if he wanted to draw her inside himself. "That was never your fault, Sandy. Never. You're the most wonderfully responsive woman I've ever made love to. I could throttle the man who made you feel otherwise."

"He didn't..." She shook her head, not certain how to explain. "I don't think it was purposeful, Garrett. Really. He wasn't a cruel man. Just... Well, I guess maybe we were both inexperienced."

He shook his head a little and let it go, but what he thought was that it didn't take experience as much as it took caring. All you had to do was pay attention to your partner's responses and care enough to follow all those subtle little hints of sounds, sighs and movements. No genius needed. And before this night was out, he was going to prove it once again.

Just then the phone rang. Sandy looked at him, startled, and hesitated. He would have reached for it, but she wasn't sure she wanted anyone to know there was a man in her apartment this late at night. This was a very small town, after all.

She reached past him and lifted the receiver from the cradle, putting it to her ear. "Hello?"

Even in the dark, he could see the tension come into her face. Moments later she leaned over him and slammed the phone back into the cradle.

"What was that?" he asked.

"Some idiot who wanted to warn me not to get Nighthawk off."

"Was that all he said?"

"Yes." She shook her head. "It wasn't the guy from last night, if that's what you're worried about. No, this was someone else who apparently had a couple of beers too many, from the sound of it. I'm not going to worry about it."

"It'll probably get worse as matters progress and the case gets a higher profile."

"Probably," she agreed, and sighed. "Heck, I wouldn't be astonished to see a TV news crew out here from one of the bigger cities. Cases like this always make headlines."

"They draw a lot of flak, too." He hesitated a moment before saying, "I've seen some pretty serious threats leveled at attorneys during high-profile cases. Usually no one acts on them, but it's not a risk you should take, Sandy."

"What am I supposed to do? Hire a bodyguard?" She was suddenly furious. The ugliness of narrow minds had filtered into the sanctuary of her bedroom and was destroying the most beautiful night of her life.

Throwing back the covers, she scrambled out of bed and grabbed her robe from a nearby chair. The mood was completely shattered, and there was no way she could lounge around in bed. She needed to move, to do something. It didn't much matter what, but she was too upset to hold still.

For the first time in her life, she wished she smoked. Lighting a cigarette and puffing rapidly on it would have provided an outlet. Instead she went to the kitchen, flipped on the light and began to clatter around making hot chocolate. Not that she really wanted it; it was just something to occupy her hands and expend nervous energy on.

What she really wanted was to throttle someone. Maybe several someones. The problem was, she simply didn't know which someones. And the truth was, she might as well admit, that even if she *had* known who to throttle, she was too law-abiding to do more than wish.

She slammed the microwave door on two cups of milk and turned it on. Just then, gentle arms slipped around her from behind and drew her securely backward against a hard chest and into a warm embrace.

"It's okay, darlin'," Garrett said quietly. "Blow off the steam, but don't be afraid. You're not going to be alone."

"I'm not afraid!" Frustration filled her, along with anger, but not fear. And now, with Garrett's arms around her, she felt a positively debilitating desire to just curl into his strength and pretend that everything would go away. The urge, fleeting as it was, infuriated her even more. She had learned a long time ago to stand on her own two feet and not depend on anyone else. It was easy and kind for Garrett to reassure her, but when push came to shove, she would be on her own. Not because Garrett would fail her, but just because that was the way life was. You had to stand up and face things on your own.

The microwave beeped, and she pulled out the mugs. "Cocoa?" she asked Garrett.

"Thanks." He let her go as soon as she started to move away, and she felt relieved when he sat at the table. His eyes never left her, but at least he wasn't within touching distance any longer. Somehow the urge to touch him seemed to weaken her resolve . . . and everything else.

She spooned cocoa into the mugs and stirred vigorously, hardly conscious of the almost emphatic way she moved the spoon, clacking it against the side of the mug. Garrett was aware, though, and the faintest of smiles lifted the corners of his mouth as he watched her.

"I don't know why," she said, "people are always so sure that the person who is arrested is the guilty one. For heaven's sake, Garrett, the most recent statistics I've seen indicated that fully thirty percent of the time the DNA samples found at the crime scene *don't* match the DNA of the accused. Which means that thirty percent of the time the wrong person is arrested—and that's just in cases when DNA samples are found. I shudder to think that percentage may apply across the board and include people who are arrested when no genetic evidence is available."

"I didn't realize it was that high."

"Well, it is! And it's estimated that ten percent of the people who are convicted are actually innocent, which is equally appalling. Despite that, people are absolutely convinced that the criminal justice system is a circus where the guilty walk free because of some legal technicality. In short, everyone is guilty until proven innocent, and even then he was probably guilty, anyway, but some fast-talking lawyer just got him off.''

''I've heard that more than once.''

''I just wonder how those same people would feel if they were being tried for something they didn't do and they couldn't even have an attorney to defend them because everyone knew they wouldn't have been arrested if they weren't guilty!''

''High-profile cases sometimes create a different impression.''

''I know that. And I can think of a number of them offhand where justice *did* miscarry. I agree it's appalling, but the bottom line is, not everyone who is arrested is guilty. And not everyone who is tried is guilty, and sometimes the jury is right to acquit despite the weight of public opinion. But whether the accused is guilty or not, he deserves legal representation, unless we want trial by kangaroo court!''

She placed the mugs of hot chocolate on the table but ignored hers, preferring to pace agitatedly. ''This perception of a revolving-door justice system really infuriates me. Good grief, we keep a higher percentage of our population imprisoned than any Western country except South Africa. That says more about our society than about our justice system. Yes, there are mistakes, but they're far outnumbered by the thousands of convicts who presently fill our prison system to bursting.''

She shook her head and wrapped her arms around herself as she came to a halt at the kitchen window, staring at her reflection in the dark glass. ''I'm sorry. I just get so angry about this kind of thing. That guy who called tonight evidently doesn't have any faith in his neighbors who'll be on the jury in the Nighthawk trial. He evidently thinks I'll somehow be able to blind them to the truth. I'm afraid I just don't think juries are that stupid. Most of the time they do a pretty damn good job of sifting through the evidence and reaching a reasoned conclusion. And it's the juries who decide, Garrett. Not the prosecutor or the defense attorney or the judge. A jury. Ordinary people, like the guy who called tonight."

She shook her head. "It's not my job to pull fancy tricks. It's not my job to distort anything. My job is to make sure that the jury reaches its conclusion on the basis of legally obtained evidence, not on the basis of gut emotions and misinformation. Yes, I'll defend Craig Nighthawk. But what a sorry state of affairs it would be if he could be tried without a chance to present his side of things. What a sorry state of affairs it would be if an arrest warrant were a conviction."

"Unfortunately, you're going to pay the price for those attitudes, Sandy."

She nodded. "I know. That's become obvious. Well, I can stick it out. I have enough savings to get me through the next few months, and I imagine folks will come around once this settles down."

"It would still be best for you and Nighthawk if we could find the real culprit."

"Goes without saying." She turned and leaned back against the counter, giving him a wan smile. "But there's hardly anything to go on, Garrett. Hardly anything at all."

"That's why I'm impatient for you to question the little girl. She might give us some little tidbit that could be really useful."

"Monday morning." She shook her head again. "I'm sorry, Garrett. That call got me really wound up."

"Perfectly understandable. Sandy, I've been guilty at times of the same attitude, complaining that some slick lawyer pulled fancy stuff and got some scum off. But the truth of the matter is, more often than not when that happens it's because the cop did something wrong and collected evidence illegally. Or there just plain wasn't enough evidence to convince a jury. And for all my bellyaching about it, I wouldn't want to see people going to jail on the basis of illegal or inadequate evidence."

"Apparently the rest of the world doesn't agree with you."

He smiled then. "Come on, that's exaggeration, and you know it. A few meatheads don't agree; that's all. And a case like this gets people really upset. Hang in there, Counselor. It'll get worse yet."

"Probably."

At last she came to sit at the table and tasted her cocoa. It was just about drinking temperature now, but she no longer wanted it... if she ever had. Holding the mug just gave her something to do with her hands. What she really wanted to do was reach out to Garrett, but she didn't feel free to do that.

The fact that they had made love really didn't mean anything, she told herself. Her insides might be quaking and her entire perspective might be altered, but Garrett could very well regard this as just another pleasant episode in his life. What did she know about his personal life, after all? He might be used to having a different woman every night of the week. Wasn't he a confirmed bachelor?

All of the questions she had refused to consider because she had been so blinded by her own fear of making love now reared their heads. Questions she should have asked beforehand looked stark and scary in the aftermath.

Aftermath. Not afterglow. The afterglow had vanished with the intrusion of the caller and his threats. She was beginning to feel very mistaken in her assessment of her neighbors, and that left her wondering about her assessment of Garrett. She'd been wrong about people before. Tragically wrong.

"What's that sigh for, darlin'?"

She looked at him, wishing she could explain, terrified that he might guess her doubts, feeling the horrifying prickle of tears behind her eyelids. Oh, God, she didn't want to turn into an emotional wreck in front of this man.

"It's okay." In an instant he was around the table, reaching for her, drawing her to her feet and into a tight embrace. "Sandy, it's okay. If you want to cry, go ahead."

"I'm not like that," she argued, even as she struggled to steady her quivering jaw.

"Not like what?" His hand found its way into her hair and stroked gently. "Not human? Is that what you mean? Look, it's three o'clock in the morning, you just got a nasty drunken phone call and...well, earlier, with me, you lowered a lot of emotional barriers. I'm not surprised all your feelings are right near the surface. It would be strange if they weren't. It doesn't mean you're weak if you cry. It just means this has been an emotionally draining night."

But she stubbornly blinked back the tears, anyway. "I'll be okay."

"Of course you will. You're okay right now."

Gently but inexorably, he led her back toward the bedroom. Soon he had them both tucked in beneath the warm blankets while wind rattled the windowpanes. It sounded so cold out there, she thought. But it was so warm in here.

It felt good to snuggle against Garrett, to feel held and protected and safe. It wouldn't last, but for right now she didn't care. It had been a long, long time since she had felt so cared for... if she ever had.

"Don't worry about a thing," Garrett whispered soothingly. Softly his hands moved over her, slowly stoking fires that seemed not to have died but rather to have become embers awaiting a breath to bring them to fiery life.

And as his hands brushed flame over her sensitive hills and hollows, one realization struck her above all others: he wanted to make love to her again. He actually *wanted* her again! The understanding rose in her like a tiny bubble of joy, making her feel light and airy and wonderful.

And it gave her courage. Reaching out with her own hands, she began to shyly explore him. At first her touches were tentative, but his husky whispers of approval encouraged her to greater boldness. How smooth and warm he felt! Contrasting textures of skin and hair pleased her palms in ways no words could describe.

His body was hard and lean, and the simple act of touching him awakened deep yearnings in her. She had nearly forgotten the textures of masculinity, had nearly forgotten how exciting a man's hardness could be in contrast to her own softness. She had forgotten, indeed, that she could want anyone or anything as much as she wanted Garrett.

"You're so sweet," he whispered in her ear. "God, Sandy, your touches are driving me wild...."

Her confidence was growing by leaps and bounds. Each touch she dared to give him met with such patent approval and such obvious pleasure that her hands began to roam in ways that just a short while ago would have seemed impossible. Hard...smooth...furry...crisp curls...a banquet of sensations.

He turned suddenly, carrying her with him, and she found herself straddling his hips in the most intimate of ways. In the faint golden light that poured through the door from the hall, she saw the smile that curved his lips.

"Here, darlin'," he said quietly, and let his fingertips brush her hardening nipples.

Instinctively she moved, and when she moved her breasts brushed against his fingers. Electric sparks shot wildly through her, causing her to move yet again and brush against him yet again in the most incredibly erotic and teasing dance.

"That's the way, honey," he whispered. "That's the way."

She forgot all her inhibitions and rocked gently back and forth, feeling his arousal pressed firmly to her, feeling the brush of his hands against her breasts, and feeling incredibly feminine, incredibly sexy. All her self-doubts slipped away on the liquid heat of desire that filled her. She was his, and somehow he made her feel as if she were the only woman in the world he wanted to be with.

"Faster..."

He must have whispered the word, for she was in control. She obeyed and dimly realized that she wasn't in control after all, that he was....

"Harder..." That might have been her voice; she couldn't be sure. Did it matter?

"Lift up...."

"Yes..."

Suddenly he was within her, filling her to her very soul, making her feel complete in a way she had never before known. She threw back her head, savoring his possession and knowing real freedom for the first time in her life.

He found her sexy. He wanted her. He liked her touches and responded to them in the most exciting ways.

He found her adequate as a woman.

She might have wept then, at last, releasing the pain that had scarred her for so many years, but already he was sweeping her past thought, up and away from all of the cares that burdened her. Carrying her far beyond to a world where nothing existed except their joined bodies.

"Now, Sandy...now..."

Whether that was a command or a plea, she hardly knew or cared. It served to unlock something inside her, something tightly wound that uncoiled swiftly like a compressed spring.

When it snapped, it hurtled her over the edge into a blinding oblivion of delight. Dimly she was aware that she didn't go alone.

Chapter 11

"How will you live with yourself if you get that creep off?"

The question was flung at her as she crossed the hospital parking lot on Monday morning. By then she was beginning to get used to it. Sunday morning she had been the topic of a sermon in which Reverend Fromberg had gently chided those who were condemning her and had reminded his flock that every man was entitled to a defense, and that everyone was innocent until it had been proven otherwise. She had appreciated the gesture, but noticed that the dark looks she received did not in any way lighten.

Grocery shopping yesterday afternoon, she had been grateful as all get-out that Garrett had decided to accompany her, because otherwise she would have been scared half to death rather than just getting angry when three cowboys hurled nasty comments at her. She didn't even know who they were, or if they were capable of carrying out their implied threats, but they looked like the type she would be defending on a drunk and disorderly charge one of these days... assuming they hadn't moved on to a ranch in another county by then.

She couldn't say she hadn't expected it, she thought as she entered the hospital, aware that Garrett was only a step behind her. She'd known she would face some of this. The problem was, she hadn't really believed it. Yes, the rape of a child was one of the most heinous acts that could be committed. Yes, the rapist ought to go to jail, preferably for the rest of his days. But until someone proved to the satisfaction of a jury that the man accused was in fact the rapist, he had to be presumed innocent. He was entitled to a defense.

And she was beginning to feel like a broken record. Even her own thoughts were running in circles on the subject. The bottom line was that if it was this bad now, it was going to get worse. Maybe her sarcastic comment about getting a bodyguard hadn't been so far off the mark.

Lisa Dunbar was sitting up in bed wearing bright pink pajamas and playing with a doll. Sam Haversham stood to one side, talking with Lisa's mother. Garrett waited out in the hallway, because both Sandy and Sam feared that the presence of a strange man might inhibit the child. Lisa's mother gave Sandy a cool nod and retreated to a corner of the hospital room, where she sat and picked up a magazine.

"This is Sandy Keller, Lisa," Sam said, introducing her to the girl. "You've seen her at church."

Lisa nodded. "Lots."

"Okay, then. We just want to ask you a few questions this morning. Later on, we might bring another person to see you, too. A court recorder. Have you ever seen one on television? The lady who sits at a tiny typewriter in the court and types down everything people say?"

Lisa nodded, but it was impossible to tell whether she was giving them the reply she thought they wanted or really knew what Sam was talking about.

"It's very important," Sam continued, "that you tell us the truth, Lisa. Do you know about telling the truth?"

These were the selfsame questions a judge would be asking Lisa later to determine if she would be a competent witness. Sandy watched the child intently.

"Mommy says to always tell the truth," Lisa told Sam and gave him the tiniest smile. "To be a good girl, so God doesn't get mad at me."

"That's right. You should always tell the truth. Do you know what a lie is?"

"When I make something up?"

"Good girl. A lie is when you tell something that didn't really happen."

Lisa nodded emphatically.

"Can you tell me a lie right now?"

Lisa tilted her head and pursed her lips. "My doggie is orange."

Both Sam and Sandy smiled. "What's the truth, Lisa?"

"My doggie's black and white. He's a damnation."

"Dalmatian," Mrs. Dunbar said hurriedly. Sandy had to choke back a laugh.

"So the truth is that your doggie is black and white, not orange at all."

Lisa nodded again. For a while Sam talked about ordinary things—school, church, what she wanted for her birthday. When Lisa seemed completely relaxed about talking with him, he began to circle in on the abduction.

"Now, Lisa, we need to talk about the bad things that happened to you. About when you were hurt. Can you talk to us about that?"

Another nod, but her eyes left Sam and became fixed on her doll.

"I know you don't want to think about it, honey, but we need to catch the bad person who hurt you, so you have to help us. Okay? Was it a man who took you away after you got off the school bus?"

Lisa nodded vigorously. "Bad man. Bad."

"Did you see what he was wearing? What kind of clothes?"

She nodded.

"Can you tell us?"

"Pants. Like mine. Jacket. Mittens."

Little by little Sam got a description of the clothes—perfectly ordinary jeans, boots, gloves. Nothing that seemed to have stuck in Lisa's mind as being interesting. As for his face, they got nothing at all.

"Did you see the man's face, Lisa?"

She nodded.

"What did he look like?"

"Mashed. Squished."

Sam and Sandy exchanged glances. Sam turned back to the little girl. "Do you know the man, Lisa?"

She stared back at him.

"Do you know who hurt you, Lisa?"

"Nighthawk."

Sandy's heart stopped dead, and the room seemed to recede as shock shook her to her very core. Nighthawk. As simply as that....

"But you said you didn't see his face, Lisa," Sam said gently. "Did you see who he was?"

Lisa shook her head. "He was wearing something funny over his face. Black."

Sandy spoke through stiff lips. "How do you know it was Nighthawk?"

"My daddy told me."

"Well, that sure as hell shoots it in the foot," Sam said a few minutes later as he and Sandy and Garrett stood in the hallway and held a low-voiced discussion. "There's no way she can testify, Sandy. No way. Her entire testimony would be suspect now! Damn it, I told those people not to discuss this with her at all."

"Maybe they didn't," Sandy said. "Maybe she overheard her dad say that to someone else."

Sam looked at her from hot eyes. "Guess who my next suspect would be if Nighthawk turned up innocent."

Sandy nodded and looked away. The father was always a prime suspect in these cases; all too often he *was* the perpetrator. "But she'd know her father. Even a mask wouldn't keep her from knowing him."

"Not necessarily," Garrett remarked. "Kids have great imaginations, and it wouldn't take much effort to convince a five-year-old that she was talking to a superhero or to a total stranger. Hell, all he'd have to do is keep his face covered and wear some funny after-shave. She sure wouldn't *want* to believe it was her dad."

"You may be right about that," Sam agreed. "But insofar as her testimony is concerned, it doesn't matter. She's a tainted witness. Useless."

Sandy agreed. "There's no way we can tell how much of what she says is accurate recollection and how much has been filled in since by overheard conversations."

"So we have to go with what she said to Nate when she was found. It doesn't help Nighthawk any."

"No, but it isn't a hell of a lot against him, either."

Sam nodded grimly. "I want a solution to this case, Sandy. Damn it, I can't stand the thought the culprit may escape."

"Me either," she agreed. "I still don't think it was Nighthawk, but I'd sure like to be able to prove who it really was."

"Before he strikes again," Garrett said.

Sam glanced over at him. "God, don't even suggest it."

"Can't you question her a little more?" Garrett asked. "I realize you can't use her as a witness, but she might know some things that would help, anyway. Like where did he take her? Does she know? When did her book bag disappear? Stuff like that. Maybe we can pick up a clue or two."

So they went back into the hospital room and began to question Lisa gently about events. Garrett stayed back by the door, but this time they left it open so he could hear.

"We went to a house," Lisa told them.

"Did you see the outside of it?"

"No."

"Do you know whose house it was? Who lived there?"

"The stinky man."

"Why do you say he's stinky?"

"Peeyew!" She held her nose.

That could mean almost anything, Sandy thought, but it sure didn't fit Nighthawk.

They questioned her further, discovering that she had seen only one room of the house, that there were a bed and a chair and a picture of an old woman in it, and that she'd been tied up most of the time while he hurt her. That she never once saw his face, and that she had been alone in the dark for long periods of time.

And that the man knew her name.

"I guess that's all, Lisa," Sam said finally. "I don't have any more questions. What about you, Sandy?"

"I think that's it for now. Would you mind if I come back and visit you tomorrow?" she asked the little girl.

Lisa shook her head slowly. "More questions?"

"Maybe." Sandy smiled gently. "And maybe we'll just play a game. We'll see. Do you have any questions for us?"

Lisa looked straight at her with a child's wide, perplexed gaze. "Why are you trying to get the bad man out of jail?"

It was like taking a punch to the stomach. She couldn't even breathe. She was saved from trying to find a reasonable answer by the arrival of the local scoutmaster, Dudley Willis. He was wearing his uniform and smiling broadly as he stepped into the room with a large beribboned box. He nodded to Sandy and Sam, then turned to Mrs. Dunbar.

"The boys took up a collection to get a little something for Lisa. Is it okay?"

The woman beamed at him. "Sure, Dud. Lisa will love it."

In fact, Lisa was already clapping her hands in excited anticipation, and the hopefulness on her face showed all the joy and delight of a child on Christmas morning. Sandy's throat tightened painfully, and for a moment her vision blurred. Right now Lisa looked the way a child should look, with none of the terrible knowledge that had been so apparent on her face but a short time ago.

When Dud Willis handed her the box, she tore at it eagerly and squealed with delight when she pulled out a beautiful and very expensive talking doll. Evidently one of her friends had one, because she needed no instructions to make it work. While she explored it, Willis stood beaming with pleasure.

Garrett slipped into the room and stood beside Sandy. "Who's he? Apart from being a scout leader."

"Dudley Willis," she whispered back. "One of our more prominent citizens."

He gave a brief nod, never taking his eyes from the man and the little girl. Willis at last said that he needed to get on back. He went to Lisa's side and bent over her, telling her to get well quick.

As he got close, Lisa flinched and turned quickly away, crying, "No!"

Willis immediately stepped back from the bed. "I'm sorry," he said, looking horrified. "I forgot she'd probably be afraid of men...." He turned with an agonized expression and hurried out into the hall.

"It's all right," Mrs. Dunbar said quickly, going after him. "Dud, it's okay. You didn't do anything."

To Sandy's amazement, Garrett went right after them and in the rudest imaginable way stepped right between them and took Willis by a shoulder. "She'll be okay," he said to the man. "I'm sure she was just startled. I've seen cases like this before."

Willis looked up at him, and after a moment he nodded. "Yeah. I just feel bad about upsetting her."

Then, just as swiftly as he'd intruded, Garrett stepped out of the way. He turned and looked at Sandy through the open door, gave a little jerk of his head and walked away. She wanted to follow and ask what had gotten into him, but instead focused on Lisa, who was clutching her new doll as if it were a lifeline and staring warily at the people in the room.

"Are you okay, honey?" Sandy asked her.

Several long moments passed before the little head nodded.

"Did something scare you?"

This time there was no answer at all, just a stony silence. Then Lisa touched the back of her doll and it began to recite a poem.

"I'll stop by tomorrow to see how you're doing, okay?" Sandy said. That elicited another nod, but Lisa didn't look at her again.

Sandy found Garrett waiting in the main lobby for her. "What got into you?" she asked him as they walked to her car.

"Just had an idea I want to check out. I'm going into the big city tonight. Want to come along?"

She hesitated and then thought, Why not? She certainly didn't have any appointments to take care of, and she didn't have to be in court again until next week, when she was handling a routine DUI. "I'd like that."

They checked into one of the better motels and shared a dinner in the restaurant. Afterward Garrett suggested they go to the mall. Though he spoke casually, Sandy guessed that this was what he had come into the city for, and she longed to ask him what he wanted to check out. She bit back the questions, though, because she was sure he would tell her when he was ready to. It wasn't easy to suppress her natural curiosity, but she respected Garrett's judgment and figured that whatever was compelling him wasn't yet clear enough to him that he felt comfortable sharing it.

The mall was busy, filled with crowds that made her think of the Christmas rush. Easter was just behind them, and now Mother's Day was very much in evidence in the card shops and a few of the department stores. Garrett seemed in no particular hurry, and if he was heading somewhere in particular, she couldn't tell. More than once he suggested they wander through one of the stores when something in the window caught her eye.

"You'd look great in that," he told her when she paused to wistfully eye a turquoise silk blouse.

She hesitated a moment longer and then shook her head. "I need to be good. I don't know when I may ever have another client."

He looked somberly down at her. "They'll come around eventually, darlin'. You're a good attorney, and I think the vast majority of your neighbors really like you."

"You could fool me. I expected fallout from this, Garrett. Truly. I expected to lose some clients, and I expected nasty phone calls. Maybe even a veiled threat or two. But I didn't expect to have my business completely collapse."

"I'm sure that's just temporary. Really." He took her hand and squeezed it, then kept it tucked warmly within his as they continued their stroll through the crowd. "I'd bet money it's just a first shocked reaction on the part of most of your clients and an instinctive desire not to have their names associated in even a remote way with this mess. Once the initial furor dies down, things'll pretty much go back to normal."

"I hope so. I hate to think of having to move away and start all over again elsewhere."

"I'm sure that won't happen."

But his reply had been a beat too late in coming, and she felt her heart give a crazy leap. Could he possibly be wishing that she would consider pulling up stakes and coming to Texas? Lord, she didn't know if she would have the gumption to start all over again—and so far away, besides! It would be so different.... No, she couldn't possibly consider it.

But she glanced up at him, anyway, wishing he would say something about it. Wishing against hope that somehow, magically, everything could work out so she could spend the rest of her life with this kind, understanding, wonderful man.

"When will you be done with convalescent leave?" she asked him finally, when he said nothing more.

"I... don't know." He turned abruptly, leading her into a lamp-lit restaurant. "Let's get some coffee and dessert."

Chocolate cheesecake was about as sinful as you could get, but she decided to splurge on it, anyway. Garrett ordered Dutch apple pie and asked the waitress to keep the coffee coming.

"Why don't you know when your convalescent leave will be over?" she asked him when they were alone. "Is something wrong?"

He didn't want to tell her. Saying it out loud somehow made it seem more real, which was utterly ridiculous, but superstition had been dogging him ever since his life had gotten out of his own control. He tried and tried not to think about it, the same way he tried not to think about how much he wanted Sandy Keller and how much that wanting scared him. He wasn't a coward, not by a long shot, but there were some things it just did no good to worry about, so a wise man set them aside and moved on to the things that *were* under his control. Besides, Sandy had enough on her plate with all this fallout from the Nighthawk case. She didn't need to be hearing his problems.

Yet he couldn't bring himself to equivocate or prevaricate. She'd been utterly honest with him, and she deserved no less in return. If he was washed-up as a cop, she deserved to know it.

"I've... had some residual damage," he told her. The words didn't come easily. "My right arm isn't as strong as it needs to be. I'm working on it, but there's no guarantee I'll be able to pass the physical."

"Oh, Garrett, that would be awful for you!" All she could think of was how she would feel if she couldn't practice law anymore. It would be like having a big chunk of her heart cut out. She longed to reach out and offer comfort of some kind, but there was simply nothing she could say that would make this any better. Regardless of whether it might embarrass him, she reached across the table and squeezed his hand. "The waiting must be terrible."

He shrugged. "Can't be helped. And, of course, every day is another day I can exercise my arm."

"Is it helping?"

"I think so." He clenched his right hand into a fist. "There's no doubt it's stronger than it was. And the tremor is nowhere near what it was. The question is whether it'll improve enough . . . and in time."

He spoke with masculine stoicism, but she wasn't buying it. She had discovered that Garrett possessed the normal complement of human feelings, and although his expression of them was subtle, that didn't mean he wasn't feeling just as intensely as she would. He would, however, probably get embarrassed if she made too much of a fuss about it.

"Have you thought about what you'll do if you don't pass?"

He shook his head, smiling faintly. "I'm a stubborn cuss, Sandy. I refuse to even consider the possibility. Well . . . not much, anyway."

Even as faint as his smile was, she found it infectious. "Was that why you were making all those references to figuring out some kind of hobby before you retire?"

"I guess so. Much as I don't want to even allow there's a possibility, it's not something I can entirely ignore."

And now she understood why he had wanted to act as an investigator on this case. Better to be busy than to sit around and brood. It was perfectly understandable, but her stomach sank anyway. So he hadn't wanted to work on the case as an excuse to be near her. It was only right then that she realized how much some little corner of her heart had been hoping precisely that. That Garrett had simply wanted to be with her.

Which was ridiculous, she told herself sternly. Utterly ridiculous. Neither of them wanted to get involved. Both of them had been burned too badly. No, it was far better that he was investigating this case for reasons that had nothing to do with her. Far better.

But it hurt a little anyway.

And because it hurt, she ate the entire slice of cheesecake instead of the three or four forkfuls she'd promised herself. Ah, well. Didn't chocolate contain the same chemical that was released when you fell in love? She could sure use a little pick-me-up right now. A pick-me-up about the size of a one-pound box of chocolates, actually. It was a silly train of thought, but the silliness picked up her mood almost as much as the chocolate.

"Have you heard any more from your sister?" she asked him.

He shook his head. "I asked a buddy of mine to look into her ex-husband's parole, though. If there's anything at all I can do to keep that guy behind bars, I'll do it. It makes me so damn mad the way these abusive guys can keep coming back at women."

"Not all of them do that, though, do they?"

"Not all. But how the hell do you know? Anyway, I'm going to make sure he doesn't get a chance at Ginny. We should know pretty quick after he gets out if he's the kind who wants to get even."

Back on the concourse, feeling as if she had eaten far too much and was going to swell into a beach ball, she was glad to be moving again. They browsed in a music store, and Sandy treated herself to a CD she'd been wanting for a long time.

And then, to her amazement, they entered a tobacco shop. "I used to smoke a pipe," Garrett told the tobacconist. "I'm thinking about taking it up again, only I can't remember the name of the tobacco I liked so much."

The man nodded to him. "What can you tell me about it?"

"It's not a widely smoked kind. I know that much. Very aromatic, but not at all sweet. Sort of heavy, and a little musty. Bitter."

The man pulled a couple of glass jars down from the shelf and removed the stoppers for him. "See if you recognize either of these aromas."

Garrett took a sniff of the first jar while Sandy wondered why he was all of a sudden talking about smoking again. He'd seemed to be proud of the fact that he'd quit, even though he often patted his breast pocket, looking for that pack of cigarettes.

"This is the stuff," Garrett told the man. "I'm sure of it."

"Latakia. One of the better Turkish tobaccos. It's not one of the most popular, because it isn't sweet at all. Would you like some?"

Garrett bought a few ounces, along with a briar pipe and the other mysterious accoutrements that men used with pipes. When they were outside, Sandy asked him, "Are you sure you want to start smoking again?"

He glanced down with an enigmatic half smile. "Only for a little while."

She shook her head. "I hear it's about the toughest addiction there is to kick. You might regret fooling with it."

"I might. But I quit once, and I figure if I could do it once, I can do it again."

"Ah, but does it truly constitute quitting if you start up again a while later?"

He laughed. "It's been three years. More than 'a while.'"

"I just don't want to see you get hooked again."

His expression softened. "Thanks for caring," he said gently. "Trust me. I won't."

"'Trust me' is always the last thing the hero says before everything goes to hell," she reminded him.

They were both laughing when they stepped out into the parking lot. The night had grown crisp, the stars were brilliant and unwinking in a black velvet sky. The air was still, however, and there was an almost hushed sense of expectancy to the world.

Garrett paused after he unlocked the car door for her. "Back to our room?"

There was no mistaking the message in his eyes. Sandy's heart quickened with excitement. It was still incredible to her that this man found her desirable. Still wonderfully impossible at the way all her doubts and fears fled when he touched her. In some inexplicable, almost magical way, she became new and fresh and untainted when he reached for her. Somehow he had peeled away all the years, all the scars, all the detritus, that had closed her away for so long.

She was also scared to death. It was terrifying to feel so open, so exposed. All her defenses were down, and there was nothing left to protect her from hurt.

And she *was* going to get hurt. She wasn't naive enough to believe there could be any other outcome. All her feelings had gotten tangled up with Garrett; that had probably been inevitable from the moment of their first meeting. Heavens, she hadn't been able to forget him in the two years since!

She would have missed him when he left if they had never made love. But they *had* made love. Gloriously. Wonderfully. Repeatedly. In a mere three nights, she had grown accustomed to his presence beside her in her bed. Had grown to love the reassurance of waking in the dark and seeing his shadow beside her in the night. Had grown to love the sound of his deep breathing, and even his light snoring in the early morning hours.

Her life, which had seemed complete and fulfilling only a brief time ago, was now going to seem empty when he was gone. A bed that had been hers alone would now forever seem lonely.

She had been foolish, she admitted, as they drove back to their motel. Utterly foolish. She had believed herself to be immune to these dangers after so many years. Even as she had felt herself slipping over the precipice of caring too much for Garrett, she had convinced herself that it wouldn't become more than she could handle. She had never for one moment realized that there was no safety in his inevitable departure, had never admitted that that wasn't safety at all.

Her only safety had been in never becoming involved at all. But she had slowly and steadily grown to care more and more... until finally she had cared enough to risk making love with him. And that had sealed her fate beyond redemption. He had shown her that she was a whole woman. He had desired her and cared for her and had made long-dead dreams come true.

How could she have failed to love him?

But now she *did* love him, and there was no hope. No ending but a painful one. He had given her no indication that she was anything more than a pleasant diversion, and he'd warned her at the very outset that he wasn't marriage material.

A sigh escaped her, but Garrett failed to hear it, and she was grateful. There was no way she could have explained her mood to him. Better to try to put a happy face on it until he was gone. If nothing else, she could preserve her pride.

It was small consolation, but it was amazing how much backbone a little pride could provide.

Garrett had registered them in a single room as boldly as if they were married, and it was a kind of illicit thrill for her. She'd never done anything like this before in her life...which perhaps said something about how limited her experiences really were.

Once they were in the motel room, Garrett turned her into his arms as easily as if he'd been doing it for a lifetime and covered her mouth in a hungry, devouring kiss. "God," he said moments later, sounding as if he were on the edge of laughter, "you've been driving me crazy all evening. Damn it, Sandy, I don't think you have any idea how naturally sexy you are! You even breathe sexy."

The gleam in his brilliant blue eyes and the humor in his tone unknotted something inside her, and a bubble of laughter spilled over her own lips. The foreshadowing of pain faded into the distant recesses of her mind, leaving her feeling open and free.

The magic of the night seemed to come into the room with them. Dark velvet feelings filled her as Garrett's hands moved over her, removing unwanted clothing, painting sensation over her nerve endings. The confidence he had been instilling in her made her bold enough to reciprocate. With unabashedly eager hands, she helped him out of his shirt and tugged away his boots and jeans. When at last they tumbled naked onto the bed, they were both laughing and breathless.

And then their eyes locked and their hearts locked and laughter became sighs and soft whispers. She felt as if she fit perfectly into the curve of his body as he held her close and explored her with gentle fingers, leading her steadily deeper into the beauty of lovemaking. She had the craziest feeling that she had been made for this man, for these moments, for this brief stolen time. As if her entire life had been focused on this mating.

Crazy, she told herself. Crazy. But she was past caring. She needed his touches and kisses to the very depths of her soul, needed to be filled with him in every one of her senses. The sound of his voice, rough with passion, was as sensual as a fur coat slipping over her ultrasensitive skin. His aromas, of soap and man and just a tinge of the tobacco he had earlier sampled, filled her nose and seemed to spread like warm waves to the farthest parts of her body. And his touches...his touches claimed every inch of her, making her feel surrounded by him, protected by him, cherished by him.

She knew it was an illusion, but she felt as if she could just crawl into him and be held safely forever. The yearning to do just that was as intense as the desire to feel him fill her body. It was appalling to realize how long it had been since last she had felt cared for, and equally frightening to realize just how much she needed to feel that way. The years behind her suddenly looked so barren, and the future held no more promise, because this man would return alone to his home in Texas.

Near panic froze her for an instant, and suddenly, to her own horror, she was weeping huge, silent tears of impending loss.

"Sandy? Darlin', what's wrong?" Garrett's concerned face hovered over her in the dusky room, and his arms changed their hold, becoming less demanding and more comforting. "Sweetheart, what's wrong?"

She shook her head emphatically and squeezed her eyes shut against the tears. She would rather face demons than admit to this man that she was crying because he would be passing out of her life.

"Don't shake your head," he said gently, his voice laced with real concern. "Did I hurt you? Are you worried about something?"

"Nothing... nothing... sorry. Guess I'm just tired...." The tears were drying almost as quickly as they had begun, leaving her feeling foolish for having shed them. She wanted to turn her face away and hide, but Garrett prevented her. He kept her cradled safely to his chest, her head upon his shoulder, and kissed away the tears he could reach.

He held her for a long time, convinced that he must have done something to upset her. He knew Sandy; she wasn't the type to burst into tears easily. Something was seriously troubling her, and since nothing had happened in the past several hours, he could assume only that he had somehow upset her himself.

But no matter how many times he played the day over in his mind, particularly the last half hour or so, he couldn't find anything that should have caused her tears. The last time a woman he'd held had cried for no apparent reason, she had been getting ready to tell him that she was leaving him.

So perhaps Sandy was planning to break it off with him. His heart lurched painfully. But of course this was coming to an end, he told himself. That had been inevitable from the outset. He had known from day one that she wouldn't abandon her law practice, and he wasn't about to abandon his career as a ranger.

But instead of the calm acceptance he thought he should feel, he was nearly overcome by a terrible sense of loss. It gripped his chest like a vise and tightened his throat until it nearly hurt to breathe. But this was just transitory, he told himself. He'd learned the hard way not to give his heart away, and he wasn't the type who forgot his lessons. No, this was just a momentary feeling, and he would be over it by tomorrow.

For the first time, he and Sandy fell asleep together without making love. But throughout the night, they never entirely let go of one another.

Chapter 12

The first thing Sandy saw when she and Garrett entered her office the next afternoon was a note taped conspicuously to her desk. Nina wanted her to know that Sam was going to depose Ben Dunbar. Could she be at Sam's office at nine the next morning? She was supposed to call Sam.

The second thing she saw was the broken window in Nina's office. Someone had hurled a large rock through it. A piece of paper was tied around the rock, which lay amid scattered slivers of glass.

"Don't touch it," Garrett said sharply. "Let's get the sheriff over here."

The Conard County sheriff's deputies were always prompt to respond, and this time was no exception. Micah Parish was walking up to her door within five minutes of her phone call. Then Sandy had to endure the incredible frustration of waiting to find out what the note said while photos were taken and the rug was marked where the rock had fallen. Only then, after painstaking preparation, did Micah put on a pair of gloves and carefully untie the note.

Written on ordinary blue-lined notebook paper, it was brief and to the point. Penciled in block letters was the message: *An eye for an eye. If you get the rapist off, you will pay.*

"Oh, great!" Sandy said in frustration. "Just great! What's next? A Molotov cocktail? A burning cross? What is the matter with everyone?"

"It's not the matter with everyone," Micah said in his deep, slow voice. "Just a few nuts. You must have expected this."

She sighed and scooped her hair back from her face with impatient hands. "Yeah, I expected it. I just didn't expect to be so scared by it! Damn it, Micah, what kind of person does something like this?"

"Generally someone who's too much of a chicken to look you right in the eye and say it," Garrett told her. "It's a cheap shot. I wouldn't worry about it, darlin'."

"Me either," Micah agreed. "This isn't a serious threat."

"What *would* be serious?" she asked. She didn't at all like the feeling that the threat wasn't being taken seriously enough. If people were willing to throw rocks through her windows, who was to say they wouldn't be willing to do something even worse? Micah and Garrett were being entirely too sanguine about all of this.

After Micah had departed with the pictures, the rock and the note, Garrett helped her tape cardboard over the broken window and clean up the glass that had sprayed all over the rug.

"This really isn't something I think you need to worry about," Garrett told her seriously. "I wouldn't kid you, Sandy. This is more of a kid's prank than a real threat."

"Well, I don't like it anyway!"

"I don't blame you. But if I'm right, we should catch our culprit pretty soon, and then this whole abominable mess will be put to rest."

She turned and faced him directly. "What's going on? And why do you keep putting me off when I ask?"

"Because I want you to observe something without knowing what you're observing, okay? Can we go to see the Dunbar girl sometime tomorrow?"

"Sure . . . I guess. Let me find out and set it up."

He smiled. "Thanks."

"This better be good, Hancock. That's all I have to say. Curiosity killed the cat, and I've got more curiosity than any cat."

He chuckled at that. "Trust me. I just want you to see what I saw, so that when I tell you about it you won't think I'm crazy, okay?"

She hesitated, wondering if he were planning something that could put her entire future on the line. Then she shrugged inwardly. Her future was apparently already on the line, and besides, Garrett was a Texas Ranger. There was no reason to think he would do anything illegal.

In the morning, Ben Dunbar's deposition did nothing to clarify matters. He'd forgotten, he said, all about Lisa being in Nighthawk's truck that morning in front of the supermarket. It just clean went out of his head until Nighthawk was arrested.

Why hadn't he come in right away to tell them about it instead of waiting until they questioned him? Because his mind was on other things, namely his little kid being so hurt, and besides, Nighthawk had already been arrested, anyway.

Why had Lisa been alone out in front of the store? "Well, you know how it is with kids. I didn't even know she'd gone off by herself until Dud Willis saw her out there. I thought she was right there while we was talking."

"Fishy as hell," Sam muttered when Dunbar had left.

Sandy thought so, too. The stenographer was quietly packing up, so she refrained from saying anything about it until they were alone. What struck her most was that Sam was apparently beginning to consider the possibility that Nighthawk wasn't guilty.

"It's making me uneasy as hell," he admitted when she mentioned it. "Basically what we have is a lot of circumstantial evidence that's beginning to look *too* circumstantial. Of course, the genetic tests aren't in yet, and it's possible they might prove the case."

"But you don't really think Nighthawk did it." She couldn't have said why, but it was somehow important to her that Sam admit doubt about the case.

"No, I don't really think Nighthawk did it," Sam said heavily. "No, damn it, I don't. I've talked to him, and the impression I keep getting is of somebody who's very decent. Of course, everybody thought Ted Bundy was a decent guy, too, didn't they?" He shook his head irritably. "I want more evidence. One way or another, I want something more to go on. It'll probably be three more weeks on the DNA matching, though."

"That long?" She'd never worked directly on a case with DNA evidence until this one and hadn't realized the analysis could take so long.

"It averages about five weeks, they tell me."

"Well, if you're so doubtful about Nighthawk's guilt, why don't you drop the charges?"

"And get myself run out of town on a rail? Be realistic, Sandy. He's the only suspect I've got, and I'm damn well going to hang on to him. The court approved the charges, and that's where we stand until something changes."

"Nothing's going to change if you don't look for anything."

He gave her a crooked smile. "You've hired a private eye, and you're not getting anywhere any faster than we are."

It was on the tip of her tongue to tell him that Garrett thought he'd solved the case, but she bit back the words. In the first place, she didn't know what Garrett suspected or what he was up to, and Sam would probably hit the roof if he thought Sandy or Garrett knew something material to the case and was concealing it. In the second place, Garrett was being secretive for a reason, and she had to respect that. For now.

So all she said to Sam was "I guess not."

"So, for lack of any evidence to the contrary," Sam continued, "Nighthawk remains accused. It's just getting to be an unpleasant feeling in my gut, that's all."

The prosecutor had an unpleasant feeling in his gut but was going to hang on to the suspect until there was something to prove the man's innocence. That seriously disturbed Sandy, but she could understand it. The *only* evidence they had pointed to Nighthawk, and it was sufficient that a judge had upheld the arrest warrant. Sam *couldn't* let Nighthawk go for no reason other than an uneasy feeling. And even if he had, from the looks of it the county would have hung him and then hung Nighthawk, so it wouldn't have done anyone a damn bit of good. Any way you looked at it, Nighthawk's incarceration was damn near protective custody.

"How'd it go?" Garrett asked her when she stepped out of Sam's office. He was waiting outside as he always was now, never leaving her alone. Like a patient watchdog. No, like a concerned lover, she amended. He was acting like a concerned lover. Too bad it was just an act.

No, that wasn't fair, either, she scolded herself. Garrett was a decent man, and his concern was genuine. It just wasn't permanent.

"Okay," she said. "I think Sam wishes he could pin this on Ben Dunbar. The man *is* behaving suspiciously."

Garrett shook his head. "No, he's acting like a not-too-bright man who's got more on his plate right now than he can handle."

"You're so sure he's innocent?"

"Sure enough to place a bet. Twenty bucks says I can prove it wasn't Dunbar *or* Nighthawk."

"I don't bet." She sniffed, but almost in spite of herself, a grin caught the corners of her mouth and tugged them upward. "Twenty bucks, huh? Doesn't sound like you're all that sure."

"Well, I'd bet a hundred without batting an eye, except that it would be like taking candy from a baby. I have *some* morals, you know."

"Not any that I've noticed," she joked, managing to purse her lips primly.

He leered. "You've been looking in the wrong places."

They were still laughing when they arrived back at her office, but the smiles faded before they finished climbing the porch steps. Spray-painted in black on the light gray wood porch floor was the warning *Justice must be served!*

"A somewhat literate vandal," Garrett remarked as he studied the mess with a dark frown. "Go get in the car, Sandy. There's probably more. I'll check things out first."

"No." Anger bubbled up from deep within her and began to boil. "Damn it, what do I have to do? Sit on my front porch with a shotgun twenty-four hours a day? Has the world gone mad?"

"No, the world hasn't gone crazy," Garrett said soothingly. "Just a few cranks, is all. This really looks like kid stuff."

Almost as quickly as it had bubbled up, Sandy's anger slipped away. "Yeah. Kid stuff. I'm sorry, I sound like a broken record. I must have asked that same question a hundred times in the past few days." She shook her head. "Now I have to have the porch painted. Maybe the whole damn house. Do you know how much that costs? I only had it done last summer...." She turned quickly away, blinking back unwanted tears. This was not the time to fall apart.

Garrett's arm settled around her shoulders, a reassuring weight. "I'll help you paint the damn place. We'll start the day after tomorrow."

Even through the closed door and windows, they could hear the phone inside start to ring. It was the distinctive chirrup of her office phone.

"Let me answer it," Garrett said as she shoved her key in the lock. "Let me handle it."

The call turned out to be for him, anyway, a friend of his in the rangers. Garrett's responses were clipped, revealing almost nothing, but when he hung up, he turned to Sandy, looking for all the world like a man who wanted to smile.

"That was Blue, my ranger buddy. I told you about him."

She nodded, remembering some middle-of-the-night conversation when he had mentioned that he'd asked a friend to check out the details of his sister's ex-husband's upcoming release. "Good news?"

"Maybe. It seems Bobby got involved in a fight. It's pretty serious, and he's in the hospital. They're not sure he'll make it." He shook his head. "Damn, it's awful to feel a man's death would be a lucky thing. Anyway, even if he does live, he's probably not going to breathe free air for a long time. They found drugs on him."

"Either way, that sounds like a reprieve for your sister."

"Yeah." He shook his head as a slow grin spread over his rugged face. "Yeah. Look the other way if I disgust you."

But she couldn't. She could understand all too well his feeling that this was news worth celebrating, and it was hardly mitigated by the fact that a man had been hurt. Your conscience could twinge, but sometimes you just felt it was justice anyway.

And speaking of justice... She looked around her office, wondering if anyone had gotten in and damaged things. The spray-painted warning out front had left her feeling...violated. Angry. Helpless. There was nothing on earth quite like a sense of helpless outrage.

"I'm going to walk around outside and see if there's any other graffiti," Garrett said. "If the phone rings, let the machine get it. I'll deal with any crap when I get done outside."

"I'm perfectly capable of answering the phone," she told him. "Actually, what I really need is a picket line out front."

Halfway to the door, he paused and looked back. "What?"

"A picket line. Put a dozen people out front with signs condemning me as the Whore of Babylon or some such nonsense because of the Nighthawk case, and I'd be as safe as a babe in a cradle."

Again that charming, lazy grin spread over his face. "You know, that's not such a bad idea. I wonder if I can arrange it."

Startled, she couldn't think of a thing to say before he disappeared out the door. She'd only been joking. Surely he didn't mean to actually have her picketed?

But she was beginning to wonder just what Garrett was capable of.

In the morning they drove out to the Dunbar ranch again, this time to talk to Lisa Dunbar, who was now home from the hospital. Garrett carried a white plastic garbage bag in which could be seen the vague outline of a stuffed doll. He also carried a box containing another doll.

"For Lisa," he said.

"I hope this isn't a nasty trick."

He put his hand over his heart. "I'm wounded. Hey, look, I promise it's not a nasty trick."

Mrs. Dunbar invited them in pleasantly enough and offered them coffee and cake. "Lisa's out with her daddy looking at the colt that was born while she was in the hospital. Ben says it's going to be Lisa's very own." The woman shook her head and looked at them from haunted eyes. "I don't want to turn into an overprotective mother, but it's not easy. I can't even stand to have her out of my sight now. How am I ever going to go back to work?"

Sandy didn't know what to say to that. Once a sense of safety was shattered, it was nearly impossible to put it back together.

"And my older girl is feeling nearly as bad," Mrs. Dunbar continued. "She's so sure that if she'd come home on the bus like she was supposed to, none of this would have happened. It *was* wrong of her to go to Johnna Willis's house after school—"

"Johnna Willis?" Garrett repeated. "I didn't know Dud had kids."

"Oh, yes, he's got four girls. His wife up and left him about three years back, never did say why. They moved into town, and Dud stayed out on the ranch. Anyhow, it was because he gave his daughter a movie that she and my girl had been wanting to see forever... Seems like forever to that age, anyway...." She smiled faintly. "Anyhow, that's what tempted my oldest to go to Johnna's house instead of coming home. What she should've done was take her sister with her, but—" she shook her head and looked away "—hindsight's always clearer."

Just then the little girl came dashing into the kitchen with a big smile on her face. "Oh, Mommy, he's beautiful, and Daddy says he's mine! My very own!"

The instant she saw Garrett and Sandy, however, her smile faded, and she sidled toward her mother. It was apparent that the sight of them had brought back memories of the past week.

"It's okay, honey," Mrs. Dunbar said gently. "It's okay. These folks just wanted to give you a present and see how you was doing. I'm right here, Lisa. You're safe."

Sandy's heart squeezed for the little girl, and the look she shot Garrett was a warning.

"Actually, I brought you two presents, Lisa. My niece in Texas loves these, so I thought I might as well get you two of them. She's always begging me to buy another one for her."

Lisa looked at him around her mother's shoulder. "Is she my size?"

"My niece? Yep. She's five years old, and she has long black hair and blue eyes like mine."

Lisa edged toward him. "What's her name?"

"Sylvia."

"I like that name."

"So do I. Sometimes I call her Silly for short."

Lisa giggled at that and apparently decided that Garrett was okay. She opened the box first, pulling forth a soft doll whose body was covered in pale pink satin. Her delight was palpable as she squealed and showed her mother, and asked Garrett if she could call the doll Silly-for-short.

"We-e-e-ell, I guess so," Garrett said, pretending reluctance. "Just don't ever tell Sylvia I said you could use her name."

Really eager now, Lisa reached for the bag as Garrett explained he had damaged the box. But when she opened it, she froze.

"Lisa?" Her mother looked instantly concerned. "Lisa, what's wrong?"

The little girl lifted frightened eyes to Garrett and stepped backward, dropping the bag as she did so.

"Lisa?" Mrs. Dunbar's voice sharpened. "Lisa, what's wrong?"

Sandy bent over in her chair, reaching for the bag Lisa had dropped. As she opened it and pulled out the doll, she understood just what Garrett had done with the pipe and Latakia tobacco he'd purchased. She shot him a furious look and then turned to Lisa.

"It smells funny, doesn't it?"

Lisa nodded.

"I'm sorry. It can be washed out, if your Mom will throw it in the machine."

"That's easy enough," Mrs. Dunbar said. Her arm was snug around the little girl, holding her close to her side. "You okay, baby?"

Lisa didn't answer.

Sandy wanted to shake Garrett, but she restrained herself and instead tried to give Lisa a reassuring smile. "Is it a bad smell?"

The small head nodded.

"Does it make you feel sad?"

"Scary," Lisa blurted. "The bad man smelled like that."

"Ahh..." The satisfied sound came from Garrett, even as the little girl looked at him warily, as if suspecting him of being the bad man. "I'm sorry, Lisa. The smell will wash out. You can keep the doll, and your mommy can fix it."

Lisa shook her head vehemently. "No. I don't want it!"

Mrs. Dunbar looked torn between chiding her daughter's rudeness and cuddling the child close.

"It's okay," Sandy told her. "Lisa has every right to refuse the doll. We'll get it out of here so it can't distress her anymore."

A few minutes later, as they were jolting down the rutted driveway to the road, Sandy exploded. "Garrett, how could you? How could you do that to that poor little girl! What if you've traumatized her all over again! Good God—"

"Willis is our rapist, and that little girl is a hell of a lot tougher than you're giving her credit for. It's just a smell, and I'm sure the whole thing is already forgotten, because nothing bad happened."

"There's no way you could have known that before you gave her the doll. No way you could be positive she wouldn't go catatonic or something!"

"I've worked on these cases before. Trust me, darlin', the child is all right. And now we have to nail Willis."

"Willis?" It suddenly penetrated her anger. "You think Dudley Willis did it? Garrett, do you have any idea of who that man is? Of his importance . . . ?"

"Important people do terrible things, too. Yes, I think it was Willis. Did you see how Lisa reacted when he came close to her bed? I don't know if you remember, but when he started to leave, I made a point of stopping him. I wanted a good look at him, in case something about his appearance reminded the kid of her abductor, but when I got close, I smelled the tobacco, and that fit better than it being something about his appearance that upset her, because she only got agitated when he came close. But I had to be sure the agitation was from the tobacco smell, not just because a man got too close. Therefore the doll."

"It was still a mean thing to do, and a tobacco odor doesn't mean a damn thing. There could be hundreds of men in this county who smoke that tobacco."

"If we were talking about chewing tobacco, I'd agree with you, sweetheart, but we're talking about pipe tobacco. About a particular type of tobacco that's usually tossed in small quantities into blends where it offsets sweetness a little. A tobacco that's smoked pure by very few people. It's too strong, too bitter and too aromatic. Anyway, I've noticed that pipe smokers don't exactly grow on trees around here. Yes, it's possible someone else smokes Latakia around here besides Willis, but I wouldn't bet the farm on it."

"It's still not enough to persuade me."

"Well, why don't you add to it the fact that it was Willis who showed up hotfoot to tell us about Nighthawk showing his truck to the little girl."

"Circumstantial. Not enough to even arrest him." But suspicious as hell, she admitted, as her anger began to seep away. Awfully suspicious. "Garrett, Willis is one of the most prominent and important people in this county. If you point a finger at him, no one is going to listen."

"Then I'll have to get more evidence. At least now I know where to look."

She turned in her seat and stared straight at him. "Don't do anything illegal, Garrett. You may be acting as a private individual here, but you're working for me. If you get up to something doubtful, I could wind up disbarred."

He nodded and glanced her way. "Haven't you heard? Honest lawyers are an endangered species and have to be protected."

"Damn it, Garrett, this is no time for lawyer jokes! If you do anything shady, I could wind up disbarred, you could wind up in trouble with the law, and Willis will get off scot-free—if he *is* the perp. I want you to walk the straight and narrow on this."

He gave her a quick, reassuring smile. "Relax. The very last thing I want to do is get you into any kind of trouble. I'm just going to talk this over with Nate Tate."

She had to be satisfied with that.

"Do you have any idea who Dudley Willis *is?*" Nate asked Garrett as they faced each other across Nate's desk.

"Yeah. Conard County's George Washington and Abe Lincoln all in one."

Nate shook his head, chuckling. "Sorry, old son. Nope, not quite. Oh, his great grandaddy had something to do with settling this county, and up until the depression they owned most of it, except for the parts owned by the Conards. But that's not who Dud is. Dud is involved in damn near every one of our community activities, from theater to scouting. He's active in the church—one of its biggest contributors, as a matter of fact—and he heads up at least a dozen charitable organizations. He's not George Washington, but I think there's hardly a soul in the county who doesn't think highly of him. *Very* highly."

Garrett stifled a sigh. "Important people do bad things, too."

"Yeah, and I'm not saying it's impossible. Just that you're going to need a hell of a lot more than a suspicion in order to hang Dud Willis, and right now you haven't even got enough for a search warrant."

"But—"

Nate waved him to silence. "The fact that he smokes a brand of tobacco that has a smell that the little girl associates with her rapist merely puts him in a class, and you know as well as I do that you can't get a warrant because somebody is a member of a certain class of people. That's like trying to get a warrant because somebody watches a certain TV program. Yeah, him and nineteen million other Americans. You put that together with him having seen Nighthawk with the little girl, and it's still meaningless. Completely and totally meaningless. And I'm never going to persuade Judge Williams to issue a warrant just because the guy smokes the wrong kind of tobacco and because he found the little girl's clothes on Nighthawk's property. Damn it, we had over a hundred people out searching that night. Any one of them could have found the kid's clothes. You know as well as I do that you have to have something that links *one* person to the crime."

"*He* found the girl's buried clothes? Damn it, Nate, you can't tell me all of this put together doesn't raise your hackles just a little!"

Nate pursed his lips and blew out a long breath. He stared hard at Garrett for several moments before rising and going to look out his office window. "Yeah, it raises my hackles. My skin is crawling, and the back of my neck is prickling. Problem is, that won't convince the judge to issue a warrant, either. Hell!" He slapped his palm against the window frame. "I would never in a million years have suspected Dud Willis of something like this. Cheating on his taxes, yeah. That I'd believe. But doing something like this? Never."

He turned abruptly. "But we still need something more to get a warrant. I'm going to put my investigator on it. In the meantime, you stay clear, Garrett."

"I understand. What you need is a reliable informant to say he saw some kind of evidence." And as long as Garrett was acting as a private individual, the Fourth Amendment didn't cover him.

Something in Garrett's eyes must have warned Nate, because he went back to his desk and leaned over it, resting his weight on his hands. "I don't want to know if you're planning anything foolish. I don't want to know a damn thing about it. Just remember—if you bring anything out of Willis's house, I can't use it."

One corner of Garrett's mouth lifted in a half smile. "By the way, I want you to know I'm giving Sandy my resignation as her investigator this evening. I am no longer working for her."

One of Nate's brows lifted, then he nodded. "I understand. I hear you. But remember, *don't touch a damn thing.*"

Garrett cooked dinner for himself and Sandy that evening in Sandy's kitchen. She felt awkward about letting someone else do the cooking, particularly a man. Never once in her entire life had a man cooked dinner for her. Her son, of course, didn't count. The thought brought a smile to her lips.

Garrett was up to something, she thought. She was convinced of it. He was planning something, and he wasn't going to tell her about it, because she would object. She

wondered if losing her entire client base wasn't the least of
the trouble she was going to get out of the Nighthawk case.

But Garrett had said he wouldn't do anything to get her
into trouble, and silly woman that she was, she wanted to
believe him. She didn't want anything to mar this evening,
and she certainly wasn't going to confront him about the
Willis idea. He'd told her that Nate had said he couldn't get
a warrant based on what they had, and she agreed. It wasn't
enough by a long shot. Garrett had seemed to accept that
easily enough, and she had to presume he planned to continue investigating in the hopes of finding enough evidence
to provide probable cause for a search warrant of Willis's
house.

Not that she thought Dudley Willis would have been stupid enough to keep anything incriminating around. She
didn't think of him as a stupid man. But then, she didn't
think of him as a child rapist, either. Trouble was, her alarm
bells were going off just like Garrett's. There was just too
much coincidence in the girl's reaction to the tobacco odor
and Willis having found her clothes buried on Nighthawk's
property. Too much. It wasn't enough to act on, but it was
enough to make her feel they had to look into it somehow.

But Garrett wasn't telling her what he was planning.
While she could have demanded some kind of explanation
or statement of intent—he was working for her, after all—
she couldn't help the cowardly feeling that it was better to
let sleeping dogs lie. He'd promised not to get her into any
trouble, and with that she had to be content.

For now.

He served up a really outstanding chili—not a bean in
sight, and hot enough to launch a rocket. It was thick with
chunks of steak and served with corn chips. While they ate,
he regaled her with tales of Fiesta in San Antonio, and
tempted her with talk of strolling along the River Walk at
the height of the holiday season. The Alamo, he assured her,
would probably disappoint her, tucked as it was in the heart
of the city, and smaller by far than most people anticipated. He chuckled as he told her that a painting of John

Wayne playing Colonel Travis was enshrined there. He also told her that Davy Crockett hadn't died the way the tales told it but had in fact surrendered to Santa Ana and been tortured to death.

"What's the deal with the saying about one ranger, one riot?" she asked him.

"The saying is One Riot, One Ranger. But that isn't what was really said, though the gist is the same. Capt. W. J. MacDonald was sent to Dallas to prevent a prize fight, and a lot of trouble was expected. Anyhow, when MacDonald stepped off the train, the mayor asked him where were the others? And MacDonald told him, 'Hell, ain't I enough? There's only one prize fight!' "

"That's a delightful story."

"I think so. MacDonald had one hell of a great attitude. Another thing he said that was drummed into us was, 'No man in the wrong can stand up against a fellow that's in the right and keeps on a-comin'.' "

Sandy somehow suspected that Garrett had had that drummed into him from a very early age by his father, who was also a ranger. It was an attitude that, to her, epitomized Garrett.

Later she was touched when he brought out his tennis ball and let her see the amount of effort he was expending in his attempt to encourage nerve regeneration.

"Another month or so," he told her. Not much longer at all. What he didn't tell her was how much trepidation that caused him. What he wanted was six more months. Months he would use to solidify his position in Sandy's life so that she would actually consider coming to Texas with him.

Or so that he might actually consider staying here with her. But there was no work for him here, and at this rate there might be none for her, either. No, he needed her to come home with him.

And he was damn near sure she wouldn't. That made him a fool, didn't it? Yeah, it did. He knew better than to get involved with a woman. All he ever got out of it was heartbreak. Well, at least this time he would get away with his pride intact, for what that was worth. He would go cheerfully to hell before he laid himself open again by asking any woman to marry him.

When he looked at Sandy, though, it was almost impossible to remember all his resolutions. This woman was becoming as essential to him as the air he breathed.

Oh, man, he was in deep trouble.

Chapter 13

Dud Willis owned an independent insurance agency, with its office located across the courthouse square from the sheriff's office. That was the first place Garrett stopped in the morning to ask when Willis was expected in. An obliging receptionist with a megawatt smile checked the appointment calendar and informed him that Mr. Willis was expected in the office at ten, but only for an hour. He would, however, be back at about two that afternoon. Would Mr. Hancock like to make an appointment?

He made one for two o'clock, thinking only that he didn't want this woman relaying to her boss that a man had been asking about his schedule for no good reason. This would make his visit appear completely innocent.

It was anything but. If Willis was expected to be in his office at ten, then Garrett could safely be at Willis's house at ten. Nobody could be in two places at once.

He knew what he was about to do could get him into serious trouble. Breaking and entering was a crime, one that could get him a jail term and cost him his career as surely as his arm might. There were a dozen valid reasons why he ought to turn his car around right now and head back into town. At least a dozen. And there were only two good reasons to do what he was doing right now.

The bad guy had to be stopped, and the innocent guy had to be cleared. It was, quite simply, a question of justice. It wasn't often that a cop really had a chance to serve justice in such a clear and important way. He'd spent his whole damn life trying to guarantee justice one way or another, and one way or another it had never seemed quite as important as it did this time.

Maybe because the crime was so awful. But he'd worked on child molestation cases before. Maybe because the bad guy was in danger of going free. But he'd worked on plenty of cases where that happened. Maybe it was because an innocent man was accused. It happened once in a while. Maybe because he really felt that there was some good that would come out of this if the bad guy was caught.

In the first place, it would keep Willis from hurting another little child. The horrifying fact was that the perpetrators of this kind of crime tended to strike more frequently and with more violence as time went on. It became harder and harder for them to get the same high, and easier and easier to quiet their consciences. The next little girl might not be as lucky as Lisa Dunbar...and wasn't that a horrifying thing to contemplate, that little Lisa had actually been lucky?

This crime also had another victim—Craig Nighthawk. That man's life was ruined until and unless the real rapist was caught and convicted. Even if the jury let Nighthawk go free for lack of evidence, the people of this county would always believe him guilty. And if he went to trial and were convicted, the injustice would be of criminal proportions.

And that didn't even take into account the losses Sandy was suffering for her belief that every man had a right to an attorney. For her belief that Nighthawk was innocent...as he was.

He shook his head irritably and hardly noticed that Dud Willis passed him going in the opposite direction. Without giving it a thought, he nodded in response to the man's casual wave and kept on driving.

* * *

Garrett had been gone when Sandy awoke in the morning. At first she didn't think much about it, other than wishing they'd had some snuggling time. He tended to be an earlier riser than she, and she'd already wakened a couple of mornings to find that he'd gone out for an early walk.

There was a pot of coffee awaiting her, and what apparently was going to be a long, empty day. Having no clients was not only a financial disaster but also an emotional one. She hated not to be busy, hated the sense of uselessness that kept trying to steal up on her. All her life she had worked, at first on her father's ranch and then at odd jobs throughout school, until finally she had achieved her lifelong ambition to be a lawyer. And since then she'd hardly ever missed a day, even for illness.

Until this. Lord, it was awful to feel useless and unwanted, and other than writing all kinds of motions to try to help Nighthawk before the trial, there wasn't a damn thing she could do except hope that Garrett or the sheriff managed to come up with something to prove who the real criminal was.

And much as she respected Garrett's judgment, she had serious trouble imagining Dudley Willis as the rapist. Of course, if she stopped and thought about it for a while, there wasn't *anyone* she could imagine doing such a terrible thing. So why not Willis?

Sitting over her coffee, she found herself wondering why Willis's wife and daughters had left him. From all she knew of the man, she would have expected him to be an exemplary father and husband. Not the kind of man a woman with children usually left.

Almost without thinking about it, she pulled out the phone book from the drawer where she kept it, and leafed through it, looking for Adeline Willis's number and address. Over on Whitcliff Lane, at the east edge of town. Making an instant decision, she reached for the phone and dialed the woman's number. Thirty seconds later, she was talking to Adeline Willis.

"Addie, it's Sandy Keller."

"Well, hi, Sandy! It's been a while. I haven't been in church much lately, I'm afraid."

"Neither have I, which I'm sorry to admit. I hate to bother you so early in the morning, but maybe you know I'm working on the case of the little girl who was raped?"

There was a perceptible hesitation from Addie, but instead of the chill Sandy expected to hear, there was only caution. "I've heard. Terrible, terrible thing that was."

"Yes, it was. Just awful. But what I understand is that the older Dunbar girl was at your house after school the day the little one was abducted."

"That's right. She came over here to watch a movie Dud gave our girl that morning. Some vampire thing they were both dying to see." She sighed and sounded indulgent. "You know how kids can be at that age. I'll never understand what can be cute about a vampire, but you should have heard those two girls squeal while they watched it."

Sandy laughed quietly. "I seem to remember being that way about a few things when I was their age."

"The Beatles," Addie said. "We were all screaming about the Beatles."

"Addie, why did you leave Dud?" There was no easy way to ask the question, so dropping it as an unexpected bomb seemed like the way to get at the truth most quickly. She hated herself for prying, but if Dud had a proclivity toward little girls, maybe his ex-wife suspected it.

Instead of being startled into blurting something, however, Addie became silent. When she finally spoke, there was no mistaking her suspicion. "Why?"

"I... just wondered."

There was another long silence, with nothing but the hum of the line stretching between them. "You don't think Dud had something to do with that little girl being hurt, do you?"

Sandy hesitated long enough that her silence was her answer.

"I see." Addie, too, fell silent.

It was then that Sandy suddenly realized that Addie wasn't behaving like someone who was outraged by her suggestion. She was being far too quiet, protesting nothing at all. "Addie, I don't know anything for sure yet, but . . . I think the wrong man is in jail."

"Oh, Lord, have mercy!" Addie barely whispered the words. "I've been so scared, Sandy! Ever since I heard it was the little Dunbar girl who was hurt. Dud made such a big deal about our girl being sure to invite the older Dunbar girl over to see that film. . . . Oh, God, I've been so worried!"

Sandy almost couldn't breathe as shock hit her forcefully. She could hardly believe her ears were hearing correctly. "You . . . you think Dud is capable of this?"

"Not trying to kill a little child. I never would have thought . . . but . . . Oh, my God! I left because . . . Oh, I don't know how to say this! I left him because there was something . . . not right in the way he touched our girls. I don't think he ever . . . But I can't be sure! I wasn't there every minute. I couldn't be! What if he hurt one of my babies?"

The cry was anguished, but there was no answer Sandy could possibly give her.

"I never thought he'd hurt somebody. Never!"

"We can't be sure he did, Addie." It was thin, and both women knew it.

A few minutes later Sandy hung up, hoping she hadn't distressed Addie unnecessarily. She was now convinced that Dud Willis must be the guilty party. She wanted to tell Garrett about the conversation, but he still hadn't returned. Feeling frustrated and excited all at once, she headed back to the bedroom to get dressed and try to decide how best to use this new information. She would go talk to Nate, she guessed, if Garrett didn't get back soon.

That was when she noticed the plain white business envelope on top of her dresser. At once her heart started hammering uncomfortably as she wondered what Garrett had to say that he couldn't tell her to her face. That he was going back to Texas? Goodbye, it's been swell, but . . .

In the envelope she found Garrett's neatly typed letter of resignation as her investigator. Effective immediately.

That was when she knew what he was doing.

And realized she had to stop him.

* * *

The Willis place was deserted, of course, and invisible from the road. Garrett pulled his Explorer around behind the house so that anyone driving up wouldn't see it. No point in advertising his presence, even to the mailman.

His heart was thundering in his chest. He was not at all deceived about what he was doing. He was proposing to break the law to catch a lawbreaker, and he knew if his captain ever heard about this, his goose would be royally cooked. It wasn't that he'd never bent the law a little, but never before had he consciously set out to commit a criminal act. His mouth was dry.

Getting in was no problem. He didn't even have to jimmy a lock. That made him even more uneasy. Surely if Dudley Willis had something to hide he would lock his doors. Even though no one out here ever apparently locked anything.

Inside he could hear the whoosh of the heater in the basement and the hum of the refrigerator. The kitchen was as neat as a pin, somehow surprising for a man who lived alone. There was even a crocheted tablecloth on the dinette.

The living room looked as if the furniture had been placed there around the turn of the century and never moved since. Maroon horsehair covered the couch, and the rug had a raised, multicolored floral pattern unlike anything he had seen in recent memory. The walls were papered in dark green, giving the whole room a musty, closed look.

Willis's bedroom was on the first floor, and the furniture there was just as old as the furniture in the living room. When he thought about it, Garrett was a little surprised that a man who was, by all accounts, quite prosperous had furnishings so old. Beside the bed were framed portraits he took to be of Willis's wife and daughters. A heartwarming touch.

He would look in the drawers later, he decided, if he didn't find anything elsewhere. Somehow he didn't think Willis would have left any incriminating evidence in his own bedroom. What Garrett *did* hope to find was the room in which Lisa had been held. The room with the picture of the woman on the wall.

And find it he did. Upstairs, at the back of the house, he found Lisa Dunbar's prison. The windows had been covered in thick black material. An iron cot stood in the middle of the room on thick padding—presumably to prevent any sound from the bed being transmitted to the room below. His little prisoner could toss and turn and shake the bed and never alert anyone who might happen to stop by. It made Garrett sick to think about it.

On the wall at the foot of the bed was the portrait of the woman. An old photograph that had been touched with color in the style of the twenties and thirties. Why the hell had Dudley left something so identifiable in plain sight? Or had he simply grown so used to it that he had forgotten it was there?

The closet was bare except for a cardboard box. Garrett had kept his thick leather gloves on when he came into the house so he wouldn't leave any fingerprints. Now he didn't hesitate to squat down and look into the box by the harsh light of the single overhead bulb.

Ropes. Leather slave cuffs. Material that could have been used for gags and blindfolds. God, he was going to be ill!

And also in the box, a tiny pair of cotton panties—white with little pink roses. And a black nylon stocking.

All the proof they needed.

Sandy's only thought was that Garrett had to be stopped before he ruined his entire future. Damn it, he could be sent to prison! And somehow she didn't think a Wyoming jury would feel any too sympathetic toward a Texas lawman who had broken the law. She thought about calling Nate but stopped herself even as she reached for the phone. Nate was a lawman; he would be obliged to go out there and arrest Garrett. No, this was one time when she had to keep the law out of it.

And this was one time when she simply ignored the potential consequences to herself. If she were found on Willis's property she could be arrested as an accomplice, and she seriously doubted that any jury would believe she'd gone out there to *stop* Garrett. Heck, they would think she was crazy not to have called the cops.

Which she was. But, after a life spent serving the law and the pursuit of justice, she found herself unable to go to the law. "I'm sorry," she heard herself telling an imaginary jury. "I just love him too much...."

She turned her car out of town toward Willis Road. "God, what a fool," she told herself. What a complete fool. It wasn't even as if Garrett reciprocated her feelings. As if she could hope for any kind of a future with him. Nope, the whole damn thing was hopeless, yet here she was, racing out to Willis Road to try to keep him from committing a crime. It was probably too late, though. He'd probably already gotten into the house. She was probably wasting her efforts, and in the process, making herself appear guilty of complicity. If she had half a brain, she would turn around and go straight to the sheriff.

But she didn't have half a brain. She was a woman in love. The thought brought a sad smile to her lips.

Garrett stiffened, thinking he heard something downstairs. The creak of a hinge? But although he listened intently, he heard nothing further. Still, it was time to get out of here and radio Nate about what he'd found so that Nate could get a warrant based on "information from an informant."

He straightened and turned out the light, then stiffened again, once more thinking he might have heard something. The trouble with being caught inside someone's house like this was that the householder could shoot you and no one would ever question his right. Least of all when the intruder was wearing a gun.

Hell! It was absolutely essential for him to get out of here without Willis knowing he had been here so that the guy wouldn't destroy the evidence.

That was when he realized he'd been a fool. Damn! Willis had passed him on his way out here, and now Garrett was hearing noises from downstairs.

Swearing under his breath, Garrett listened intently, absolutely convinced that Willis was somewhere in the house. The man would have seen Garrett's car out back and would guess that Garrett was somewhere in here. If he suspected that Garrett was on to him, he'd want to shoot Garrett as a trespasser and destroy the evidence before the cops arrived. Yep. So Garrett had to somehow get out of the house and draw Willis with him so that the evidence would be preserved. And then…well, a little rope would probably solve the issue. And get him sent up the river for unlawful imprisonment, along with the breaking-and-entering charge.

But none of that mattered next to getting an innocent man out of jail and putting a guilty one away before he could hurt some other little girl.

But to do that, he had to live. Which meant coming up on Willis before Willis came up on him.

It also meant pulling his gun from its holster, and just the thought of doing that made him pause. It had been a while since he'd tried to hold his gun, and he was extremely reluctant. What if it shook visibly in his hand, the way it had the last time, right after he'd got out of the hospital?

But he had to risk it. It might be his only defense against Willis. Slowly, with a hand that suddenly felt like lead, he unsnapped his belt holster and palmed the butt of his 9 mm. He held it barrel-up by his shoulder and absolutely refused to check if his hand was trembling.

Wishing he'd had the sense to wear jogging shoes, he began to move toward the hallway, taking care to set down his feet as gently as if they were puffs of down. Even the slightest sound suddenly seemed deafening.

There were no further sounds from downstairs, and he began to wonder if he'd simply heard the noises any old house makes, and not someone moving around downstairs at all. Yet, if he were Willis, he would wait downstairs, knowing the intruder would have to come downstairs sometime. Easy enough to play cat and mouse and wait for your intended victim to try to ease down the stairway.

That was when he noticed another sound, the distant drone of an approaching engine. It crossed his mind to wonder why he hadn't heard Willis approach. Then he wondered again if anyone else were in the house at all. Maybe he'd imagined it. Maybe if he got out of here now, Willis would never know he'd been in the house.

But no, that wasn't the drone of a truck engine, and Willis had been driving a full-size pickup. This was the sound of a smaller four-cylinder engine. Like Sandy's.

All of a sudden his heart was in his throat. Damn, he'd never imagined she would come after him. Never! He'd known she would figure out his intentions when she read his resignation, but he'd believed she would stay clear, which was what he had wanted her to do.

Now this. Moving carefully, but as quickly as he could, he went to the window and pulled the dark curtain aside, trying to see down the driveway. The angle was sharp, and he had to press his cheek flat against the window in order to see the driveway at all. But there it was, sure enough—Sandy's car. Only by the greatest effort did he keep from swearing out loud. The question now was whether Willis was really downstairs, and if he was, whether he would send Sandy on her way, figuring she knew nothing about this, or whether he would be sure Sandy was Garrett's accomplice.

Probably the latter. His stomach clenched into a tight knot. What now? He couldn't let that bastard hurt Sandy.

When Sandy pulled up, the house appeared to be deserted. No cars were parked out front. Maybe Garrett hadn't come out here after all. But no, if he were going to break into someone's house, he would have the sense to hide his vehicle from casual view.

But still she hesitated, uncertain what to do next. She could get out and go ring the doorbell. If by some strange circumstance Willis answered, she could excuse her presence by saying she needed to ask him something more about his statement. On the other hand, if Garrett was inside, alone, no one would come to the door. That was hardly going to get him out of there.

But if he was already in there, the crime had been committed and there was nothing she could do now to stop him.

In fact, all she could do was make herself an accomplice. She ought to turn around right now and get out of here.

But before she could move, she saw Dud Willis come out the front door, carrying a shotgun' casually cradled in his arm. At once every one of her alarm bells went off. Her instinctive reaction was to get out of there, but even as she reached to release the hand brake, she realized it was too late. If he wanted to hurt her, he was close enough to blow her away with his shotgun. The only thing to do was brazen it out.

So she rolled down the window and leaned out with a bright smile. "Dud! I was hoping I'd find you here. I have a couple of questions, if you wouldn't mind answering them."

"Sure." He smiled. "Come on in. I'll make us some coffee."

Obviously Garrett couldn't be around, Sandy thought, or Dud wouldn't be inviting her inside for coffee. Now she had to get through this charade as quickly as possible and get out of here. Where could Garrett have gone?

Keeping her smile firmly in place, she switched off her ignition and climbed out of the car. "Thanks. Coffee sounds great."

But as she started to walk toward the house, he moved in behind her, and she felt something hard press into the small of her back, right against her spine.

"Don't move, Sandy," he said quietly. "One shot here will make you a paraplegic if it doesn't kill you. Hold your hands up where I can see them."

She could feel icy sweat bead on her brow almost instantly. Slowly and very carefully, she lifted her hands. "Dud, what's wrong? Why are you doing this?"

"You know damn well why. That investigator of yours is inside my house. Damn fool left enough tracks for an idiot to follow. Some Texas Ranger."

"Why would he do that? Dud, this is ridiculous!"

"Nothing ridiculous about it, lady. He thinks I hurt that little girl. Is that what you came out here for? To help him?"

"I came out here to talk to you! I told you that."

"And I'm a brass-plated fool. Walk straight up to the door, and don't try any funny stuff, lady. You're trespassing, and no court'll hang me for protecting my property."

"That's not true! It's—"

He interrupted her ruthlessly. "Shut up. Just shut up and keep walking. This gun is loaded, and I'll use it."

Garrett heard the door slam and knew that Willis had indeed been in the house, and that now he was going outside to meet Sandy. And that scared the bejesus out of him. Forgetting everything else, he hurried down the stairs and out the back door, taking care not to let it slam shut. Then, exercising every talent he possessed for moving silently, he crept around the house to the front.

What he saw when he peered around the corner nearly stopped his heart dead. Sandy, hands held high, with a shotgun at her back, was walking slowly toward the front of the house.

There was no question in his mind now that Willis knew what was up. And there was no question in his mind that Willis would kill them both rather than be exposed as a child molester.

At least his eyes hadn't been affected. He could clearly see that Willis had his finger on the trigger of the shotgun. That brand of gun didn't have a hair trigger, but that was scant help. If anything startled him, Willis might well pull that trigger, and Sandy wouldn't stand a chance in hell.

Halfway between her car and the house, Willis told Sandy to stop. Then, keeping the gun firmly planted at her back, he hollered, "Come on out, Hancock. I know you're in there. I've got a gun pointing at Keller's back."

He had a clear shot. Problem was, he didn't trust his hand, and besides, if he shot Willis, the man might well squeeze that trigger. If he could just get him to turn . . .

Willis called out again. "Come on out, Hancock. You wouldn't want me to get mad and shoot her."

"No, I certainly wouldn't."

Garrett stepped around the corner of the house as he spoke and leveled his automatic at Willis. As he had hoped, his appearance from a different direction startled Willis into turning, and as he turned, Willis brought the barrel of the shotgun around with him. It was an instinctive movement, one he would have remedied immediately.

Except that Garrett was faster. He aimed, vaguely noticing that his hand was rock steady, and fired before Willis could fully assess the situation. An instant later, Willis crumpled to the ground, moaning.

"Run, Sandy! Around back. Call the sheriff!"

She took off, those long legs of hers eating up the distance as if she were the wind, and vanished around the other side of the house. Then Garrett cautiously approached Willis.

The shotgun was still within the man's reach, and he couldn't be sure Willis was down for the count. He might reach for the gun....

But Willis had more important things on his mind...such as survival. "Don't shoot me," he begged between moans. "Oh, God, don't shoot me again."

Garrett kicked the shotgun away and then squatted by Willis, who was holding his side. Blood oozed darkly between his fingers.

"You're going to live, you son of a bitch," Garrett told him roughly. "You're going to live so you can pay."

Chapter 14

Nate scowled at Garrett. "You know what I could charge you with."

Garrett nodded. "Plenty. Believe me, I thought about all of it."

"And Willis could make a case that he was just protecting his property, and that you had no business shooting a man who was just trying to protect his own."

"Except that I was there, Nate," Sandy said quickly. "Damn it, he asked me to get out of my car and come in for coffee, and then he put a gun to my back! With the evidence against him on the Dunbar case, nobody's going to believe Willis was just trying to drive off trespassers."

"That's not the point," Nate growled. "The point is that this fellow here ought to know better! He's a lawman, for heaven's sake! A little patience would have gone a long way!"

"Not for Nighthawk," Garrett said flatly. "An innocent man was in jail. Were we going to wait for another rape to happen, one while Nighthawk was in jail, so we could be sure he didn't commit it?"

Nate's scowl didn't lighten much. "It's messy. Damn messy. Messier than I like. Be that as it may, Sam agrees we're not going to charge you. I think he'd like to wring your neck, though. It's a damn good thing Willis decided to confess to everything, because there's some question about whether using you as a reliable informant to get a warrant would have stood up. He keeps muttering that someone could have made a good Fourth Amendment case and gotten all that stuff thrown out."

"I doubt it," Sandy said. "I seriously doubt it. Garrett wasn't acting in any official capacity. Since he was acting as a private individual, the Fourth Amendment doesn't cover him."

Nate shook his head. "I somehow suspect that would have been argued until the sky fell. Anyway, it's over and done with, and we have a signed-and-sealed confession, and all I want is for you to quit acting like the Lone Ranger in my county. Enjoy your vacation and keep your nose clean." Then he grinned. "And thanks. I just won't say for what."

Outside, the sun was high and the air as clear as crystal, so clear that the mountains looked close enough to touch.

"I'll walk you back, Sandy," Garrett said. "You can fill me in on exactly what Willis told Sam."

"Most of it I guess you figured out. He planned the abduction in advance, and he bought the movie for his daughter because he knew how much she and the Dunbar girl wanted to see it. He delivered it that morning so that his daughter couldn't watch it until after school, and he made a really big point about how she had to invite the Dunbar girl over, because he'd promised her she could see it, too. Anyway, that's how he separated the sisters. I talked with Mrs. Willis that morning before I came looking for you, and that's pretty much the way she told it, too."

He nodded. "When we get to the part about you coming after me, remind me I want to holler at you."

"Somehow I think you'll remember," she said dryly. Inside, though, she was aching with fear and anticipated loss. Now that the case was over, this man wouldn't have any reason to spend time with her. In fact, now that he knew he could shoot his gun without any trouble, he was probably chomping at the bit, wanting to get right back to Texas and pass his reinstatement physical.

"Yeah, I probably will. Okay, so the girl was separated from her older sister."

"That's right. He wore the nylon stocking you found to conceal his face and drove an old car that Lisa wouldn't have recognized, because she's always seen him in his truck. He took her to his place and kept her until just before dawn. He dumped her, buried her clothes on Nighthawk's property, then left the book bag out on the road, figuring some-one would call the cops about it. In the end, he got too worried about the girl dying, so *he* called to report it."

"I was wondering if that was him." Garrett nodded, sat-isfied, and smiled down at her from those amazing blue eyes. "Not too bright."

"He was also the one who called me that night, as you suspected." She smiled at his nod and tried to ignore the way her throat kept wanting to tighten.

"But why did he want to frame Nighthawk?" Garrett asked. "Just because the guy had been seen talking to the girl?"

"No, that's more interesting. Nighthawk bought a parcel of land that used to be in the Willis family. I don't know if you've heard, but the Willises used to own one of the big-gest spreads in the county. Anyway, the land that Night-hawk bought had belonged to Willis's aunt, who lives in Cheyenne. She had some kind of grudge against Dud and refused to sell him the parcel, though he'd tried more than once to buy it. She sold it to Nighthawk instead, and Nighthawk refused to sell it to Willis. So Willis decided that if he could frame Nighthawk for this crime, the land would eventually come onto the market as a foreclosure, and he could get it then. It was evidently some kind of an obses-sion with Dud, but according to Sam, the map will show you why. Nighthawk's property is evidently a big hole in Wil-lis's spread."

Garrett nodded slowly. "That makes a perverted kind of sense."

"And there you have it. Nighthawk probably wouldn't have been involved at all, except he had the misfortune to own a piece of land Dudley Willis wanted. Kind of chilling, isn't it?"

"To say the least."

At the office, Nina was back behind her desk, busily taking messages and calling clients, trying to fill up the appointment book once again. Sandy appreciated her efforts, but the bottom line was that this whole affair had left a very bad taste in her mouth, and she wasn't sure if she wanted those clients back. She had thought of them as her friends, but it seemed they weren't her friends at all. They had turned on her the instant they objected to another one of her clients. That was their right, of course, but it didn't leave her feeling eager to deal with them.

"Messages," Sandy said, handing her a small stack of pink slips, and handing Garrett one.

"Well, hallelujah," Garrett said as he scanned his. "My ex-brother-in-law is being charged with criminal possession of a controlled substance with intent to deal. The feds are going to put him away for a good long time, if he ever gets out of the hospital. I think Ginny will be safe for a while now."

"That's good news." Sandy tried to smile but couldn't quite manage it. The corners of her mouth were developing the most distressing tendency to tremble and pull downward. Surely she wouldn't cry? Not now!

She forced herself to look down at her own stack of messages, and all of a sudden, despite her proximity to tears, she couldn't prevent a laugh. "Will you look at this? The phone company is ready to put the tap on the line. Do we still want to do it?"

Garrett and Nina both chuckled.

"Oh, and look, the tribal police have contacted Nighthawk's sister. She'll be calling tomorrow morning at ten." Sandy looked at Nina. "Try to get hold of Nighthawk and ask him to be here in the morning. I think he'd like the chance to talk with his sister. My treat."

And that, she thought, wrapped up all the loose ends but one: her heart.

"Nina," Garrett said, "you'll have to excuse us, but I need to yell at your boss for a few minutes about risking her lovely neck."

Sandy looked up at him. "Didn't you already do that?"

"No, I only told you to remind me when we got to that part of the story, and then you managed to avoid it. So I'm going to do that right now. Here or upstairs. Your choice."

She picked upstairs, because if she burst into tears she didn't want any witnesses. It would be humiliating enough for Garrett to see it.

And she very much feared she was going to cry. She had been a blind fool for a couple of weeks now, ignoring her deepening feelings for Garrett, refusing to consider the eventual cost when he left. Focusing all her attention on the case, while her heart ran amok behind the scenes. Well, now she would get exactly what she deserved for her foolishness. If not this very day, then soon, when Garrett headed home.

Upstairs, she put on a pot of coffee and joined Garrett at the dinette. "So yell at me," she told him.

"Nah, I'm not in the mood anymore." He gave her a faint smile. "I guess you'll put your practice back together pretty quick."

She shook her head and looked away. "For some reason, I really don't care if I do or not. I've got the sourest taste in my mouth about it."

"About the way so many of your clients bailed out?"

She nodded slowly. "There isn't a one of them who wouldn't have expected me to handle their defense if they'd been accused of something, rightly or wrongly. To have them turn on me for doing the same thing for someone else makes me feel . . ." She hesitated, trying to find a word that adequately described the mixed sense of betrayal, disappointment and hurt—not to mention an inescapable feeling of disgust. "I guess I found out who my friends really are."

"If that's how you want to look at it."

"What do you mean?"

"Just that these people didn't so much betray you as register a protest, which they're entitled to do. It would be nice if everyone were able to adhere to high-minded moral principles, but most of us just can't. It's all well and good to say you believe in the First Amendment, but lots of folks got really sick to their stomachs when the American Civil Liberties Union defended the American Nazi Party's right to march in a Jewish suburb. The courts upheld it, but an awful lot of people couldn't escape the feeling that it was inherently wrong."

"I know. I backed the ACLU, but it wasn't easy. I choked on that one."

He smiled. "See? Well, these folks weren't thinking about constitutional rights as much as they were thinking about a truly horrible crime. Try not to take it too personally."

She sighed and nodded slowly. "I know you're right. But it's going to be a while before I feel the way I used to about the people in this county. Somebody spray-painted my front porch, someone threw a rock through my window.... I guess this isn't the kind of place I thought it was."

"There are people like that everywhere, honey. Just write them off."

Honey. Oh, how she wished he meant that! But it was just a casual endearment, and she swallowed hard against the lump in her throat.

That was when she realized that she was avoiding a confrontation that had to occur sooner or later. By evading the questions that meant the most to her, she was merely postponing the inevitable conclusion of their relationship. What could that do except draw out her agony in exchange for a few more moments of stolen bliss?

Feeling suddenly determined, she opened her mouth to say something, when Garrett forestalled her.

"You know," he said, "about those two women I was engaged to."

It was as if her heart stood stock-still. Was he about to give her all the reasons why he would never get involved again? Oh, God, that was exactly what he was leading up to! She tried to tell herself it was for the best, but the truth was that she would have jumped off a cliff without a parachute if it would have kept Garrett with her. "I know," she managed to say.

"Well... Oh, hell. You know what they say—once burned, twice shy. I swore I was never going to care about a woman again."

"I know. You told me." And this was it, she thought. It was over. He was prefacing his farewell with his reasons.

"Hell," Garrett said again, in almost impatient exclamation. "What I'm trying to say is that I've been a total ass!"

Astonished, she felt her jaw drop. "About what?" Yes, this was it. He was about to tell her that he'd been incredibly insensitive to have started a relationship with her when he had no intention of permanence, that he ought to be strung up or shot or whatever it was he would feel was suitable punishment for his transgression. Bottom line: she was being dumped.

"I knew from the start that you wouldn't consider giving up your practice here," he said. "It's your home and always has been, and I'd have to be an arrogant jerk to even suggest it. But the trouble is, I knew it was impossible, but I went and fell in love with you anyway."

Her heart began to hammer so hard that she thought it was going to explode right out of her chest. "Garrett..."

But he plunged ahead, heedless. "I thought about giving up the rangers, but... darlin', I'm sorry, but I'd be as useless as warts on a hog if I came up here, and I can't stand to be useless. It'd kill me. And I can't ask you to do what I won't do—"

"Why not?" she interrupted him.

He froze, his mouth open on a word that never emerged.

"Why not?" she repeated.

"Because you've worked so hard to build all this," he said.

"So?" She shook her head. "Just exactly what did I build, Garrett? A practice that evaporated the very first time I took a controversial case? A safe little hiding place where I didn't have to deal with real life—until it walked up and grabbed me by the throat?"

"I think you're being a little hard on yourself, honey. Really, you invested a lot of time and effort—"

"Yes, I did. And it's gone. Just like that, it's gone. And you know what? That's fine. Because now I'm free to do any damn thing I want. I've been wondering for some time what would have happened if I'd had the guts to stay in Cheyenne. Well, actually, I've been trying not to think about it, but I've had this inescapable sense of being...cheated, I guess. Like I've missed things I really wanted to do."

Garrett's expression changed slowly, gradually shifting to one of uncertain hope. "What did you really want to do?"

"Way back when, I wanted to specialize in criminal work. The prosecutor's office didn't have any openings, which is why I went to work for my husband's firm and found myself doing family law. But I always wanted to be a criminal lawyer."

Now it seemed Garrett was the one holding his breath. Finally he released it. "Would you consider coming to Texas? I'm sure you'd find plenty of work."

Everything inside her suddenly became hushed with joy. "Come to Texas with you?"

He nodded, a smile spreading across his face. He rose and came around the table, tugging her gently to her feet. "With me," he said huskily. "As my wife. If you think you could stand living with a cop."

Her arms slipped upward to close snugly about his neck. "What I absolutely couldn't stand, Garrett, is life without you. Of course I'll come to Texas with you."

His blue eyes grew bright. "It gets hotter'n Hades in the summer, and I tend to get obsessed with the job."

"Heat sounds good after all the cold winters I've had, and I get obsessed with the job, too. We'll work it out, Garrett."

Suddenly he threw back his head and let out a loud whoop of joy. And Sandy burst into happy tears.

* * * * *

Get Ready to be Swept Away by
Silhouette's Spring Collection

Abduction

Seduction

These passion-filled stories explore both the dangerous
desires of men and the seductive powers of women.
Written by three of our most celebrated authors, they are
sure to capture your hearts.

Diana Palmer
Brings us a spin-off of her Long, Tall Texans series

Joan Johnston
Crafts a beguiling Western romance

Rebecca Brandewyne
New York Times bestselling author
makes a smashing contemporary debut

Available in March at your favorite retail outlet.

ETERNAL LOVE
by Maggie Shayne

Fans of Maggie Shayne's bestselling Wings in the Night miniseries have heard the whispers about the one known as Damien. And now the most feared and revered of his kind has his own story in TWILIGHT ILLUSIONS (SS #47), the latest in this darkly romantic, sensual series.

As he risks everything for a mortal woman, characters from the previous books risk their very existence to help. For they know the secrets of eternal life—and the hunger for eternal love....

Don't miss TWILIGHT ILLUSIONS by Maggie Shayne, available in January, only from Silhouette Shadows

HE'S A LOVER...
A FIGHTER...
AND A REAL HEARTBREAKER.

Silhouette Intimate Moments is proud to introduce a new lineup of sensational heroes called **HEARTBREAKERS**—real heavyweights in matters of the heart. They're headstrong, hot-blooded and true heartthrobs. Starting in April 1995, we'll be presenting one HEARTBREAKER each month from some of our hottest authors:

Nora Roberts
Dallas Schulze
Linda Turner—and many more....

So prepare yourselves for these heart-pounding HEARTBREAKERS, coming your way in April 1995—
only in

Return to the classic plot lines you love, with

January 1995 rings in a new year of the ROMANTIC TRADITIONS you've come to cherish. And we've resolved to bring you more unforgettable stories by some of your favorite authors, beginning with Beverly Barton's THE OUTCAST, IM #614, featuring one very breathtaking bad boy!

Convict Reese Landry was running from the law—and the demons that tortured his soul. Psychic Elizabeth Mallory knew he was innocent...and in desperate need of the right woman's love.

ROMANTIC TRADITIONS continues in April 1995 with Patricia Coughlin's LOVE IN THE FIRST DEGREE, a must-read innovation on the "wrongly convicted" plot line. So start your new year off the romantic way with ROMANTIC TRADITIONS—only in